DRIFTING

Krause's expression was grim. "Just between you and me, Mac, I want to move this ship."

"Move?"

"Ever since the accident, we've been drifting like a lame duck. If someone planned to hijack this ship, they'll know exactly where we are. I'm going to use the auxiliary bridge to dip us in and out of hyperspace again. When *Starbright* is hidden somewhere, we'll wait and see if hijackers show up."

"But it someone planned to disable *Starbright* and hijack it, why haven't they made an appearance?" Mac asked.

"My guess would be they're waiting. If you were a hijacker and had wrecked a starliner with a thousand passengers, would you want to be right in the middle of hijacking and have rescuers show up?"

"So you think that if this *is* a hijack attempt, the hijackers are sitting back and waiting to see if anyone will come and rescue us? And if no one comes in a week or whatever, then they'll make their move?"

"Maybe," Krause said grimly. "If we're being hijacked, it has to be the work of another country, another race, or another civilization. If that's the case, we may have a problem."

STARBRIGHT

Damon Castle

"Starlight, starbright,
First star I see tonight,
Wish I may, wish I might
Have the wish I wish tonight."

LEISURE BOOKS ✖ NEW YORK CITY

A LEISURE BOOK

Published by

Dorchester Publishing Co., Inc.
41 E. 60 St.
New York City

Printed in the United States of America

CHAPTER ONE

". . . We would like a more comprehensive analysis of the Algorian natives. This should include pertinent facts from interviews with the colonists, and government reports, commercial articles or new items. During our stay at Beta Crucis we heard several rumors that the Algorians are cannibalistic. It may be that the colony governor and planetary enterprises such as Brach and Unipex have taken steps to prevent public knowledge of this condition until after our agreement to build the three new Synpla process plants there. Suggest you check with Communications and obtain the number of grams received from colonists per month during the entire lifespan of the colony and compare the average with that of colonies on other planets. Mahoney and Lyons in Central should be able to suggest other methods of analysis. We appreciate your prompt attention to this matter. Sign it 'Best, Alex' and send it now."

Gwenna rose as she shut the minirec off, turned, and headed toward the Gram Room. She could have asked one of the hostesses to take the message, but she knew from past experience that Alex preferred her to deal directly with the radioman.

The lounge was crowded at this late hour in the evening and she felt the curious gaze of at least a dozen passengers. At times she glanced at some, only to be greeted by an unwavering stare. Many of the men were watching the flash of her long, shapely legs. She was a beautiful woman but had always considered herself only moderately attractive. She had been a dedicated worker since sixteen and ambition had turned into obsession. Many eyes were turned in her direction, and she attributed that fact not to her own appearance, but to curiosity, because she was a secretary for the richest man in the universe.

"He's alone now."

"No. His Centrol man is at the bar. See? MacPherson is his name. And two of his SS men are at the adjoining table. See the two who look like college kids? One of his top SS men is at that booth in the corner, the one with the blonde, and God knows how many more there are. They'll be watching closer now that he's by himself. This would be the wrong time to approach him. His secretary must be going to the Gram Room. Why don't you tag along and send a hello to your friend in New York? Maybe you can get acquainted with Gwenna and work in from that angle. Finish your drink. Don't rush. Go out the other door."

"OK, boss." Lila obediently finished her drink and then left the lounge. After the door closed behind her, she quickened her steps. The hallway appeared endless, stretching into infinity with the rows of brightly colored metapla doors making it a strange geometrical rainbow.

The pot of gold at the end of the rainbow, she thought with detachment. It had started by winning a local beauty contest. At eighteen she had known she was attractive but had never dreamed of becoming an actress. Life in the small town of Greenville had, in its way, given her equally small ambitions. She'd placed the trophy on the fireplace mantel; her father had given her a kiss on the cheek, her mother an affectionate hug, and she thought that would be the end result of being born pretty—except perhaps marrying the boy she loved.

6

But then she'd received the phone call from the talent scout in Hollywood. He'd seen her photograph on a video tape, thought she had possibilities, and asked if she would come to Hollywood for some coaching and a screen test, all expenses paid.

She had asked her parents' permission. Her mother had agreed with one restriction. She had to be with Lila at all times.

That stipulation had been met with several moments' silence, then, "*All* the time?"

Her mother had been pressing her ear close to the phone. At that point, she had taken it and said, "We will only agree if I can be with my daughter every single moment. When she's being coached, rehearsing, acting, eating her meals, changing costumes, talking to directors or producers . . . and my daughter and I will sleep in the same room. Have I made myself clear?"

"I'm afraid that wouldn't work, Mrs.—uh, Mrs. Pollard."

An hour later the talent scout had phoned again. "I think it *will* work, Lila. We can make you a modern Grace Kelly. Tell your mother I'm agreeable."

"Who's Grace Kelly?"

"A popular actress centuries ago. I'll explain when you get here. Ask your mother if the two of you can catch the next jet."

Her first movie, *Bright Promise,* had proven prophetic in title. The public had swung into another nostalgia obsession. Her mother stayed with her constantly, as promised. The publicity department had emphasized this and, shortly before the worldwide premiere, someone in Public Relations had created the blurb, "As pure as untouched snow on the peak of a Tibetan monastery."

The description of her life-style had seemed humorous, almost ridiculous, but the public loved it. Her first movie catapulted her to stardom. Her father came to Hollywood and, besides being constantly in view, or nearby, was given the title of assistant manager. He guided her career with surprising skill. As her popularity grew, the crowds increased until it was necessary to hire armed guards to accompany her. No one had ever attempted to harm her, but the sheer masses of the crowds were physically dangerous and the guards had sometimes used their stunners to restrain the masses of admirers.

Acting had come more naturally than she expected. Her agent assured her she was a born actress. After a few years and one successful movie after another, she had acquired several million dollars.

She and her parents gradually became aware of the syndicate. Whispers, hints, insinuations.

The syndicate was a shadowy organization of businessmen and professionals who, on the surface, performed no illegal acts. It was said that their predecessors were gangsters—men who killed with guns and engaged in every illegal operation imaginable. By evolution, they were no longer overt. It was sometimes difficult to ascertain who belonged to the syndicate and who did not. But, as her fame and fortune increased, she became acutely aware of events—causes and effects. If certain people did not follow desired paths, they died mysteriously—either in "accidents" or by heart failure. It was rumored that the syndicate knew how to eliminate a person by seemingly natural causes.

Her father had died in a jet accident that also killed two hundred others. Her mother had died of a heart attack when she heard the news. It seemed incredible that the syndicate would have killed two hundred people to eliminate her father's influence upon her life. It was equally unbelievable that they could have poisoned or weakened her mother's physical condition so that the shock of the news would cause a heart attack.

Yet, shortly after her parents' deaths, she had been approached by wealthy and influential businessmen who wanted to form a corporation and act as her guardian. Numbly, she had agreed. She had done anything and everything they suggested.

She had married, at their suggestion, one of the richest men in the world, the inventor of the hyperdrive. He had died by a heart attack, supposedly from overwork.

Now they wanted her to become acquainted with Alexander Stauffer. The richest man in the universe. Her task was to win his confidence—become his wife if possible. The bits of information that she would gain and the subtle influences she could exert from such a position would make her one of the most powerful women alive.

Because of the long, horizontal V-style mirror behind the bar, MacPherson was able to watch both the customers in the lounge and the everchanging stars beyond the ship's hull. Both were equally fascinating.

The passengers represented the elite of their society. The average citizen could not afford the interstellar fare. Someone had once said that only the rich and the celebrated could travel from one planet to another. This wasn't far from the truth, MacPherson felt. There were a few others: the most adventuresome, gamblers, some entrepreneurs, and occasionally rarities such as a religious zealot, a professional man, or an assassin. He knew from past experience with interstellar travel that most of the women who traveled between the stars were exceptional in some way. Usually they were sexually above average—both in desire and performance. He was sure there were good sociological reasons for the phenomenon—such as the species' instinctive projection of its most fertile and promiscuous females into new territory—but, scanning the array of sensual, beautiful women at the tables and booths, it was hard to be concerned with the whys when the end result was so pleasing.

Finishing his drink and signaling for another, he studied the upper half of the V-mirror, watching the flicker of star clusters and galaxies. Most of the starboard lounge's ceiling was the skylight. Although it gave the appearance of a huge windshield or porthole through which the passengers could see the stars, he knew the skylight was nothing more than a projection from a camera somewhere in the observatory.

He tasted his new drink, watched the mirror above the glass's rim. A spectacular spiral nebula faded slowly to complete darkness, gradually replaced by a new image of a star cluster that dominated the screen with the nebula to the extreme left. He scoffed inwardly—he

9

knew the jumps through subspace were not so gradual or smooth. The ship's passengers were being given a carefully edited version of the scenery.

Glancing over the sea of faces once more, he wondered which one would try to reach Alexander Stauffer. He felt a strange sensation. He closed his eyes, ran a hand across his forehead. The new sensation was difficult to identify at first, but it grew until there was no denying its texture. It was a new hunger, an acquired taste that only struck a few. He told himself it wasn't reasonable, but he knew the seed had been growing in his soul for years. It had matured now. Born of frustration and strain and smoldering hatred he, for the first time in his life, felt the urge to kill someone.

Anyone.

"She's beautiful, isn't she?"

Mac turned toward the voice and saw the round-faced man by his side nodding toward the blonde leaving the lounge.

"Not bad."

"Do you know who she is?"

"Lila Hartnett."

"Right. I saw all her movies before she married Hartnett. What an angel. They described her as pure as untouched snow on the peak of a Tibetan monastery. Oh. I'm Jeff Gunther."

The man extended his hand. Deciding that his bar partner had reached the stage of intoxication at which everyone automatically seemed a friend, Mac shook his hand and said, "Mac."

"Glad to know you, Mac. This your first starflight?"

"Ninth or tenth. I can't remember which."

"My first. Makes me feel like a kid. A famous actress, now a millionairess. And Stauffer. . . . Did you know he's here too?"

"I know."

"Richest man in the universe. Wouldn't you like to have his money? He can buy anything he wants."

"I think he already *has* everything."

Gunther laughed and signaled the robotender for another drink.

As an afterthought, he nodded to indicate he would buy Mac one too.

"I'm an engineer," Gunther volunteered. "I was one of the first students at the Electrotherapy Education University of Pennsylvania. Amazing. You know, the whole time I went there, I didn't read a single book or write a note or listen to a lecture or study. For two hours each day, we wore eduhelmets on our head, and sat there with our brains steeping in knowledge."

Mac felt a tingle of resentment. He had been forced to study to earn his diploma. It had been hard and tedious work. He resented the new system that poured knowledge and skills into minds like pouring liquid into bottles.

"How did it feel?"

"The eduhelmets? You don't feel anything. You sit there and stare at a wall without any sensation but when each session is over, you know you have knowledge about whatever subject they fed you. Believe it or not, I can repair ninety-nine out of a hundred machines. I could take this spaceship apart and put it together again. Or fix anything that went wrong with it."

Since the man had not *worked* for his skill, Mac could not feel any admiration. He said, "Do you work for Stauffer?"

"I wish I did. I'm employed by Unipex. They have a planet on Algor. I'm relieving a guy who's been there four years. I'll be on a two-year hitch." Gunther smiled. "The guy's wife talked with me. . . . You see, I'll spend a few days with him while he briefs me on the operation there. Then he'll catch a flight home. You know what his wife said? She said, 'Tell him I said I love him.' How in the hell can you tell a guy something like that?"

"Simple. Say, 'Your wife told me to tell you she loves you.' "

Gunther shrugged his shoulders. "That's stupid. They been married twenty years. Anybody stays married that long has to be in love or crazy or both." He gulped his drink. "What kind of work do you do?"

"Secret service."

Gunther eyed him carefully. "If you're in a secret service, should you go around telling people?"

"The people who *shouldn't* know, do know. If a person doesn't know, it's because it doesn't matter to him or her. I'm known because I've been in the business so long, the word has gotten around. But . . . we do have secret service agents that are strictly undercover . . . ones even *I* don't know. Are you a secret service agent?"

Gunther frowned and the man's momentary confusion amused Mac. "No. No, I'm not. I'm an engineer."

"You can tell me if you are. You can trust me."

"No. Really. Are you a secret service agent for the government or a corporation?"

"That's a secret."

When Gunther's eyes widened and his jaw sagged slightly, Mac repressed a smile.

"If it's not a secret that you're a secret service agent, then why is it a secret *who* you're one for?"

"The reason is confidential."

As Mac sipped his drink, he watched Gunther in the bar mirror. The man blinked and shook his head as if to shake away his confusion.

"Hans Steiger, the philosopher, is aboard too. Did you know that?"

"I know."

"Ever read any of his books?"

"I don't believe in philosophy. Excuse me, I just noticed some friends at a table. . . ."

Hans Steiger sat in his compartment, alone, eyes closed, a tall, lean man with a deeply etched and wrinkled face. His long hair was as white as snow but there was never a hint of age in his mannerisms. He had published two dozen books of philosophy for the masses. Unlike almost every previous philosopher of any importance, he had aimed all his books at the bluecollar and deskjobber millions. Although many of his writings were merely observations and thoughts that ranged from ordinary to poetic, he filled a position in society that had never been occupied before. His followers and devotees had made him rich. While he repeatedly preached that the best things in life were mental appreciations rather than physical treasures, he had almost all the luxuries that wealth could purchase.

A suction cup held a electrode firmly against his temple, a thin green wire trailing down to the waiting thinkwriter. When he felt he had composed his thoughts sufficiently, he fed the machine a combination of numbers to activate it, and it began to type on a roll of white paper:

It occurred to me today that most of the men and women aboard this ship do not really know where they are. Mankind, in its ignorance and conceit, sees the universe as a place with a certain number of inhabitable worlds that can be reached by seldom-traveled but well-known paths.

It seems that most people conceptually envision the universe as a rather large Texas or Earth or solar system. I visualize this greatest environment as unthinkably huge. We are, comparatively, less than ants on a vast plain . . . ants on an endless continent. The paths are not clearly defined. Star routes are comparable to trails through unexplored jungles in uncharted lands. No one knows what lies hidden on the countless unexplored worlds that have been discovered in the past few years. Mankind has reached a new era. It is much more than the physical accomplishment of space travel itself. Whereas the unknown has for many centuries been microscopic and beyond man's reach, mankind now has a cosmic unknown at its fingertips.

It would need some revising but he was well satisfied with the range and content. They needed jolting from their blind nests. Make them see the vastness of space. Many gave lip service to the "New Vista," saying they understood the tremendousness of the universe while still emotionally visualizing it as a large public park. He wanted to make them realize the full import of the hundreds of worlds that the explorers had discovered. Every time he made his followers see something they had not seen before, he strengthened his position.

13

MacPherson carried his drink to the booth where Krause and Eva were sitting. Smiling briefly at Eva, he said to Krause, "Did you see the blonde follow Gwenna?"

"She didn't *follow* Gwenna. She went out the other door."

"I know. But she and the bald businessman type with her were watching Alex and Gwenna. I think the blonde will try to work her way to Alex through Gwenna."

Krause fiddled with his empty glass. "She's Lila Hartnett. Widow. Twenty-eight. Her husband was Henderson Hartnett, inventor of the hyperdrive. The interstellar transport arm of the syndicate bought his patents, put him on a fat salary, and gave credit for development of the hyperdrive engine to a man named Sloan. No one knows why, except that the syndicate must have had Sloan wrapped up good, and they must've had plans for him." He paused and frowned as he lit a cigarette. "But they treated Hartnett good. He had millions when he died and now Lila has them. She has too much money to be an ordinary shill."

"True. When I learned her name was on the passenger list, I asked for Centrol's file. Here it is."

He passed the cartridge to Krause who placed it against his temple and pushed the button. He closed his eyes, frowning several times as he received the steady stream of images. When he finished, he gave the cartridge to Eva who listened to the recording while she sipped her drink.

"Any more like that aboard ship?" Krause asked.

"Six or seven, but none as successful. Lila may be the only syndicate girl."

"Do you *know* she works for the syndicate?"

Mac shrugged. "Who else could make a famous ex-actress with millions of dollars pursue a man like Alex?"

Eva laughed. "Men, men. Don't you know money isn't everything? There's such a thing as prestige."

Ignoring Eva's remark, Krause asked, "Do you have anything on the bald businessman at the bar?"

14

Mac nodded negatively. "As far as we know, he's only a computer manufacturer, but . . ."

"Will someone be gentleman enough to order me another drink?"

Mac glanced at Eva and then began to study her when he noticed the glazed condition of her eyes. Her mouth was slack and her face flushed. "Shop talk," she complained. "I get so tired of shop talk."

"What would you rather do?" Mac inquired in a bitter tone. "Do you feel more in the mood to get drunk?"

Eva smiled and raised her empty glass. "Didn't they tell you? My job in the SS is to be a lush. I'm the best paid lush in the world."

At first Mac thought it was only a quip but then he saw Krause shrug helplessly. "That's right. She's under instructions to stay plastered as long as possible each day on this trip and then continue when we reach Algor . . . until the Synpla process plants are finalized one way or another."

"I'm a real professional," Eva bragged. Krause had signaled for three more drinks. When the waitress brought them, she took her drink from the tray—not waiting for it to be placed on the table. Mac watched as she drank quickly and smoothly. Her hands were long and slender and soft. The velvety lines of her throat pulsed as she drank. Her red lips were moist when she lowered the glass. She giggled and winked at Mac.

Krause leaned closer to Mac and said in a near whisper, "If the syndicate plans to throw Lila Hartnett at Alex, why don't we throw Eva at him? He knows she's on his SS staff and he'd be polite. If Eva can get chummy enough with him, she can upset any move on Lila's part by keeping him too busy for outside diversions.

"Well . . ."

"It's been planned as a tentative countermove."

Mac nodded consent. Both men looked at Eva. She gulped the remainder of her drink. "I resent the terminology. You make me sound like a bone thrown to a dog!"

Krause placed a hand on hers. "Alexander Stauffer is far from a dog and you're not exactly a bone. Sorry. I should have said, 'Let's keep it in the family.' "

"That's better." The red mouth tightened briefly. She took her purse and stood. "Well . . . consider me thrown. Wish me luck. You guys be good."

After Eva had left the table, Mac said, "What the hell *is* she?"

"She's a real lush; it's not an act. She's been in Synpla's secret service two years. Remember that skirmish in the Pleiades? When the Pleiadesians attacked the colony, her husband was killed. During the conflict almost all the medical supplies were destroyed. Her baby contracted one of the local diseases and there was no way to stop it. She had to watch her son die slowly. She started hitting the bottle and never stopped. She makes a good SS agent because the cover is perfect. She's a Synpla secretary, so she has a reason for always being near Alex."

Mac sipped his drink and lit a cigarette. He was a tall man with graying hair at the temples and deceptively mild gray-blue eyes. He had worked his way up from a job as one of the millions of nameless clerks in the Synpla industry to the Centrol board. Although his position paid well and carried considerable responsibility, the job was not what he'd hoped it would be.

He had visualized working at Centrol as an executive, evaluating data and making important decisions. He had envisioned a large desk with a gleaming top in a luxurious office, attended by a pretty secretary. Instead—one of the damnable Synpla computers had declared he was best suited for this type of work.

He was a glorified bodyguard and a liaison between Synpla's central intelligence and its secret service division. He had more rank than the somewhat mysterious SS, but his main job was simply to keep a wealthy man from being unduly influenced.

And everybody and his brother wanted to influence Alexander Stauffer. Among the ten wealthiest men his value could not be precisely estimated due to the huge complex of corporations that fluctuated daily in their financial positions—Alexander Stauffer was often referred to as, "The richest man in the universe."

The trouble was that Alex was a lunatic. Aside from some startling eccentricities, it was absolutely insane for a man with Alex's wealth to travel so much. He should stay safely out of sight as the fabled Howard Hughes had done, and not constantly expose himself to the flotsam and jetsam of the universe!

Mac watched as Eva stopped at Alex's table. He listened in on the SS telecom. She was saying:

. . . can a standby secretary have a drink with the boss?

He couldn't hear Alex's thoughts but he knew from the expression on his face that the answer was more than a polite yes. As Eva sat at the table, she crossed her legs and Mac studied the lengths of thighs and curves of calves. Not bad, not bad at all. She wore a pale blue dress that hugged her hips and breasts.

"Another drink?" Krause offered.

"Make it a double. I think I'll see if I can work my way up to a position as a male SS lush."

They drank steadily for an hour and then Krause said, gazing over Mac's shoulder, "They're leaving."

"Fast worker."

"Maybe he wants to dictate a letter."

Mac did not comment.

"They might be going to the observatory or one of the other lounges."

"Or the ship's library to pick up a book on Chinese poetry." It was then that Mac realized he was nearly intoxicated.

"Let's stay here. I'll give the signal for the kids to follow them."

By *kids*, Krause meant the two college boys that had been sitting at the table next to Alex's. They were trained SS killers, in effect. If anyone so much as lifted a finger to harm Alexander Stauffer, one or both of them would probably kill the offender on the spot. The SS had a reputation for killing would-be assassins swiftly and efficiently. Not many had tried to harm the richest man in the universe, and those that had had not survived to tell the tale.

The Synpla lawyers can make anything right, he thought bitterly.

The SS can kill a dozen people on a crowded street corner and make it look like they died in an elevator accident.

Mac and Krause ordered sandwiches and coffee. When the waitress arrived with the tray, Mac looked up, nodded his thanks, but suddenly her blue eyes were covered with the redness of blood. He instinctively reached for the gun in his pocket holster, thinking someone had tried to kill Krause and himself in a fantastic attempt to eliminate Alex's protection.

His hand never touched the gun. As his ears were filled with a deafening whistle of escaping air, he felt himself being shoved violently by an invisible force. The table turned on its side and came crashing against his chest. He fought for balance, saw that everyone and everything was being hurled to one end of the lounge—men and women flying through the air or grotesquely skidding across the long, smooth floor.

He slammed against a wall of bodies and others were hurled against him. Something crashed against his head and he lost consciousness briefly. When he could see and hear again, he found himself part of an incredible pile of men and women . . . some dead, some dying, some unconscious, many seriously injured. He felt the stickiness of blood on his right hand but did not know if it was his or someone else's. The shrill whistle of escaping air had stopped but now the room was filled with screams of pain and terror. He placed a hand down and tried to force himself erect—finding he had placed his hand squarely on a woman's leg. The woman kicked spasmodically. As he managed to rise to his knees, someone toppled against him and forced him down again.

When he finally managed to struggle erect, he saw the sparks from the electrical board at one end of the bar. It had been neatly concealed by artificial wood, but something during the explosion had ripped the paneling away and torn into the maze of wiring. Sparks erupted and, as he watched in unbelieving horror, a girl staggered toward the smoldering tangle, turned and leaned into it. Her eyes were closed. She ran a hand across her forehead. Her lips parted but the sound was lost

18

in the turmoil of screams. He leaped to his feet. . . .

Her shoulders touched the wiring. Her plaskirt melted and, for a microsecond, she was clad only in what appeared to be cotton panties and a bra. In the next instant she became a mass of charred flesh and the room plunged into darkness.

Mac stumbled toward the door he had seen for a moment in all the confusion, his mind focused on its now invisible location.

He knew that only one thing could have caused this disaster: The energy screen had failed somehow. A meteor had punctured the ship's hull and a large quantity of air had escaped. The auxiliary screen must have activated automatically—too late to prevent the loss of air but quick enough to prevent total disaster. The failure of an energy screen was something that happened only once in a hundred flights. Sometimes with no deaths—sometimes with appalling losses.

There were only two ways that an energy screen could fail. Accidental mechanical failure or deliberate sabotage.

He realized numbly that he had his gun in his hand. He was more than a Centrol man—as liaison with the SS, Alex's security was his prime responsibility.

CHAPTER TWO

When Gwenna reached the Gram Room, she was both flattered and annoyed at the attention the radioman gave her. As he stood on the other side of the counter and pretended to read the message a second time, he was actually watching her from the corners of his eyes.

He was a young man with a flawless complexion and a very faint hint of beard on his cheeks and chin. When he looked up into her face and told her how much the gram would cost, he was blushing and his eyes flitted from her mouth to her nose, as if he could not gather the courage to look directly into her eyes.

He thinks I'm beautiful, she thought with a flutter of excitement. She had grown accustomed to appraising glances and polite flattery and calculated advances, but this was something much different—this was an inexperienced young man who must find her extremely attractive.

"Will you ask for a receipt acknowledgement and let me know when the message is delivered? I'll be either in the starboard lounge or my cabin . . . number twenty-six."

When she turned away from the counter she almost bumped into Lila Harnett. She smiled and walked quickly down the corridor, thinking that she had handled it just right. If the young radioman could summon enough courage, he could use the receipt acknowledgement as an excuse to see her again.

"Wasn't that Alexander Stauffer's secretary?" Lila whispered.

"Yes, it was."

"I wanted to discuss something with her. I wonder . . ." She stepped to the bend in the corridor and saw the other woman opening the pink-colored door that led to the ladies' room for that particular corridor. She winked at the radioman. "I think I'll send that gram later."

Since the corridor was empty, she waited a few mintues before opening the pink door—pretending to be searching for something in her purse, just in case someone should appear unexpectedly. Then she opened the door and stepped inside. Gwenna was sitting at one of the vanities, combing her long, dark hair.

"Hello. Aren't you Gwenna Hill, Alexander Stauffer's secretary?"

Gwenna nodded, amazed at the other woman's manner. She had imagined that Lila Hartnett would be coolly sophisticated, but she acted much like a friendly small-town girl.

"I'm Lila Hartnett . . ."

"I know. I've seen you on the TViews many times."

"Oh. Then you must have a good memory for faces. I haven't been in the news very often since my husband died." They were exchanging the Lib handshake. Gwenna wondered if Lila was active in the Lib movement or if, as in her own case, she used the handshake only because it was currently fashionable.

"Will you excuse me a moment? I have to make some repairs . . ."

Gwenna watched as Lila sat before the vanity, withdrew an expensive makeup machine from her purse and ran it across her face as her fingers expertly tapped the miniature keyboard. She felt a bit of jealousy—her own life had been one of letters and reports and never-ending responsibility almost as far back as she could remember. She was not very adept with a makeup machine and her life had not been even one-hundredth as exciting as Lila's.

21

She had followed the private lives of a half-dozen playgirls—it had been an almost pitiful attempt at pleasure—and Lila had been one of the few whose experiences she had enjoyed in a small, vicarious way. It seemed that Lila had been everywhere and done everything. She was always among the first to know the latest Paris styles. For the first time during their conversation, Gwenna paid close attention to her companion's attire—a silver butterfly hair ornament, diamond necklaces, earrings and bracelets. She wore a tan corduroy mini with a gold chain belt, pendants of jewels and coins. Somehow, all the jewerly did not seem ostentatious on Lila. It all blended together smoothly, beautifully, tastefully.

"I've been looking for a personal secetary and I've been considering you," Lila Hartnett said as she finished with the makeup machine. "Are you interested?"

Gwenna felt numb for a moment. She had received other offers in the past, but never so abruptly. "I'm satisfied with my job at Snypla."

"But the pressures and responsibilities must be tremendous." Lila shrugged as she replaced the makeup machine in her purse. "As my secretary there wouldn't be any pressures and I can afford to pay you more than Alex."

"Well . . ." How could she say no swiftly and politely? "I'm afraid I'm not interested. I certainly appreciate the offer. . . ."

Lila crossed her legs and lit a cigarette. Her diamond bracelet caught the glow from the lights above the vanity mirrors and glittered softly. Gwenna remembered reading that Lila's favorite bracelet had been valued at an amount higher than the average man's lifetime income. "There's more than a good salary involved," Lila said. "I like to travel, so you wouldn't be confined to an office nine months out of a year as you are at Synpla. Your expense account would be unlimited. As my secretary you would also be my traveling companion and your wardrobe would have to be appropriate. That would be my expense, not yours. And . . ." Gwenna watched Lila's mouth turn softly into a sly smile. "Some of the fringe benefits may intrigue you. . . ."

When she did not continue, Gwenna laughed and shrugged her

shoulders. "You're very persuasive. But I've spent years working for Alex. I wouldn't—"

"Let me buy you a drink and tell you all the other advantages."

"Well . . ."

"Ask Alex's permission, if you wish."

"Perhaps I should." Turning toward the mirror and studying her hair to make certain it was perfect, she said silently through the telecom, *Alex, do you mind if I take half an hour or so for personal business?*

Take the remainder of the evening.

She nodded at Lila.

"Good. Why don't we find a quiet booth in the main lounge?"

CHAPTER THREE

Sam Parker had been watching the tall, slender redhead for almost an hour as she sat alone in the booth. The mirror on the other side of the bar afforded an excellent view of that particular booth. She had the prettiest red hair he'd seen in ages. Dimpled knees. She wore a mid-thigh, emerald-green, sequined dress that sparkled beneath the lounge lights. She was a beckoning jewel, an irresistible temptation.

She seemed aware of him—at least she had glanced in his general direction several times, as if studying him from the corners of her eyes. Women were masters at the art of peripheral vision—able to study you intently while appearing to be looking at a dozen other things.

The redhead left the lounge. She might be going to the port or main lounge. It would be an opportunity to meet her. If she went to one of the other lounges, he could tag along a few yards behind and open the door for her—as an excuse to speak and introduce himself. She was alone and might be deliberately seeking a companion for the three-week trip.

Sam finished his drink, the cocktail glass almost lost in the large muscular grip of his hand. He was a huge, burly man with wide shoulders and long, powerful arms. Because of his square jaw, gray eyes, and his crewcut, strangers often thought him to be one of the fighters that were currently so popular on TViews.

He was, actually, more fortunate than the fighters who battered each other to entertain audiences; his profession paid more than most. His family had been bluecollar for generations and he had held the classifications of Operator First Class and Mechanic First Class since the age of nineteen. Having started work at sixteen, now thirty-two, he had spent half of his lifetime working with and repairing machinery. As the oper and mech professions grew rarer, his salary had increased tremendously. It never ceased to amaze him that the males of his society were turning increasingly toward deskjobbing.

Glancing around the lounge, he fought the familiar surge of contempt as he studied the other men. He did not *want* to feel contemptuous, but the sensation was often difficult to overcome. Although many men might have a better education than himself, there wasn't a single man in the room he couldn't beat to a pulp. Most had hands as delicate as a woman's—most had only toyed with computers or pens or thinkwriters all their lives. He doubted if a single one knew how to change a valve in a chemical process line or replace an energy plug in a mobile. He doubted if any of them had ever used a hammer or wrench. Most of them probably wouldn't be able to find the oiler on an engine.

As he slid from his stool to follow the redhead, the starboard lounge erupted. A relay between his mind and body clicked. Whereas most others saw the turmoil as a fleeting incomprehensible whirl, Sam Parker's quickened reflexes allowed him to see the sequence of events as one might see a slow-motion film. While all other occupants were floundering beneath the shock wave of the unexpected force, he hurled himself from the room with only a few scars and bruises. He was the first one on *Starbright* to recover from the catastrophe, the first to make and execute a decision.

In the corridor, as he clung to the edge of a doorway for support, he felt the sudden reappearance of gravity—perhaps the ship's secondary gravitational system activating. He had no way of knowing what

25

exactly had happened but he imagined that a meteorite had punctured the ship's hull and they had lost some air. Perhaps the grav system had been damaged, the auxiliary system kicking in after the ship's computer realized the emergency.

The redhead sat against one of the doors. She rubbed her forehead dazedly and stared at him as he approached. "What . . . what happened?"

He helped her to her feet. "Struck by a meteorite, I guess. Are you all right?"

"I . . . I don't know." She blinked rapidly.

Having a closer look, Sam decided his first evaluations were right. She was a beauty and, as far as he could tell, it was the real thing, not a product of some damned cosmetic machine. He held her hand, half-dragging her down the corridor.

"Where are we going?"

Her question did not contain any alarm. The shock of the great ship shuddering had been large enough to make all other matters seem small by comparison. He wanted to help her—she must sense that. "I saw an emergency station somewhere along this corridor," he answered.

She was silent as they continued on down the corridor. He found the station and pulled her inside. He closed the door behind them and studied the racks of spacesuits and other emergency equipment.

"Are you certain it was a meteorite?" the woman asked. "I thought ships had safeguards against them."

"I think we witnessed a safeguard that didn't work," Sam murmured as he opened a box of oxy pills. He studied the green sequined dress that clung so tightly to the curves of her body. "Do you have any pockets in that thing?"

"No. Why?"

He gave her three of the pills and stuffed the remainder from the box in his pockets. She was staring at the pills in her hand, baffled.

"You don't know what they are?"

She nodded that she didn't.

"Put one in your mouth . . . up in your cheek. If we're hit by another meteorite and you feel the air rushing away, bite it like you would a piece of candy. It'll give you enough oxygen for five or ten minutes . . . enough time to get into a protective suit."

Understanding suddenly brightened her eyes. "Oh. It's one of those oxygen pills." She looked up at him.

He nodded. "They're not magic but they're better than nothing, and they might save your life if the ship is struck again.

"You think we'll be hit by other meteorites?"

"We might be passing through a belt. Who knows? Have you ever put on a spacesuit before?"

"No."

He selected one from the rack and gave it to her. "Practice."

During the next half hour, he watched as she practiced getting in and out of the suit. He noticed that she slid the two extra oxy pills between her breasts, beneath her blouse. He showed her all the shortcuts he knew about getting into one of the suits, but didn't show her the easy and efficient way of peeling out of one. It was interesting to see the contortions she went through in her struggles.

"Is that fast enough?" she asked wearily. She was sweating, her red hair was ruffled, and her lipstick was smeared from sliding the helmet on and off her head.

"It's your life. If you can do it fast enough to save your skin, it's good enough." Immediately after the words left his mouth, he regretted their curtness. He had spent too much time working with men, only men. Deskjobbers were around women constantly; they learned the habit of treating women differently. On Ganymede and many other jobs, he had been out of contact with women except on weekends. *It's your life, buddy.* That was the typical answer given when one man instructed another in the safeguards against a hazard on a particular job. The sudden expression on her face told him the reply was too rough.

"You did fine," he corrected himself. "You learn fast."

Something in her eyes changed. He didn't take the time to evaluate what was going on in her pretty head. He heard voices in the corridor.

He took two of the suits and rolled them up, handed them to her, taking two others for himself. "Let's get out of here."

He stepped out of the compartment. Four or five men brushed past and he reached for the woman's hand, guiding her down the corridor. He could see others headed for the emergency station. He was amazed it had taken most of the passengers so long to arrive at the same conclusion. *But,* he reminded himself, *deskjobbers aren't used to worrying about their skin.*

"Spacesuits are going to be valuable from now on," he told the woman. "Everyone will want at least one and most of the passengers will want two or three. Some nuts will walk around in the things all the time if nobody stops them."

"But . . . is there *still* danger from meteorites?" She glanced at her tiny wristwatch as if checking a timetable.

"Who knows? The hull and bulkheads have been weakened by the first contact. One of them might collapse under the strain at any moment. You see . . ." He nodded at the men and women crowding into the emergency station behind them. "They've started to realize that." He added quickly, "Where's your room?"

"This way." He followed her into an elevator and was surprised to find it still operating. Either the ship's main power plant hadn't been damaged or the ship's captain hadn't decided to conserve energy and make the passengers use the stairs.

In the woman's cabin, he locked the door. When he saw the expression on her face, he shrugged. "Just a precaution. Twelve years ago I was on a ship that had a similar accident. Some of the passengers went berserk, going from cabin to cabin. If we have any nuts aboard, somebody will stop them before they do too much damage. Meanwhile, we keep them off our backs."

He lit a cigarette and studied the room. It wasn't much different than his own except it had been done in pastels and was slightly larger. He said, "Can you think of a good place to hide one of your suits?"

28

She was still holding the two spacesuits and seemed puzzled by his question. He explained, "Later on, someone might try to steal your suit. If you hide one and keep one in an obvious place, they might take only one and think that's all you have."

He sat in a chair and finished the cigarette as he watched her hide one of the suits in the closet behind her dresses. She hung the other one on the door where it would be evident. She said, "You've done a lot to help me. I don't even know your name."

"Sam Parker."

"My name is Diane," she said as she turned toward him, smiling. "Diane Russell."

He could tell she felt awkward. He studied her legs and breasts, remaining silent.

"Would you . . . care for a drink?"

"Anything wet and strong."

She mixed two drinks. Her hand trembled slightly as she handed the glass to him. For a moment he was deep in thought as he realized the captain had not made any announcements over the ship's intercom system. Had he been killed? Was he so disorganized that he didn't know what kind of announcement to make to his passengers? Or had the ship's intercom network been disrupted?

Diane sat nervously on the edge of a chair, her head tilted to one side as if listening for sounds in the corridor beyond the cabin. "I don't know how to thank you for all the help you've given me. I'm rather inexperienced in space travel. Some of the things you've taught me might save my life."

He thought, *Centuries ago, air passengers were never instructed in the use of parachutes, and ocean liner passengers were never taught the use of lifeboats or jackets. . . .* Gulping his drink and watching her eyes to see what they would do, he said, "I know how you can thank me."

Her eyes were veiled, hiding her thoughts, although he suspected she might know how it would end.

"You can give me a date," he explained.

29

Her smile was quick and sincere. "I'd like that. As soon as we reach •
Algor . . ."

"We might not get there." He grinned. "Maybe we should have the
date before that, so we don't miss it."

"Well . . ."

As she frowned, he anticipated her thoughts. "Tonight might be too
late, also. We might both be dead before we could keep the date. Besides . . . the starboard lounge was a hell of a mess when I left it. I
doubt there'll be any dining and dancing there tonight."

"I—Do you mean? . . ." She started to blush.

He said, "Maybe we shouldn't waste any time. You're a beautiful
woman and I'd hate to miss a date with anyone like you. Maybe we
should have that date a few minutes from now, when we finish our
drinks."

He watched her reaction, amused and pleased at the way her face
reddened still more. He gulped the remainder of his drink and set the
glass on the chair arm. "I finished my drink."

She had risen from her chair. He went to her and slipped his arms
around her waist. He could see a tiny excited pulse beat in the smooth
length of her throat. Her red lips were slightly parted and he leaned
forward, kissing her, crushing the supple curves of her body against
him. He moved a hand up—

His cheek stung. He stepped backward, uncomprehending for a
moment. When he realized she had slapped his face, a flood of unreasonable anger poured into his system. He reached for her dress,
intending to rip it away.

He saw her grasp his arm. The room spun. He struck the floor so
violently that stars danced before his eyes and he lost his breath. He
struggled to his feet, instinctively reaching for her again.

The second time was worse. He hit a wall upside down and fell
straight on his head, his body toppling and twisting as it fell. He lay
motionless, breathing deeply. She must be a Virgin. A *Virgin!* He'd
heard of them but had never met one personally. There were several
hundred thousand of them on Earth . . . the females of the families

30

religiously and zealously guarded their virginity. The mothers taught the daughters a special hybrid jujitsu that enabled them to guard and preserve their valued chastity. The beliefs were passed from generation to generation. The Virgins were anachronistic but dedicated and deadly. He had read accounts of young Virgins actually *killing* would-be attackers. Oddly enough, kissing was an acceptable facet of the Virgin religion. Anything other than kissing was accomplished only after marriage.

He groaned. "My God." He practiced breathing again.

"I'm sorry, Sam," she said softly. She was kneeling by his side. "Did I hurt you very much?"

He nodded. "You almost killed me!"

She extended her hand as if wishing to touch and comfort him but her fingers hesitated inches away. She placed the hand on her knee. "I'm sorry," she repeated. "I . . . I'm not used to that."

"I'm sorry, too. I . . . uh . . . sort of lost my head."

"Are you all right?"

He shifted to a sitting position and rubbed the back of his skull. It ached. His neck felt as if it had broken and accidentally reset itself with the uppermost vertebra a fraction of an inch off center. When he saw the frown-wrinkles in her forehead and the concern in her misty eyes, he decided to emphasize his injured role. He groaned again and slowly struggled erect, massaging his neck. "I don't *feel* all right. I think I'll concede, take my pieces to my room and see if they all fit together." He hobbled toward the door.

"I *am* terribly sorry." She shrugged helplessly. "It was . . . so automatic."

"I understand." He opened the door.

"Are you mad?"

"No, no." He stepped into the corridor.

"I appreciate everything you did to help me."

"Don't mention it."

She bit her lower lip. She attempted a smile but it faltered. "I *would* like to see you again. . . ."

This is crazy, he thought. *First she throws me around like a ragdoll and then she says she'd like to see me again.* He looked into her eyes and then at her red lips, his gaze sliding down to the ripe curves of her body. "Maybe we can have another drink together someday," he said. "But . . . next time let's tie my hands or yours!"

CHAPTER FOUR

By turning to his left, Jimmy Franklin could see the girl in the scanner at his elbow. The eye on the desk beside her gave him a wonderful profile view. She was young and pretty—much prettier than the one named Gwenna; she reminded him of Judith.

She had that young, fresh, thoroughly innocent complexion that could not be duplicated by all the cosmetic machines in the world. Her eyes were clear and sparkling, there wasn't a single wrinkle in her face, not even at the corners of her eyes, and her mouth had the full red-soft look of a sweet fruit. Her honey-blond hair had been done in a bouffant style—the shade was very much like Judith's and Judith had often worn her hair that way.

When he stood at the counter while she wrote down the gram she wanted to send, he'd noticed her waist—so small that you wondered how that slight space could contain all the necessary bodily organs. By contrast, her hips were flared, not overlarge but generous.

She couldn't see her image in his scanner because he'd turned it so only its side faced her. After he finished sending the gram, he sat for a few minutes studying her profile. She was chewing the end of the cheap wooden pencil, looking at him. He wondered if she was studying his hair or head or shoulders, or merely looking in his direction while deep in thought.

He glanced at the carbon of the gram she'd sent:

DEAR MOM,
WE ARE ON OUR WAY AND I HAVEN'T BEEN SPACESICK AT ALL.
HOPE YOU ARE WELL.
DO YOU REALIZE I AM FAMOUS?
I WILL BE THE FIRST PROFESSIONAL RECEPTIONIST ON ALGOR!
HAVING A WONDERFUL TIME. . . .
LOVE,
FAUSTINA

He didn't like her name. It sounded clannish. But it was the only thing about her that didn't appeal.

After composing the first gram, she had said, "You can send that one and I'll be thinking up one to send my sister."

Glancing at her profile once more, he saw her take the pencil from her mouth and write quickly.

"Thought of something to send your sister?" He turned around and reached for the carbon of the first gram.

The control console crumpled. He closed his eyes as he felt sharp stings throughout his body. Plastiglas was shattering and he heard the whistle of escaping oxygen. He gripped the edge of the console and that was the very instant he felt a sudden weightlessness. He held tighter—felt his chair float lazily beneath him.

He tried to see.

Something wet and sticky fogged his vision.

Gravity returned.

He fell to the floor, struggled to his feet, knuckled the stickiness from his eyes.

The room had contained numerous plastiglas statuettes and globes to represent the various worlds between which the *Starbright* trav-

34

eled. All the plastiglas ornaments were broken and some force or object had smashed the gram console.

The room was red . . . bright. He frowned at the color and went around to the other side of the counter.

The object on the floor was barely recognizable as a human being. His mind slowly reconstructed the events. Faustina Sewell had been standing directly in the path of the plastiglas objects when they shattered. A quirk of inertia of centrifugal force or some other impetus had sent the fragments of plastiglas against her body like sharp edges of a thousand knives.

During the period of weightlessness, the blood must have poured from her mutilated body like a crimson waterfall.

Jimmy Franklin felt suddenly dizzy. He stumbled out of the gram room and made his way toward sick bay.

Alexander Stauffer lay quietly in his cabin. The woman named Eva had fallen asleep. The cabin was one of several completely self-contained with its own gravity and air-recycling systems. In the past it had seemed an unnecessary precaution since there hadn't been an interstellar ship struck by a meteorite for years, but now, listening to MacPherson's telepathic report, he was glad his suite functioned independently of the ship. According to Mac, there had been some sort of accident, a temporary and partial loss of both oxygen and gravity. There had been some deaths in the starboard lounge and other parts of the ship.

Find the captain and tell him I want to know the extent of the damage.

He placed a hand on Eva's shoulder and shook her. She moaned. "Wake up. There's been an accident."

While Eva slowly rose to a sitting position, he closed his eyes and concentrated on the flow of telecoms from his employees.

The extent of the damage was considerable. The ship was completely disabled. A sizable portion was airless—the meteorite had been so large that the automatic hull-sealers could not function. The bridge had been wrecked and all crew members there at the time of the accident had died. The number included the captain, the executive officer, the chief engineer, the steward, and many others.

Mac, find the next in command. I want to talk to him.

Yes, sir.

He opened his eyes. Eva did not seem alarmed—she did not yet know the extent of the accident. "What is your supervisor's name?"

"Krause."

He closed his eyes again. *Krause!*

Yes, sir.

Why didn't you report shortly after the accident?

I've been busy, sir. Mac said he'd report. I listened in on your conversation with him, so I knew you were all right.

Are you sure I'm all right?

What do you mean, sir?

How do you know this goddamned accident isn't part of a plot to kill me?

I doubt that, sir. If someone had the capability to sabotage the ship's protective devices and then penetrate the hull with a meteorite, they would have the power to demolish the ship completely and kill all of us instantly.

I love your logic.

It's the truth as I see it, sir.

I suppose you're right. Have you had anyone under surveillance?

Only two passengers. A woman named Lila Hartnett and a man named Charles Greene.

Background?

Lila was an actress. She married Henderson Hartnett, scientist, inventor of the hyperdrive engine. Since her husband's death, she's been what you might call a playgirl, hopping from planet to planet. Greene was president of Interstellar Electronics. They manufacture computers and he owned more than half the stock.

Where are they now?

Greene was killed during the accident. That was one of the things I was checking on instead of reporting.

I apologize for my reprimand. Where's Lila Hartnett?

She's with Gwenna in the main lounge.

Thank you. His head had started to ache. It was not the situation or the complexity of events, it was the telecom messages themselves. He had consented to have the operation that permitted him to communicate telepathically with some of his employees, but telecom conversations of more than a few minutes' duration had always given him a headache. His physicians had tried various methods to alleviate what he considered a weakness but it seemed his brain was constructed in such a way that telecoms were a strain.

Gwenna!

Yes, sir?

Are you still with Lila Hartnett?

In the main lounge. We were having a few drinks together. Are you all right, sir?

I'm fine except for a goddamned headache. Turning to Eva, he said aloud, "Get me that bottle of pink pills in the medicine cabinet . . . and a glass of water." *Gwenna, what were you discussing with Lila Hartnett?*

Hesitation. Then his secretary's answer: *She wanted to hire me as her personal secretary. Mac told me there'd been an accident and some of the passengers had been killed. We didn't feel the effects here in the main lounge.*

Krause! Mac! Wasn't the main lounge affected?

They answered simultaneously, the two replies bursting in his mind in a jumble:

No, sir. The main lounge wasn't damaged at all.

No. The emergency grav system functioned perfectly for that section of the ship.

Eva had returned with the glass of water and pills. He swallowed two and gulped the water to speed the dissolution in his stomach. His head throbbed with fire. He knew from past experience that the pills would dull the pain but not suffocate it completely. He would have the headache for hours.

37

Gwenna. Make an excuse to leave Lila. Come to my suite. I want you to start handling some of the telecom messages before they make this headache worse and drive me crazy.

Yes, sir.

Don't tell her where you're going.

He felt Gwenna's telecom equivalent of *yes*. It was more than the word *yes*. It was like a soft murmur, a nod of her beautiful head. He had not experienced it with anyone else and he knew it must be a result of their long, close association.

"Eva, this headache is killing me and there are some matters I have to attend to. I don't want to seem abrupt, but will you find Krause and see if you can help him with security? I'll see you later."

After Eva left, Alexander Stauffer closed his eyes once more and tried to weigh the scraps of data.

Rare accident to an interstellar ship—one of a type that hadn't occurred for years.

The accident had occurred *after* he reached the safety of his self-contained suite.

Some of the passengers had died. Charles Greene, the president of Interstellar Electronics could have been a member of the syndicate.

Lila Hartnett could be a member.

Greene had been killed. Was it possible that someone above Greene had engineered the accident so that Greene would be killed and Lila Hartnett would live?

It would probably be days or weeks before they were rescued. The stock market would zigzag when news of the accident reached investors and speculators. Someone with foreknowledge could make billions by selling and buying the right stocks at precisely the right time.

Could the answer be that simple?

He thought, *No, it isn't.*

After thinking about the matter several more minutes he said fretfully, *Mac, are you investigating the cause of this shipwreck?*

Krause and I are working on that now. We're on our way to a conference with two of the ship's engineers.

Please give me your report as soon as possible.

He stretched out on the bed in the room, once more closing his eyes, resolving not to use the telecom again today. With luck the headache might be gone in an hour or so and Gwenna's telecom apparatus was such that she would automatically intercept messages to him and could relay them verbally.

I know what the answer will be, he thought. *Someone has arranged this as part of a plan to kidnap me.*

CHAPTER FIVE

Technician 1/C Natalaie Farrell was awakened from a deep sleep by the sound of the insistent alarm on the other side of the small cabin. She rose quickly and stood for half a moment before the monitor, staring at the flashing words and symbols with a mixture of near disbelief and shock. The ship had been struck by a meteor, the bridge destroyed, and the ship was losing considerable oxygen—rapidly. And then, abruptly, the loss of air stopped. The secondary energy shield had activated automatically, or the damaged compartments had been sealed off, or the hull had sealed itself. Or a combination of the three. *But,* she thought without panic, *this means we could all die—in the next minute or the next hour.*

And how many were aboard, counting both crew and passengers? Five hundred?

Natalaie was a small dark-haired woman. Her slenderness and youthful appearance had often led to her being mistaken for a very young girl. During her off-duty hours she frequently and mischievously delighted in dressing as a teenager, relishing the fact that, at thirty-two, strangers frequently guessed her age at sixteen.

She had been born and raised on one of the frontier planets that were populated by only a handful of Earthmen. Her father had been a radio technician and had signed for a ten-year tour of duty on an unpopular planet named Settle. She had been the only child to be conceived and born on the arid planet at the edge of a galaxy far from commercial routes. She had spent her childhood with almost no toys—none except the ones made by her father and mother. Since both were engineers rather than artists, they had made her numerous mechanical toys. One of her earliest memories was that of playing with a miniature robot designed by her mother and built by her father. She had learned how to disassemble and reassemble the toy in minutes, pleased when her father congratulated her on her mechanical aptitude and dexterity.

Settle had been described as an "Arizona type of planet." True—there was little humidity and the terrain was much like that of Arizona, but Natalaie had decided there was something inexplicable happening at Settle—something in the atmosphere or water or soil or plants. She had been nine years old when her parents returned to Earth for a one-year vacation. Playing with other girls her own age, she had noticed startling differences. She had been deeper-tanned because of the relentless suns which Settle revolved around, but she had also been shorter, smallerwaisted, stronger, more athletic. The mother of another girl had described Natalaie as a, "bouncing brown baby," because of her deep tan, energy and small size. She and her parents had returned to Settle for another ten-year tour of duty and when she returned to Earth next time, Natalaie, at the age of twenty-one, discovered that she, by Earth standards, looked exactly like a girl of sixteen. And the appearance had remained for the next eleven years, so that she now looked approximately half her age.

Natalaie had grown accustomed to loneliness during her twenty years on Settle. She had turned it into a friend rather than an enemy. She could read microbooks for a whole day or a weekend—reading not only for the facts and events as most readers seemed to do, but reading also for the feel and sensations and moods and imageries projected by the author. She had taught herself how to write and had sold forty novels, all under pseudonyms—some reaching the bestsel-

41

ler lists and earning impressive sums of money. She had also become a part-time inventor and had sold her inventions for considerable sums.

After receiving several engineering degrees through correspondence courses, when she and her parents returned to Earth for the last time, she had taken a short vacation and then applied for a position as a technician on the *Starbright.*

She had been accepted immediately and given the position of recycle engineer, rapidly becoming a Technician First Class. She loved the huge hulk of the *Starbright,* the largest starliner out of Earth. She relished the long flights through subspace and across uncharted galaxies. Somehow the prolonged journeys reminded her of the loneliness of her room on Settle, the emptiness that she had managed to make interesting and comforting.

As one of the technicians in charge of the recycle equipment, her small cabin adjoined the compartment that contained the recyle controls and much of the actual equipment. The three other recycle technicians also had cabins that bordered their specialized work area and the concept of technicians living a step away from their work had been followed throughout the ship in its original design.

Turning off the alarm only seconds later, Natalaie unlocked the door of her cabin and stepped into the recycle control room. Lamar was not there. *Lamar should be on duty now,* she thought angrily. *He shouldn't have left without calling someone to replace him!*

Seating herself behind the familiar maze of control consoles, she watched the ship react to the emergency.

Starbright was so heavily computerized that it could act like a living entity. It reacted to emergencies. It made decisions. It could think. It could even talk to you under some circumstances. You could ask its opinion on this or that—and in some cases it would talk to you on its own initiative.

The ship was handling everything nicely. Perhaps no corrections would be necessary. Except—

The meteor had obliterated the bridge, damaged and weakened

surrounding bulkheads. Oxygen was escaping from some of the compartments peripheral to the main control room. *Starbright* was not programmed to make certain decisions that could mean the death of humans. Natalaie, however, noticed the massive air leaking from more than a dozen seldom-used areas. On an impulse, she began the shutdown of each compartment. First she stopped the supply of air into endangered zones, then started the suction back from each area.

Fingers poised above the buttons that could lock the necessary doors, she flickered her way through the intercom system, sending her voice to each compartment and inquiring:

"Urgent! Is there anyone in this zone?"

In each case she waited for an answer and when none came, she pushed the buttons that locked the doors. In a few minutes she managed to seal off the damaged territory and then returned her attention to the recycle equipment itself. It was laboring under the new tasks presented by the emergency, hovering near some breakdown points. She quickly stopped all filtering processes, shutting them down and then opening the valves that bypassed the filters, lessening the strain on the equipment. The needles swung back to the normal zone.

We can filter out the cigarette smoke later when we're sure we're going to live, Natalaie was thinking when she saw movement from the corner of an eye and glanced in that direction to see Lamar.

He looked terrible. Pale, frightened, trembling. Lamar was, she knew, the son of a wealthy businessman, but, oddly, had none of the characteristics that such a young man usually possessed. She had known him for half a year and he had always seemed somewhat unsure of himself, indecisive. She couldn't imagine why he had decided he wanted to be a technician aboard a spaceship. She had, however, found herself liking Lamar for some strange reason, despite the facets of his character that she considered flaws. Although he might seem weak and indecisive, he had also seemed gentle, considerate, and sensitive—three characteristics that she liked in a man and yet did not find in many.

"I was looking for Shaw and Alan," Lamar explained as she stared

43

at him questioningly. "I went to get them to help as soon as the meteor struck but they weren't in their cabins."

Why should he go for help when he could have handled the emergency by himself? she wondered and thought angrily, *He was on duty!*

Without taking her eyes off Lamar, she activated her telecom with the central *Starbright* computer and inquired:

When was the automatic SOS transmitted?

Starbright answered. *The automatic distress signal was not sent due to mechanical failure.*

When did the captain transmit an SOS?

The intergalactic radio is not functioning.

What is our location?

When the ship informed Natalaie that they were in an uncharted galaxy and their navigational equipment was not functioning, she felt her eyes widen with understanding. She asked *Starbright* a few more questions and reached the conclusion that they could be stranded in the uncharted galaxy, drifting aimlessly . . . forever.

"Why were you looking for Shaw and Alan?" Natalaie demanded. "Why not handle the emergency yourself?"

"I didn't know how to handle it," Lamar confessed. He lowered his eyes and went on, "I'm a fake, Natalaie. I'm not qualified as a recycle engineer."

"But—?"

"My papers were faked. I studied recycle engineering—the fundamentals—and learned just enough to put up a front. I wanted a vacation. I talked it over with some friends and they came up with the idea of using my father's influence to get me this position. They said why worry, if anything important happened that I couldn't handle, there would be three qualified recycle engineers to handle the situation. You know, Nat, the equipment *does* run itself under ordinary circumstances. . . ."

She nodded numbly. It was true. The recycle equipment was operated by its own computer linked to the other ship computers. She had often thought of the human element as only necessary for any "fine tuning" or decisions that the computer could not or would not make. So . . . Lamar had been sitting out his shifts, doing nothing essentially, except watching the gauges and printouts. Maybe he hadn't even bothered to do that much.

Rising from the seat, she started back toward the cabin, deep in thought, but gradually became aware that Lamar was staring at her.

She was nude, she realized abruptly.

Since she first heard the alarm, she had thought of nothing except the ship's "wound" and how to heal it so far as her own specialized profession was concerned. She knew that crewmen throughout the ship would be working frantically also, but each to his own skill. She had no intention of trying to help in realms where she knew nothing. But she had been sleeping nude as was her custom and had responded to the alarm instantly, shoving everything else out of her mind.

Inside her cabin, she turned to see that Lamar had followed her. He was staring at her naked body with obvious appreciation.

"What's going to happen to us?" Lamar asked shakily. His gaze traveled from her ripe round breasts to her V of pubic hair.

"I don't know," she answered tonelessly. She closed the cabin door and locked it. The monitor inside her cabin would warn her of any extreme difficulty in the recycle system. *I have to get dressed*, she thought. *If the captain is still alive, he may want to have a conference when everything settles down.*

She opened her wardrobe and selected a pair of pink panties. As she slipped into them, Lamar was saying, "The ship is damaged so badly, something else could go wrong before we're rescued. We could all die . . . any minute . . ."

Natalaie shrugged. "Time will tell," she answered coolly.

"You're fantastic. How can you stay so calm?" Lamar came closer and placed his hands on her shoulders. She looked up at him and could see he was trembling. When he spoke again, his voice was down to a near whisper, "Someone said you're a member of the Sex-

45

ual Liberation party."

"I joined some years ago." She shrugged her shoulders and smiled crookedly. "But I'm not a fervent member."

At the age of twenty-one, when she returned to Earth for the last time, she had been a virgin. Circulating into society again, she had been deluged with requests for dates. On one of the first dates, a handsome young man had expertly aroused her through gifts, flattery, wine, dancing, kissing, and fondling. At his apartment, to the accompaniment of dim lights and music, he had taken her virginity. She had enjoyed the sex so much she had spent the weekend with him.

After a series of lovers and affairs during which she found sex stimulating and pleasant, one of her girl friends had described the Sexual Liberation party and suggested she join. Natalaie had attended some meetings, joined for the sake of trying something new, and had tried some of the programs. The majority of the programs had turned out to be group sex parties and a much smaller percentage had been sex experiments of one nature or another. She had enjoyed the group sex, the casual promiscuity, but not in the same way that most of the girls did. In the end she had decided it pleased her because she had spent most of her life essentially alone. The Liberation party was, for her, like a starved person being invited to a feast.

"I want you," Lamar said thickly, reaching out and fondling her breasts with trembling fingers. In the next moment he was holding her against him, crushing her against his body.

Natalaie started to say, *This is a hell of a time for it,* but held back for several reasons. The Sexual Liberation party had not only advocated the freedom of women to invite men to bed but had also stressed acquiescence on both sides. If one member of the party expressed a sexual desire for another member, that member was expected to comply. When Natalaie's girl friend explained this facet, she had said, "That doesn't mean you have to spend all night in bed with someone—or even spend an hour with someone—not unless you want to. Unless they're really well acquainted, the male members of the party never expect more than a short union. A few minutes and

46

it's over. A true liberation in its own way . . . and fun once you get used to it."

During her membership, Natalaie had had brief sex with dozens of members. The times she remembered most vividly were the times at the club building where a male member would say something or touch her in a certain way and she had "acquiesced" in hallways or in the elevators or by the pool or in many other places—most often not remembering the man's face, many times not knowing his name—but relishing the easy sexuality, the pleasures of being desired and giving satisfaction to the opposite sex quickly and without complex and enduring emotional involvement. Somehow the episodes had made her feel more *alive,* more *human.*

"Are you a member of the party?" she asked, pulling her mouth away from his. She had remained more or less aloof from other *Starbright* crew members, rarely socializing, spending the majority or free time in her cabin, reading and writing. She had even avoided Lamar and the other recycle engineers as much as possible.

"Yes," he said huskily, dropping a hand between her legs and fondling her boldly.

"Liar."

He grinned. "Well . . . I'd like to become a member. Maybe you could show me the ropes. Who knows? This may be our last chance to make it with *anybody.*"

She began pushing him away and was about to tell him to go to hell when several thoughts occurred simultaneously.

He was right about this possibly being their last chance to make love with anyone. If the energy shield had broken down once to allow a meteor to penetrate the hull of the ship, it could do so again and the second time could be instantly fatal.

Lamar said he had not been able to locate Shaw and Alan, the two other recycle technicians. If they should be dead, that would mean that she and Lamar would have to work closely during the coming period, whether it be hours or days or weeks or months. If he wasn't properly qualified on the equipment as he said—and why should he

47

lie about *that?*—it would be wisest if she taught him some more of the operational essentials, especially the ones that applied to emergency situations. In that case, it would be best if they kept resentments to a minimum.

"All right," she said, turning away and hooking her thumbs in the waistband of her panties, rolling the garment down from her hips and thighs. "Let's take five minutes . . ."

She stepped out of the undergarment and went to the narrow bunk, stretching out and spreading her legs. Lamar undressed quickly. She glanced in his direction but her mind also wandered to the ship, wondering what the future would hold . . . if *Starbright* could survive this disaster.

Lamar climbed above her and she closed her eyes. She held her breath when he plunged into her. He was large and as hard as a steel bar. She lay very still, letting him set the rhythm, letting him use her body.

He used long slow strokes and she could sense he was trying to hold back, to make it last as long as possible. She wondered if the storage cylinders of compressed and liquefied oxygen had been damaged. Had the auxiliary engines been damaged?

Lamar was unable to restrain himself any longer. With her eyes still closed, she felt him become very excited, moving faster and faster. He exploded suddenly and was very heavy and limp upon her.

"You're so beautiful," he murmured, running his fingers through her hair. "So very beautiful . . . I've wanted to do that since I first met you . . ." He paused, covered her face with kisses and repeated, as if he thought she hadn't heard him the first time, "You're so beautiful."

"Thanks," Natalaie replied almost absently. She was not conceited in the ordinary sense but she had grown accustomed to compliments from men. She'd had some difficulty weeding out the insincere ones from the sincere ones. A majority of the men who'd had sex with her had complimented her either before, during, or after the mating. In many cases, she'd sensed, the men had thought it obligatory.

Lamar began kissing her again. She was about to say they should

48

get up, shower, and return to the recyle control room when he murmured, "I love you." He didn't say it as if he expected an answer, and he said it over and over, a dozen times. Natalaie became aware that he was hardening again—rapidly rising to a full erection—and then he was making love to her again, violently, passionately. She mentally noted that this was the first time a man had stayed with her and obtained a second erection while still inside her. Did that mean Lamar was really in love with her? Was that a sign of true love? Or only a sign that he was a very virile person? Could she find the answers in any microbooks in the ship's library?

That puzzled her for a while but then, as Lamar made love, her thoughts shifted to the recycle equipment. If they were stranded for a considerable length of time—months? years? decades?—there would be ways to make the equipment last forever. Alternating the engines and shutting down periodically for inspection and lubrication were only two of the ways the feat could be accomplished. The systems of lubrication on some of the engines could be changed to more efficient systems. Part of the equipment was not cooled. The heat buildup was not excessive, but the bearings and shafts and other moving parts were subjected to continuous heat that eventually wore the equipment down earlier than necessary. The reasons, of course, were a mixture of planned obsolescence, economy, and priority. Expert industrial engineers had estimated that certain types of equipment aboard every spaceship would be obsolete after a certain number of years. And then recycle machines were within that classification along with a dozen other types. The logic: Why try to make something last ten years when you'll be replacing it within five years while it's still operational? Economy—it was cheaper *not* to cool a machine that would survive an appropriate length of time without the luxury. They had actually mentioned in the recycle maintenance course that it was more important to distribute water to the passengers' showers than to machines. *But* she thought excitedly, *if we could cut down on the number of showers and other facilities involving water—and reroute the water through plastic lines to the equipment, we could add years*

49

to the equipment life. In some cases air could be used to cool . . . and there are other coolants to increase the lifespan.

She became so engrossed in thinking about the equipment and planning ways to increase its lifespan that she was startled that Lamar was still above her. Looking back through the unconscious memory of her mind, she realized she had lain there as lifeless and expressionless as a mannequin while he passionately made love to her.

And, she could see, anger was spreading across his face as he slowly withdrew.

"You're a cold bitch, aren't you?" he growled. "I tell you that I love you and you don't even blink. Twice—for me—and you didn't even twitch a muscle. What's the trouble? You don't believe me when I say I love you. Doesn't it matter that someone loves you, or—his face twisted more grotesquely as his anger reached a peak—" have you screwed around so much that it was all just another fuck to you?"

He slid off the cot and grabbed at his clothes. Natalaie knew she had drastically misjudged Lamar during their acquaintance. He had often spoke to her and sought her company aboard ship. He'd invited her to ship parties, to attend the *Starbright* theater, asked her to accompany him to various affairs involving the crew. He had always been polite and pleasant, and she had somehow assumed his intentions to be platonic rather than romantic. She had never known "love" before—not in the sense of a man saying he loved her. There had been sex but not emotional love, and she knew she had become a master at cutting herself off mentally and emotionally from the man mating with her. This, however, according to the expression on Lamar's face—and his violent reaction—was something entirely new in her life.

As he started to dress, she slipped from the bed and went to him—felt the sting of tears in her eyes. How long had it been since she last cried? The only times she could remember shedding tears were back on the planet Settle when she had been a child and done of her favorite mechanical toys had broken beyond repair.

But, here she was, crying because a human being had spoken

50

harshly—a relationship had been damaged, not a mechanical toy.

I hope this damage can be repaired, she thought fleetingly.

She placed her hands on his shoulders, wanting to slip her arms around him and hold him tight, but somehow unable. More tears rolled down her cheeks before she could stop that physical response.

"I'm sorry, Lamar," she said, "It's—I don't know how to explain it. It's the emergency. . . and my childhood . . . the way I had to live as a child. I know I'm cold. I can't help it . . . at least so far I haven't been able to change . . . perhaps because I didn't have any reason to try to change myself. I wasn't rejecting or ignoring your love. Please believe me." She managed to stop the tears and unconsciously bit her lower lip. She hoped she didn't sound like something out of one of the ancient soap operas. She felt like a child exploring new territory, but forced herself to add, "Why don't we spend some time checking the ship's equipment and crew. Then, when we need a rest, we can come back and I'll explain why I am the way I am. I think you'll understand."

He was staring at her intently, and he nodded his head briefly before slipping into his clothes.

As Natalaie reached for her own clothing, she heard the faint, smooth hum of the *Starbright* through the walls and knew the truth.

How could she gracefully explain to Lamar that, because of her childhood and background, machinery was the real lover in her life? Machinery meant more than men.

CHAPTER SIX

In the flight engineer's control room, Krause and Mac introduced themselves. The two engineers on duty seemed impressed, Mac thought. *Maybe they should be,* he realized. *We're emissaries from the richest man in the universe!*

The engineer named Sheffield had the highest rank, Mac noted—and the most years in service according to the service slashes on the sleeve of his spotless white uniform. Krause had taken charge of this conference. Mac had no objections. If Krause asked the right questions, he could relax and concentrate on the answers.

The small control room was filled with the faces of computers and complicated electronic equipment along with hundreds of control buttons and levers. Mac had seen the bridge of this ship during one of the security checks and it seemed there were more controls in here than there had been on the bridge. Sheffield and Reynolds were seated on rollaround swivel chairs. There were two other rollaround chairs in the room but Krause and Mac had remained standing.

Krause was directing his questions at Sheffield, who seemed concerned but confident.

"So . . . the two of you were on duty when the accident happened?"

"That's right."

"What happened exactly?"

"The energy screen failed. A portion of it, that is. The portion protecting the ship's bridge. A starship energy screen can fail altogether or a portion of it can fail."

"But—*Why? Why* did the screen fail and let the meteorite damage the ship?"

"I don't know why," Sheffield said evasively.

"*How*, then? If *why* isn't the right word . . . *how?*"

"I don't know the answer to that either," Sheffield admitted.

He must be in his forties somewhere, Mac thought absently. He was a man of medium height, medium weight—as near as Mac could determine since the man was sitting. Gray hair—calm gray eyes. A good tan—as if he spent most of his time on beaches between flights.

"It wasn't a mechanical failure," Reynolds said abruptly.

Everyone turned to stare at the junior engineer. According to the rank symbols on his shoulders and the service slashes, he was of lesser rank than Sheffield and with less time in service. Mac glanced quickly at Sheffield to see his reaction to this statement. The senior engineer's face was impassive. He turned slowly to look at a control panel and make an adjustment in one of the processes.

"Do you have evidence it was not a mechanical failure?" Krause prodded.

"We do *not* have evidence that it *was* mechanical trouble," Reynolds said.

Mac studied the man more closely. He was younger than Sheffield. Far younger. And he had one of those pinkish round faces like a baby's. His eyes were blue. A bright blue. Reynolds looked masculine enough, but those eyes were a shade of blue that would have looked great on a blonde.

Krause repeated slowly, "You do *not* have evidence that it *was* mechanical trouble."

"That's right."

Krause groaned, wiped a hand across his forehead and, as if too

53

weary to look around and see if there were no smoking signs, inquired, "Is it all right to smoke in here?"

"It doesn't make any difference in this compartment," Sheffield replied. "If you want to, you can build a fucking bonfire on the floor and toast marshmallows. It won't hurt the equipment."

The statement—delivered casually and seemingly without malice or sarcasm—relieved the tension in the air somewhat, bringing some brief grunts of amusement.

Krause lit his cigarette, inhaled deeply and then waved it in an obscure gesture. "Maybe I'm too tired . . . maybe I'm having trouble thinking. Forgive me if I'm dense. I want to get this straight. We have more than a thousand people aboard this ship and I'm partially responsible for the safety of many of them." *And especially Alex's safety,* Mac thought. "So . . . I'm damned concerned whether it was an act of nature or the act of a murderer that sent that meteor through our hull." Taking another drag on the cigarette, he looked at Reynolds again. "You said it wasn't a mechanical failure. And then you said you do not have evidence that it *was* mechanical trouble. Can you explain that?"

Reynolds appeared almost frightened at Krause's belligerent mood. He explained falteringly, "If a generator had malfunctioned temporarily, or a relay had failed, that would have shown on the control boards. There is no 'board' evidence that any of the equipment failed."

"And yet . . . part of the energy screen went down a moment— which means that part of the equipment failed or did not function properly. How can you explain how that happened without being evident?"

Reynolds turned to look at Sheffield. He squirmed in his chair nervously, waiting for the senior engineer to take the ball.

"Only variations of one basic method," Sheffield replied. He was staring at a spot in midair, his eyes blank with concentration. "Most people think a computer always tells the truth. It won't if it's been programmed to lie." He waved a hand at the electrical nerve endings of

54

the ship that surrounded them in the small compartment. "All these computers and controls could lie to us if they were programmed to lie. And they could also be made to conceal the fact that they *had* lied."

Sheffield was silent awhile. "Keep talking," Krause said quietly.

"Someone could have programmed the energy screen over the bridge to shut down when the ship passed through a meteor stream. And programmed it to activate itself again as soon as the sensors detected a meteor had passed through the hull."

"Correct me if I'm wrong," Krause said when Sheffield paused again. "That would be the same as saying that someone sabotaged the ship . . . planned to kill everyone on the bridge."

Sheffield nodded.

"That's incredible," Krause said.

"But possible," Sheffield stated. "Remember the Cepheus incident?"

"Vaguely."

"The colony at Cepheus declared its independence. Two decades later it was in need of food and tools and equipment of every kind. The president refused aid in lieu of pursuing a balanced budget. Why give supplies to a colony that had officially become a separate government? A ship to another colony was hijacked. A ship that carried more than a hundred women—wives and daughters of the men establishing the roots of a primitive planet. With them about twenty men and boys, and all the tools and equipment that the Cepheus colony needed. The ship was disabled by a passenger who programmed the computers to lower the energy screen around the bridge when a meteor struck that area. The screen flicked off and back on. Just long enough to kill everyone on the bridge—everyone in command—and destroy the nerve center of the ship. Similar to what has happened to us. Then the ship drifted through space, a Cepheus ship transferred the passengers and cargo. The 'hijacked' ship was blown up and the truth wasn't discovered until fifteen or sixteen years later."

"I remember hearing part of that story," Krause said. "I'd heard about the hijacking but I hadn't heard how it was accomplished."

"That's the way it was done. They made a movie about the incident. A movie starring Lila Pollard. In the movie—for some reason—the hijackers are shown as men with submachine guns who shoot the crew. Maybe the director thought that would be more dramatic."

Krause, as if suddenly aware of Mac's presence, turned in his direction. He did not speak, but his expression clearly said, *Do you want to ask a question?*

Sometime during the conversation, Mac had settled into a chair, making himself comfortable while Krause remained standing. When Krause turned to look at him, the two engineers turned also.

They were all looking at him now as if expecting him to say something important. Mac shrugged as if to indicate, *What can I say?* But, he thought, the conference should be summarized as concisely as possible.

"Is this a fair summary . . ." Mac began, leaning forward in his chair, studying the two engineers. "Since there is no evidence of a mechanical failure, that lack can be taken as indication that the ship was sabotaged?"

"That's right," Sheffield supplied. "We have no proof, but the lack of data pointing to an 'ordinary' mechanical failure can be taken as a strong indication that *Starbright* was deliberately sabotaged."

CHAPTER SEVEN

Josef Kaiser had been roaming the ship's corridors for an hour before the perfect opportunity came. A dozen men and women left a cabin where they had apparently gathered for a party. It was two in the morning and all the partymakers were drunk—some stumbling silently along the corridor while others sang and babbled noisily. They reached the door to the main lounge and he saw one try to open the lounge door, then kick at it when he discovered it locked. The bar staff was observing interplanetary regulations despite their shipwrecked status and, Josef knew, the lounge had closed.

The group turned from the lounge as a whole and, forming a small group at the opposite end of the corridor, progressed toward him slowly and waveringly. He killed four of them before they knew they were being attacked. A woman was the first to realize what was happening and he chopped her scream in half with two bursts from the laser. The rest tried to flee but found themselves at a dead end. The pleas and screams ended one by one. A young girl fell to her knees, sobbing hysterically, begging to be spared. He tore her throat apart with a well-placed shot. The last of the group tried to claw his way through a solid wall.

When all motion had ceased, Kaiser dropped the tiny weapon in his jacket pocket and went to each of the bodies, checking pulse and heartbeat. All were silent except for one—he shot him twice through the chest and then rechecked for a pulse.

Returning to his cabin, he hid the weapon, poured a drink and settled into a chair to make further plans.

Josef was a stocky man with wide hands and thick wrists. His gray eyes, at a casual glance, appeared calm, but men and women who knew him well were more inclined to think of his eyes as cold and calculating. He had been a mercenary in a dozen intergalactic wars—had survived all with many medals for bravery, plus considerable financial reimbursement. He had never thought of himself as a brave man. He knew that, somehow, someway, he had grown with a lack of fear. He was not afraid of death, and killing others did not disturb him. His lack of fear had been replaced by a cold reasoning as devoid of emotion as any computer.

It had occurred to him that if they were shipwrecked for a long period, the question of food and oxygen could become crucial. Therefore, if he eliminated some of the other passengers, he would automatically increase his own chances of survival until rescue. If they were not rescued, every person he killed would, nevertheless, lengthen his own lifespan.

Killing the dozen men and women in the corridor had been satisfying and practical but he knew he could not risk killing such a large number of people again. Carrying the laser would be dangerous. The starship police would probably start searching for weapons. Some men and women would start carrying lasers in self-defense, but the possession of the weapon would focus attention on himself. From now on, he reasoned, it would be wisest to continue eliminating the passengers one by one.

He would have to be careful, he knew, not to eliminate some of the essential crew members with their irreplaceable technical skills. In the future he would have to *know* each person he eliminated—be certain that he or she was not essential to the ship's maintenance.

Two other thoughts occurred.

Starbright was a huge starliner with more than a thousand passengers. Hundreds of the passengers were "singles" with no relatives or close friends aboard. If the body of each "single" could be eliminated somehow—discarded into outer space or deposited in the ship's incinerator, the person would not be missed and he could operate more freely. Yes—he should *know* each person he killed.

Last but not least, it would avert suspicion if he was not identified as a loner. He needed a traveling companion, preferably a woman.

CHAPTER EIGHT

"Who would have an opportunity to sabotage *Starbright?*" Mac inquired.

"That may be a logical question," Sheffield answered, "but there is no way to answer it."

"Well . . . could a *passenger* have done it?"

"A passenger could have . . . if he'd been thoroughly trained. But access to the necessary equipment would be almost impossible. We, the crew, have keys to vital areas. A passenger would have to obtain the right keys and avoid being seen by the crew members. I doubt a passenger could pull it off."

"Then it's your idea that it would be more likely the ship was sabotaged by a crew member?"

"Right."

"And," Reynolds volunteered, "only certain crew members would have the necessary knowledge to sabotage the energy screen."

"Which crew members have that knowledge?" As soon as Krause asked the question, he suspected the answer.

Reynolds hesitated, his eyes widening slightly as he glanced at his companion. Sheffield answered, "*We* could have done it. And Harrison and Darnell had the understanding of the equipment."

"Who are they?" Krause asked curtly.

"Harrison and Darnell are our relief operators. *Were*. They were both on the bridge when the meteor struck. If they did it, they committed suicide."

Mac was surprised when, as Krause smoked a cigarette, apparently reflectively, he spoke to Mac by telecom, *I'm going to have a couple of men come here to keep and eye on these two.*

Placing them under guard, Mac translated in his mind, but did not answer the telecom. Instead, since the two crew members were not looking in their direction, he acknowledged by a brief nod of his head. Sheffield and Reynolds might resent being placed under guard. It would sure as hell be a clear indication they were under suspicion.

"If someone sabotaged the energy screen," Krause went on, "is there a certain area or areas where there might be evidence of tampering?" He shrugged. "Places where someone might leave fingerprints?"

Mac admired the question. Krause was digging into the matter expertly and relentlessly.

Reynolds licked his lips. He looked increasingly nervous.

"The maintenance corridor," Sheffield said.

"Can you give me some more information?"

"What we call the maintenance corridor is a narrow passageway behind much of the equipment you see here. It's kept locked. It's used only for routine maintenance, inspection, and the occasional replacement of a component. No one has any reason to go in there except for a scheduled inspection—or unless there's an operational problem of some kind. If you find evidence that someone was in the corridor after our departure, I would take that as direct evidence of sabotage."

"I have a man who can check that area for fingerprints," Krause stated. "I'll send for him."

The verbal conversation died away. Sheffield and Reynolds were busy watching their equipment. Krause said to Mac by telecom, *The guards will be here in a minute.*

When the two guards arrived, it all went much smoother than Mac

61

anticipated. Krause introduced everyone casually. The fingerprint expert arrived a short time later carrying a black attaché case.

"Now," Krause said, "if you'll show us the maintenance corridor . . ."

Sheffield led the way out of the control room and down a short hallway to an inconspicuous hatchway. He turned a key in the lock and also placed his right thumb on the identipad. As he opened the hatchway and went inside, Sheffield said, "I'd forgotten about the identipad. It's programmed to allow only crew members in here. It wouldn't do a passenger any good to steal a key unless he could get around the identipad somehow."

They walked a distance—Sheffield leading the way and frowning as he studied the maze of access panels. Many of them were color-coded in addition to the small printed labels signifying the purpose of the equipment. Mac had the feeling they were moving behind the heart of the ship. He knew instinctively that a madman in this area could kill everyone—instantly. A laser beam, a bomb, perhaps something as simple as ripping some wiring apart—would stop a vital function of the ship.

"Here we are," Sheffield said, stopping suddenly. "This is the access panel to the energy screen computer and equipment. If you find fresh fingerprints here, you'll have the culprit."

They were at a large green panel. After a moment of silence, Krause said, "Thanks. You can leave us now."

Mac watched as the fingerprint expert went to work. He held a machine the size of a small portable radio that sprayed a violet ray. The fingerprint machine clicked and hummed.

"Can you tell the age of the fingerprints?" Krause asked the expert.

"The machine can," the SS man said humorlessly, "The oils dry and deteriorate. So the machine can tell the difference between a print that's a year old, or a month, or a few days. Hello." He peered at the gauges on the machine and said again, "Hello. Prints. Fresh prints. Two sets."

"By two sets you mean two people?"

"Right."

"How fresh?"

"Since takeoff."

As Krause and Mac watched, the fingerprint expert finished his work and returned the machine to the attaché case.

"Let me know who made those prints. Immediately."

As they returned to the control room, Mac remembered that every passenger's fingerprints were on file along with his or her passport. And the ship's records would have the prints of every crew member. He wondered how long it would be before they knew the answer.

In the control room again, Krause spoke to Sheffield and Reynolds, "Have either of you been in the maintenance corridor since takeoff?"

Reynolds answered nervously, "N—No."

Sheffield said calmly, "Maybe we should have inspected the equipment from the corridor, but we didn't."

Let's get out of here, Krause said to Mac by telecom.

As they headed toward the passenger area, Mac said, "Reynolds acts guilty as hell."

"I noticed. I don't think he's guilty of anything. I think his problem is he's a chicken and he's unnerved. And maybe he suspects something . . . something that's worrying him."

"What do *you* think?"

"Maybe we're being set up for a hijack. Maybe Sheffield hit it when he mentioned the Cepheus incident. We have the richest man in the universe on this ship. And millions of credits in diamonds and currency, not to mention equipment and a thousand other items. Do me a favor? Have someone check in the ship's library . . . check on the Cepheus incident. Meanwhile . . ." Krause's expression was grim. "Just between you and me, Mac, I want to move this ship."

"Move?"

"Ever since the accident, we've been drifting like a lame duck. *If* someone planned to hijack this ship, they'll know exactly where we are. I'm going to get somebody to use the auxiliary bridge to dip us in and out of hyperspace again. I want to leave some cameras and junk in this location. Then . . . when *Starbright* is hidden somewhere, we'll wait and see if hijackers show up."

"This may be a stupid question," Mac said. "But if someone planned to disable *Starbright* and hijack it, why haven't they made an appearance?"

"My guess would be they're waiting."

"Waiting for what?"

"If you were a hijacker and had wrecked a starliner with a thousand passengers, would you want to be right in the middle of hijacking and have rescuers show up? Wouldn't that be embarrassing?"

"So you think that if this is a hijack attempt the hijackers are just sitting back and waiting to see if anyone will come and rescue us? And . . . if no one comes in a week or whatever, then they'll make their move?"

"Maybe."

"Who would . . ." Mac had started to ask who would attempt to hijack a ship as large as *Starbright*, but the realization began to occur before he could finish the question.

Krause guessed his thinking and put it into words. "If *Starbright* is in the process of being hijacked, then I sure as hell doubt it's the work of a few individuals. There are too many elements involved in hijacking a ship this size. *If* we're being hijacked, it has to be the work of another country, another race, or another civilization. If that's the case, we may have a problem."

Hans Steiger sat quietly in his cabin, watching the new thinkwriter machine several yards away. It displayed the words of his thoughts in a continuous moving line, appearing at one side of the screen, disappearing at the other end as the thoughts were recorded in the thinkwriter memory bank:

When the salesman announced he was selling a new style of thinkwriter, I immediately decided I didn't want to buy one. He insisted on a demonstration. To be polite, I allowed him into my cabin.

"I know you use a thinkwriter now," the salesman said. "What is the point that you like least about your current machine?"

"The suction cup with the electrode slips off my head sometimes," I answered. "And I've broken the green wire to the machine several times accidentally—you know, forgetting about it and getting up to get a cup of coffee or answer the phone."

"Aha," the salesman replied. He showed me the new model. "See? This machine does not need the antiquated suction cup. It is attuned to your particular brainwaves. There is no green wire to be broken. It is entirely independent. It has a range of a hundred miles. That means you can dictate to it while traveling. It is programmed to respond to code words or numbers, whichever you prefer."

I didn't want to buy the machine but I had heard of the new models. They'd been around for years but this was the very newest model of the new styles, so I agreed to purchase one. The salesman gave me the instructions and we established the code numbers for the various processes. I was about to sign the sales agreement—I had the pen in my hand—when the ship shuddered. I ran to the cabin door and opened it. The air was filled with screams and a great sound of rushing air. I knew Starbright had been struck by a meteor.

"My God," I said, "We've been struck!"

The salesman was jumping up and down with excitement. I was stupefied, paralyzed by shock. "First things first," he screamed. "Sign the goddamned contract!" I signed the contract and he folded it, placing it into a pocket, saying, "Thank you." He left.

As I wandered around the ship, I discovered we had indeed been struck by a meteor and lost a quantity of oxygen although the energy screen was once again functioning.

The passengers were milling around in confusion, on the fine edge of panic. People were asking each other, "What happened?" and there were wild guesses. When someone asked me what had happened, I said, "I think we were struck by a small meteor, but they're repairing the damage now. Everything will be all right."

The word began to spread. In a crowd I could hear people telling

65

each other, "Everything will be all right," and everyone gradually calmed. Hell, I didn't have the slightest idea whether everything would be all right or not. We might lose the rest of the ship's air in the next minute and all die. But human nature is such that everyone looks for comforting words. The injured parties were carried away to the ship's dispensary for medical treatment. The passengers with the most courage came forth to comfort the ones with the least courage. The stewardesses were extremely busy and adept in caring for the in-jured and frightened. For a while I watched the ebb and flow of hu-man emotions until everyone calmed.

We may all die during the coming weeks, but I firmly believe, if we do, we will pass away with a maximum of dignity.

Senior Stewardess Brenda Gibbons was on her way to her cabin when the man passed her in the corridor. She had seen hundreds of passengers during the flight and thousands during her career, but something in the man's manner struck her as slightly odd. She did not look directly at his face but her peripheral vision registered the wrong-ness.

Am I cracking up? she wondered. It had been a long day—full of screams of pain and fear, soothing the passengers mentally, emotion-ally, and physically. She could hear a group of "stews" behind her in the corridor—heading toward their cabins also. The man seemed in-decisive. For a moment she had the feeling he wanted to stop and talk to her but suddenly, as the voices of the other stews grew louder, he hurried down the corridor. She turned a corner, a sliding door opened automatically, and she stepped into the short stretch of hall opposite the lounge. As one of the senior stewardesses, she had the dubious honor of having her cabin directly across from one of the main passenger-gathering points. The theory was that if a passenger needed attention, she would be close at hand even on her off-duty hours. Some of the other senior stews had cabins that were strategi-cally located throughout the ship.

Her thoughts froze as she turned another corner and saw the

sprawled bodies.

A dozen men and women.

Instinctively rushing forward to see if she could be of assistance, she saw this had not been an accident at all. They had all been shot with a laser weapon.

And they were all dead.

CHAPTER NINE

Gwenna had not liked Troyan from the moment she first saw him three years ago. He had come to Stauffer Industries with excellent references and an impressive employment history. He had sought the position of office manager for one of their companies, a comparatively lowly position, had been interviewed by Alexander personally, hired, and risen rapidly through the ranks to the position of a special assistant to Alexander Stauffer, technically with the title of administrative assistant.

Why is it that I don't like him? Gwenna asked herself as she studied the man sitting beside her desk. *It can't be professional jealousy can it?*

He had risen so rapidly that in far less time than she'd been with Alex, Troyan now had more power than herself. Alex not only *listened* to Troyan's advice, he actively *sought* it.

Troyan was physically a small man with narrow shoulders, mousey brown hair and a timid manner. *But the eyes are as cunning as a fox's,* she thought. *Or a rat's?* And, as a special administrative assistant to Alex, he wielded more power than some men with more important-sounding titles.

"I've just come from a conference with Alex," Gwenna said. "He's instructed me to ask you to hire as many of the passengers and crew members as you can—as rapidly as possible."

"His reasoning?"

Gwenna hesitated. Troyan had a habit of asking questions with few words, sometimes only a single word, most often an incomplete sentence. And she could not quite understand why the man's habit annoyed her.

"His reasoning is multifaceted. He reasons it will distract the passengers, encourage them to a certain degree . . . and help organize the available labor resources."

"Salary?"

"Alex would like to hire each passenger and crew member if possible for a sum ranging from one thousand to ten thousand credits a day during this emergency."

Gwenna waited for a sign of reaction in the man's expression. Alex had already increased the salary of every existing staff member to a hundred thousand credits a day for the duration of the emergency. Each senior staff member would receive ten times the amount of the new staff members. But, relative to the economy, the offer of one thousand to ten thousand credits a day was still a fortune to be offered to new employees. Troyan's expression, however, did not change.

"Duties?"

"Alex thought you would have some ideas about the duties of the new employees."

"Recording this conversation?"

"Yes."

"Advise Alex that I would recommend the formation of several committees. First, a 'Survival Committee,' to determine ways out of this emergency. The passengers may not have any worthwhile contributions, but we can keep them busy and make them feel as if they're contributing. Secondly, an 'Entertainment Committee.' If there's going to be a delay before we're rescued, new methods of entertainment should be devised to occupy everyone's time and lessen impatience and fear. I have some other ideas for special committees. Well, rather than making you type out a report, let me write them out for Alex."

Gwenna watched as the small man withdrew a pad from an inside jacket pocket. He wrote at length, took an envelope from another inside pocket, put the paper in the envelope, sealed it, addressed the front with the name *Alex* and handed it to Gwenna.

"I'll give it to him as soon as we finish our meeting."

"Anything else?"

Gwenna had been dreading that question. And she had known Troyan would ask it. He always did as their meetings neared a conclusion. She took a deep breath and said, "Alex would like you to determine the passengers who might make good hostesses and furnish him with a confidential list."

She fought the physical reaction but found herself blushing nevertheless. *Hostess* was the term that Alex used for women who were willing to go to bed with him. He always went through some flimsy camouflage of throwing occasional parties with the women acting as hostesses, but in the "training" for the parties, they were actually bedded. She knew that Troyan had been a procurer for Alex before, but the two men had always dealt directly in the past. She resented being even a middle person in Alex's excesses.

"That was one of the other committees I listed," Troyan offered with a faint smile.

Two minutes later, staring at the door that Troyan had vanished through, Gwenna breathed deeply and slowly regained her composure. She rose and moved toward Alex's private quarters with the sealed envelope in her hand. *He had to seal it, the bastard.* Among all the other reasons for her dislike for Troyan, she suddenly realized another primary reason: The bastard was a skilled brown-noser.

"My childhood was very unique," Natalaie said. "Settle's total population never exceeded two dozen people. I was the only person ever born on the planet. I didn't see anyone my own age until, at the age of nine, my parents and I returned to Earth for a vacation. Dad was an engineer, in charge of the intergalactic radio relay station on Settle . . . and also the maintenance man for some mysterious recording equipment. I think some of it was to record cosmic rays and some, I guess, recorded weather conditions on Settle. I don't know why. No one ever cared about the weather . . . not even the few people who lived there. Maybe some of it was 'make busy' work or whatever they call it. Regardless . . . Dad was not only mechanically inclined, he loved machines more than he loved humans. That may sound harsh, but that's the way he was."

Natalaie and Lamar had worked for nearly twelve hours, discovering that most of the recycle equipment was intact, but their fellow engineers, Shaw and Allen, were missing. They had apparently been on the bridge when the meteor struck and their bodies, along with those of a dozen other crew members, had not been recovered. It was assumed that the bodies had been blasted into outer space during the rupture of the ship by the meteor. Returning to her cabin, Natalaie had begun the explanation of her childhood, as she had promised Lamar, to explain her seeming coldness.

She felt as if she were being excessively defensive but still, she knew, it was a stance she had assumed of her own volition—perhaps because Lamar was the first man ever to declare his love for her.

I must care for him, she thought, *to want to explain to him why I am the way I am . . .*

She went on to paint a verbal autobiography of the first twenty years of her life, describing her growing love of mechanical toys, since she had no human playmates. She described how the childish love of mechanical toys had gradually led to an adult love of science and machines. She tried not to sound apologetic and attempted a summary that would not sound idiotic. With a shrug she said, "And that's the way I am. I didn't have any human relationships with anyone other than my parents until a few years ago. All my relationships with the opposite sex have been . . . casual. Partly because of my background and basic nature, and partly because I joined the Liberation party. The truth is . . . although I want to change . . . although I know I can change in time . . . am changing . . . at present I am more emotionally involved with a love of machines rather than a love of mankind."

71

Having made this explanation which she considered rather revealing and startling, Natalaie waited for Lamar's reaction. She felt as if
she had admitted to having leprosy. She had been watching Lamar's
expression from time to time during the talk and knew he had been
listening to her intently, his mind not drifting elsewhere. Now she
looked at his face again, wondering if she would see mild disgust or
faint shock—or a blend of similar emotions.

He appeared thoughtful. That was all—other than an obvious af-
fection and strong interest, which he made no attempt to conceal.
She waited for him to speak, wondering what his comments would
be.

"What is Settle like?" Lamar asked. "It sounds like an interesting
planet."

Not one comment on what she had said about her personal nature . . .

I suppose that means he accepts me the way I am? . . .

"Settle isn't a popular planet," Natalaie explained.

"Why?"

"It's an arid planet. Only two small oceans that would be classified
as lakes on most planets. Very few lakes and rivers. Most of Settle is
flat with vast stretches of desert."

"Any good fishing?"

"My father did some fishing and I went with him a few times. He
said the fish are *weird,* so I suppose the answer is no, the fishing isn't
good."

"What were the fish like? Do you remember?"

"*Do I?* In my teens I was always searching for new hobbies and
once I had an idea of keeping some fish live in aquariums in our
home. My father and I made the aquariums ourselves. On Settle
there is a sturdy type of fish much like an eel. We named it, 'Blue Eel.'
We caught some and brought them home. We learned they glowed in
the dark. Like neon. So then we renamed them, 'Blue Neon Eel.' The
first night that we had them at home in the aquariums, I was awakened by my mother's screams. I found her in the kitchen, screaming

72

her head off. There were no lights except the fish. They had slipped out of their tanks and found their way to the kitchen where they were busily devouring a bowl of fruit. My mother later said they looked like glowing blue snakes. Father and I renamed them, 'Walking Blue Neon Eels.' There are some other 'walking fish' on Settle, although, I think, on Earth there is only one type of 'walking fish'. . . a cat-fish? . . ."

"That's a funny story," Lamar said, laughing briefly. "Tell me more about the fish."

"Later. I'm tired. I need a shower and I need . . . want . . ." She hesitated. They were sitting very close with their thighs almost touching. She turned and looked at him, their eyes meeting. She thought, *I need to make love with him again.*

They kissed. He fumbled at her clothing and she fumbled at his. They made love with a hungry passion. This time she was active, wanting the union and, instead of thinking about the ship's machinery as she had the first time they made love, she was thinking of giving him the most pleasure with her body—also concentrating on the pleasure within her own flesh. He held back on his climax and she knew he was doing it deliberately so she could reach her orgasm first. The idea excited her. Few men in her life had ever been so considerate . . .

"You first," Lamar said. He kissed her forehead, moving his body in a manner to give her more sensation. She had an orgasm. He finished a short time later and she felt a new emotional satisfaction in addition to the physical satisfaction.

They showered and ate. Lamar suggested that he could move his bunk into her cabin and they could place the two bunks side by side, so sleeping would be more comfortable. She nodded yes but inwardly felt some reservations that made her feel tense and nervous. It was a good feeling to know that he loved her—or at least desired her enough to call it love—and good to feel that she was falling in love with him, but he was now, in reality, moving into her cabin, moving into her life. After being alone so many years, it was a strange sensation that made her feel vaguely uncomfortable . . . To lose all one's privacy . . .

Should I tell him no? Stop it now before it goes too far?

An hour later they were lying side-by-side, talking, awaiting sleep.

"Tell me more about Settle," Lamar suggested.

"I said it was arid . . . very arid. Sandstorms. The climate has always been so hot and dry that most people have no desire to travel to Settle." She laughed. "There isn't anything to do when a person gets there."

She fell into a long silence and Lamar waited patiently for her to continue. She remembered reading a book titled *Human Relationships and How They Work*. And somewhere in the chapters she had read that one of the elements that made a relationship function properly was the sharing of past experiences, dreams, goals, and what a person ordinarily considered secrets.

Remembering the passage in the book, she suddenly decided to share her dreams and goals and secrets with Lamar—to give them to Lamar, the decision being made in much the way she would have decided to oil the gears of a machine that appeared in need.

She told Lamar about the books she had written and the large amounts of money she had earned from them. She also mentioned the inventions she had patented and how the sale of the patents had brought more income. She was slightly embarrassed by his open admiration. She had not sought that reaction—had sought only to share.

"And what are you doing with all your money?" Lamar inquired half-jokingly.

Natalaie hesitated again and then decided to share one of her most important secrets:

"I'm buying Settle."

"Buying a planet? That's fantastic."

"Other people have done it. I'm doing it."

"Who are you buying it *from*?"

"Settle is in a solar system of five planets. Since there is no intelli-

74

gent life native to the planet, it, according to interplanetary law, belongs to the most intelligent and advanced race in the same solar system. On a planet named Maridia, the fifth from the double sun of the system, there is a halfway intelligent race. They look like beetles and their society is unappealing to Earthmen, but they are legally the owners of Settle. The planet means nothing to them. They haven't achieved spaceflight yet, so they've never seen it in person. They couldn't live there. Through the equivalent of a real estate agency on Maridia, I've been buying portions of Settle. Other people have bought a total of ten percent of the surface—as a purely speculative investment, I suppose. I own seventy-five percent. Next year. . . if all goes well, I'll have the money to buy the remaining fifteen percent. That will give me ninety percent possession of the plannet." She shrugged. "In time I might be able to buy the outstanding ten percent but that's not really important. I will be the controlling owner."

"That's remarkable," Lamar said, grinning broadly in admiration. "I've heard of people investing in property on other worlds, but you're the first person I've met with the ambition to own a *whole planet*."

"Under the conditions it's an achievable goal. If I tried to buy one of the popular planets, it would be impossible . . . I would never make enough money in a lifetime."

"I understand it's achievable . . . but why are you doing it? The planets that people usually invest in are considered valuable for one reason or another. You were just saying that Settle is unpopular. I assume it's not along the trade routes?"

"No."

"It can't be rich in ores. I would have heard about it through my relatives. They're always discussing good investments."

"No. Settle isn't rich in natural resources."

He studied her closely. "I can't believe you'd invest so heavily for sentimental reasons . . . just because it's your home planet."

She held back from telling him the truth. She was the only person born and raised on Settle. At the age of thirty-two, she had the body of a sixteen-year-old girl. As far as she could tell, she was aging but at

75

a rate far slower than that of people born on Earth and other planets. Unless there was something freakish in her genes, the environment of Settle acted as a "fountain of youth" or the equivalent of a longevity serum. When that fact became general knowledge—and it might become generally known only when she made the disclosure—the value of land on Settle should soar.

"It's a hobby," she attempted and could not keep a mysterious smile from her lips.

"I can't believe that."

"Personal reasons," she said. "I might tell you some day."

CHAPTER TEN

Eva awoke in her cabin and could not remember how she had gotten there or what had happened during the previous hours.

Or was it days?

She stirred on the narrow bed and searched her memories, recalling vaguely that she had been with Alex Stauffer for a while and that he had been good to her.

If I wasn't so dumb and such a drunk and so plain, I might've had a chance of working my way in as one of his steady mistresses. If I had any possibilities at all, I probably blew it . . .

Her head throbbed painfully. She shifted to a sitting position and the room swam. She felt sick in the pit of her stomach and her nerves were jittery. When she ran a hand through her hair, it trembled.

One cure for that.

She crawled on her hands and knees to the liquor cabinet, took one of the bottles at random and sat on the floor with her back against the wall. As she lifted the bottle to her mouth, she was suddenly and acutely aware of the fact that her body needed to urinate. She could not stop the forthcoming function and knew she was short on time. She had time enough to dash to the private bath—or take the drink. One or the other. A choice was necessary and she needed the drink so badly she decided to drink.

As the alcohol went down her throat and warmed her stomach, she urinated. As the warm liquid soaked into her underwear and skirt, she suddenly became aware of the fact that her clothing was already soiled with her excrement.

When did I do that? I must have done that while I was asleep or passed out. Why didn't I notice it as soon as I awakened? Now I will positively have to go to the bathroom before too long.

She took another drink—and another—and another.

I might as well finish the bottle before I go to the bathroom.

When the bottle was empty, she began thinking that this was a new low for her. She'd been drunk thousands of times—she'd experienced alcoholic blackouts and hangovers and made a fool of herself in a hundred ways—but this . . . *this* . . . sitting here, drunk, in her own excrement was a new, new low.

And everybody used to say I was so beautiful, so poised, so competent, so organized and squeaky clean.

I'm sure as hell not squeaky clean now, am I?

How did all this start?

What are the reasons?

Is it because I like booze psychologically — or need it physically — or need the emotional release? . . .

A few years ago she'd had a first degree psychoelectric mnemonic erasure. She'd been seeing a psychiatrist because of certain emotional and mental problems. After the first degree erasure proved only half effective, her psychiatrist had recommended a second degree psychoelectric mnemonic erasure.

She had agreed and underwent an operation that was medically termed electrical brain surgery although the brain tissues themselves were not physically altered. It had been explained to her that first degree mnemonic erasure meant that certain disturbing memories would be shielded from easy association and recall. That part of your past would be there in your memory but you'd have to concentrate hard to remember it.

Second degree psychoelectric mnemonic erasure retained the memories within the brain but were reachable only by painful concentration. If you wanted to remember the particular painful portion of your life for one reason or another, you could recall it only by enduring a physical pain similar to an intense migraine. She remembered her psychiatrist's explanation, "The memories will be there—if you ever *need* to recall them for one reason or another, such as having to testify in a court of law. Or if you ever *want* to review them for any personal emotional reason. But you'll have to endure the pain for the necessary length of time—like deliberately giving yourself a migraine. The pain varies with the person and the physical pain index. It's a middle ground that's effective in most cases. After that, of course, there would be nothing left except third degree mnemonic erasure which is a *total* erasure."

"I've heard that changes the personality," she'd replied.

"That's right. Not drastically in some cases."

"I knew a girl who had the third degree erasure . . ." Veronica. Lovely, lovable, shy Veronica. "It changed her . . . horribly. She'd always been such a shy, nice girl. The erasure made her a totally unlikable extrovert."

The psychiatrist had shrugged. "The result of a third degree erasure is sometimes unpredictable."

The second degree mnemonic surgery had proven helpful apparently, but now she wanted to know what was hidden in that dark corner of her mind and deliberately strained to remember. Her head exploded with pain. She whimpered with the intensity of the pain but went on and on for what seemed hours until at last she burst through all the barriers and found the truth.

She'd married at the age of twenty. Julian Rivero had been one year younger than herself—dark-haired, energetic, handsome, muscular, virile—and so boyish he acted like a kid of fourteen or fifteen. But she'd loved him and they'd been happy. She had been, she remembered, vivacious, bubbly, innocent in many ways, unmarked by life. The worst thing that had happened in her life had been the death

79

of a pet cat when she was twelve.

Shortly after their marriage, Julian had suggested they volunteer to be colonists on one of the planets in the Pleiades. He'd brought home literature on a world called Prettyplanet. Looking at the color photographs, she had been entranced. It was a beautiful planet with green fields and valleys, rocky mountains and pale blue lakes with splotches of wild vegetation as colorful as any carefully planned and tended flower garden. She had agreed and they'd filled out application blanks, thinking they would have only a chance in a million.

They'd been accepted. Later she had learned that the government had been looking for newly married couples and there were only so many newly married men and women who applied to be colonists.

She had their baby at the end of their first year on Prettyplanet and life had seemed idyllic except for one element: the natives.

The Pleiadesians were not troublesome, but they were frustrating and irritating at times. On this, the most beautiful of all planets, the only natives were ugly—resembling four-legged dogs but with an addition of two tentacles that served as arms and hands. The Pleiadesians were little more than savages, barely above the bow-and-arrow stage, unable to communicate with the human colonists except by the most crude sign language.

No trouble had been anticipated, but then, during their fourth year at Prettyplanet, the Pleiadesians attacked the colony with bows and arrows.

I remember it now . . .

All the horrible images returned. It was noon and, according to their custom, they were all having what they called a picnic lunch to divide the working day in half. The air was abruptly filled with arrows and screams of pain and anger. In minutes the battle was over. The colonists had been caught completely off guard. The men who were not killed in the initial attack were slaughtered after the colonists surrendered. Eva had found herself separated from her son, Danny, found herself tied hand and foot and carried, along with five other women survivors, to a camp in a nearby valley.

Rape came as a completely unexpected shock. Their clothes were torn away and they were tied to two tree trunks that had been placed together at a level of approximately two feet—tied into a kneeling position.

The Pleiadesians had raped them repeatedly, with a casualness that only alien animals would have been capable of.

Julian was dead. She had seen two arrows strike him in the chest, seen him fall. Their son had been snatched from her arms and taken away. Hysterical from the sorrow and shock of such sudden loss, she had numbly endured the physical pain and emotional humiliation of the raping.

The Pleiadesian males were heavier than the females of their race, their average weight fifty or sixty pounds above that of the average male human. The Pleiadesian male sexual organs were nearly identical in shape to that of a human male although considerably larger than average. During the first entry, Eva had felt as if she would be torn apart by the thrusting member that seemed as hard as an iron bar. Some of the women were screaming hysterically, others were crying. Eva made no sound. She felt dead inside and counted mechanically the number of the aliens who raped her . . .

One, two, three, four . . .

Five, six, seven, eight . . .

She fainted and regained consciousness only to find herself still being raped, to know by the sensations in her body that she had been sexually assaulted repeatedly while unconscious.

That night they remained tied in the kneeling position. By the flickering glow of the campfire, they were occasionally raped by lone Pleiadesians who would wander into their "prison." She was raped twice in the semidarkness and heard the other women being attacked countless times. She could not sleep and the next day they were forced to travel with the tribe.

Tribe? They were all males. Hunters, it seemed, out scouting the countryside for food. Why had they attacked the colony?

The following weeks were an incredible nightmare. Yvonne

81

Bassler went insane, her eyes wild. As if she had become an animal, one of them, her body responded to the sexual intercourse with the Pleiadesians. She would groan with pleasure at her orgasms, moving her body in rhythms to satisfy her alien attackers the way she would have moved to please a human lover. The Pleiadesians freed her and she crawled around their camp each day, indulging with any who wanted sex. It was no longer rape in her case but Yvonne Bassler had become a mindless animal.

Helena Morrow went insane in a different way. She screamed for two days and two nights and then become absolutely withdrawn. The aliens freed her. She would remain as motionless as a dummy unless prodded in one direction or another. Her eyes were empty, her expression blank. The aliens used her body as they would have used that of a lifeless dummy.

A week later Eva saw pretty Terry Keane pretend to be mindless, a convert like Yvonne and Helena. She was freed but her eyes were not empty. . . they were filled with a strange and crafty cunning. She did not speak to anyone—she acted as if insane and indulged with the aliens freely, either enjoying the unions or pretending to enjoy them. She was free and Eva began to wonder if it was her way of maneuvering so she could eventually escape.

Sally Benson went totally insane from the attacks. The aliens kept her tied because her behavior was unpredictable. Eva remained a bound prisoner for over three weeks, and then they were rescued by members of a colony on a nearby planet.

Her son was found alive in a camp with a dozen alien females. Alive but dying from one of the strange native diseases. All the colony's medical supplies had been destroyed during the initial attack. During the days that followed, she had watched helplessly as Danny died. An hour after his burial, she had been contemplating suicide when one of the male rescuers introduced her to alcohol. Down at the bottom of the bottle she found delightful restful oblivion. Not the sliding sharp hard edge of a knife kind of nothingness but the muted fuzzy liquid mind-changing oblivion in which nothing mattered.

She had been transformed into an alcoholic and had been one for many years now.

That's how I got here. Now that I've remembered why, I'll have to go to the bathroom, shower, clean up. Or should I clean up first and then take a shower? Whatever you do, you'll have to take these filthy clothes off first . . .

She made it to the bathroom by using the wall for support, sliding along it as she performed something approximating walking.

In the bathroom she closed the door and started to lock it but then realized there was no one to intrude accidentally.

She stared into the spaceship medicine cabinet mirror that was much like the mirrors in medicine cabinets anywhere on Earth. *You look horrible*, she said to her image. And then added as she remembered the nightmare memories she'd unlocked from that far corner of her mind: *You are horrible.*

The image in the mirror was frowning. The nightmares were dying in the back of her mind. That damned second degree mnemonic erasure. It would slip away. She would forget. She knew that now. She'd forget how those sickening aliens had raped her—forget her dead husband, dead son, all the things she had lost.

I wish I was dead, she thought suddenly.

But the ironic thing was that if she didn't kill herself immediately, she would forget she wanted to die. She would walk around like all those horrible things still in her past—raped by dozens of filthy alien animals—but *not remember*. She would be as horrible as ever but beneath a facade of forgetfulness.

Now or never.

She seized the bottle of sleeping pills and saw it was three-quarters full. She remembered hearing someone prophesy that mankind would keep its sleeping pills until the end of time, no matter how advanced their technology. There was such a thing as the electronic sleep-inducers but they never worked too well with her and usually gave her a headache.

Until the end of time.

She filled a glass with water and used it to wash down a handful of the pills. Another handful and then another until the bottle was empty. She carefully placed the empty bottle back into the cabinet, quickly slipped out of her clothes and shoved them in the ship's laundry chute. They would be cleaned in the main laundry room and returned to her cabin spotless and pressed. She showered quickly and slipped into a robe.

She was crossing the floor of her cabin, heading toward the bed when—with one of the steps—it seemed she was suddenly stepping into an infinity of nothingness.

Early this morning I was approached by a man named Troyan who stated he represented Alexander Stauffer.

I learned that Stauffer is hiring a majority of the passengers and when Troyan made an offer, I, too, accepted. Enlisting everyone into Stauffer's employement appears to be mostly an organizational maneuver. Since we are all primarily concerned with survival at the moment, the move on Stauffer's part is appropriate and ingenious. We will be extremely well paid in our natural and instinctive efforts toward survival! This has an amazing soothing psychological effect upon the passengers.

When asked what my duties would be, Troyan suggested that I get in touch with a man named Krause.

I located Krause and learned he was busy on a confidential project. We had a brief talk and, apparently impressed by my background, he gave me the details of the project and asked for my advice.

The gist of the matter is that Krause thinks Starbright may have been wrecked in a hijack attempt. His thinking is that the hijackers will wait awhile to see if we are rescued.

He wants to send a visual SOS signal, but at the same time he is concerned that we may be in unfriendly waters. He told me some stories of starships that ventured into unexplored galaxies, encountered difficulties, and sent distress signals that attracted scouts from alien civilizations. In nearly half of the cases, the Earth ships were destroyed—or the Earthmen were murdered. This tendency of alien races to eliminate representatives of our race has been kept from the general public. In many cases the information was gathered years or decades after the fact—from tapes or material evidence. When I asked Krause why these events had been kept from the public, he said the main reasons were political and financial. Support for interstellar projects would be much less, he said, if everyone knew that quite often the stars are not friendly.

Krause's scheme was to devise some way to do everything at once: Move the ship to another location, hide it in space or subspace, send a visual SOS signal—and wait to see if either hijackers or alien scouts appear. He wanted to leave cameras and "junk" at the scene of our shipwreck to give the impression to alien scouts that our ship had been blown apart. Krause asked my advice on how I thought we might jettison all the material while still keeping the purpose a secret from the passengers. The project he had in mind would entail the efforts of a considerable number of people over a period of time.

I suggested that we tell the passengers we wanted to collect unwanted and unnecessary material to jettison, to lighten the burden of the artificial gravity system and to conserve energy. I said that, that way, we could ask every passenger to turn over his or her "junk" and enlist the help of the passengers in the discharge.

Krause seemed impressed by the suggested subterfuge and agreed to use it. When I asked him how long he thought we might have to wait for our hijackers to show up—if there are any hijackers at all—he laughed and said anywhere from a week to a year.

CHAPTER ELEVEN

Mac considered the possibility of going to the ship's library personally to check on the Cepheus incident. He'd been there once before during their preflight inspection. He remembered the place was comfortable and as quiet as any library on Earth. Almost every book in the world had been made available by the library's computer and microdot system. Checking into the Cepheus incident could be a pleasant change of pace rather than a chore.

I'd better keep myself available for other things, he decided. His personal secretary had remained on Earth, to take a well-earned vacation. Gwenna, in addition to being Stauffer's secretary, was also in charge of a small secretarial pool. One of the girls in the pool would be loaned to him without question.

When he went to Gwenna's offices, he found her reception room flooded with a maze of people who wanted to see Alex Stauffer for one reason or another. She was deftly routing them to other Synpla executives and during a break in her manipulations, he asked if he could see the personnel folders on the secretarial pool. There were only five. After studying each briefly he selected a girl named Beverly Haney. She was attractive without being beautiful or striking. In her file photo she appeared studious and serious-minded. She had been a scretary for some top executives on Earth. She was also, according to the confidential information in the folder, destined to be the personal secretary to the new district manager of the Synpla plants on Algor. The manager had not yet been appointed—that was one of Alex's reasons for traveling to Algor—to make that final decision.

Now it looked as if they would never reach Algor but the very fact that Beverly Haney had been chosen for such a difficult job spoke highly as a recommendation.

"Gwenna, how can I get in touch with this Beverly Haney? I need her for a security project."

"She's writing a report for Alex. A profile on the passengers. Nothing urgent but I don't want her off that too long. How long will your project take?"

"An hour maybe. Two hours at the most."

"I'll give her a call. Where do you want her to meet you?"

"Some place where we can be alone."

"What about the conference room down the hall?"

"Fine."

"Do you want her now?"

"The sooner the better."

"Why don't you go on down to the conference room? She should be there in a minute."

While waiting in the plush compartment, Mac had the eerie feeling that he was back on Earth again. Gwenna's office on *Starbright* was very similar to her office on Earth. This room with its long table and comfortable chairs and carefully blended colors with tasteful wall decorations was like dozens of others that he had been in at one time or another. *Mankind takes his familiar and comfortable shell with him wherever he goes.* Their ship had been badly damaged and they were stranded in space but it still had an air of unreality so far. It had the strange feeling of a game being played and the designers were not telling all the rules . . .

Beverly Haney appeared in a few minutes. She was dressed in a conservative suit and wore horn-rimmed glasses. In an era when contact lenses had been so perfected that they were completely comfortable, external glasses were worn as a decoration more than anything

87

else. Mac was aware that some women wore glasses because they made them look more attractive somehow, emphasizing certain lines in their face or certain features. The horn-rimmed glasses *did* something to Beverly, he had to admit. They made her look like a cute and thoughtful owl. Nice legs, he noticed as she came into the room. Nice shape. Short. She came only to his chin when they stood facing each other.

He had seen her before, he remembered suddenly. At one of the company parties. But no one had introduced them previously.

"Good to see you again," Mac said quickly. "Have a seat. Gwenna tells me you're busy on a project for Alex. I don't want to take you away from that too long, but I do have a highly confidential matter and I think you're the right person . . ."

She turned a chair around and sat facing him, crossing her legs and resting her elbows on the chair armrests, clasping her fingers. She reminded Mac of how a high school teenage student might look when called for a talk with the school principal. He pulled out a chair and sat facing her.

"Have you heard of the Cepheus incident?"

She nodded yes.

"How much do you know about it in a general way?"

'Not too much. I know it involved the hijacking of a starship. The book became a bestseller and it was made into a movie. Lila Pollard was the star. She's Lila *Hartnett* now. Not many people remember her maiden name . . ." *I didn't*, Mac thought. *Sheffield mentioned her starring in the movie. And — Lila is a passenger on this ship. That's an odd coincidence. First a movie and now a real life incident . . . That can't mean anything, can it?* "I read about it in the papers and I saw the movie," Beverly finished.

"Did you read the book?"

"No."

"One of the crew members pointed out the similarity between the Cepheus incident and what happened to *Starbright*. He thinks there's a possibility we might be in the process of being hijacked. Will you go to the ship's library, find all the material you can on the Cepheus incident — without letting anyone know what you're doing — and then get back to me with the pertinent details?"

The secretary said thoughtfully, "You'll be looking for similarities . . . indications that we *are* being hijacked?"

Mac nodded his head affirmatively. "But I want this little bit of research to be kept confidential. I don't want to start a panic."

"Most of the passengers are past the panic stage, I believe," Beverly commented. "They've adjusted to the idea of being shipwrecked but, although they're past the panic stage, they're certainly not past various stages of insanity and emotional instability."

When she made the statement, Mac noticed, she made it without emotion—as if impartially discussing the rise and fall of the stock market.

"As a matter of fact," she added, one thin eyebrow arching slightly, "one of the rumors going around is that we have been hijacked."

"Oh? I wasn't aware of that. What's the general reaction to that possiblity?"

She had an attractive mouth and now it spread into a faint smile. "I believe most of the passengers would *prefer* to be hijacked. That way they might be kept prisoner . . . mistreated some, perhaps, but . . . *kept alive.* The possibility that the shipwreck was a pure accident could mean that we will all die shortly."

"Well," Mac said. "Regardless . . . I'd rather you keep your research confidential. Let the passengers have their rumors, but let's not feed them. If the rumors are not fed, everyone will more or less believe what they *want* to believe."

Beverly nodded that she understood the reasoning. "How do you want me to make my report? Written? Memo tape?"

"Let's not put it in writing or on tape. When you've gathered the data, contact me and we'll have another meeting."

As Beverly left the conference room, Mac received a telecom from Gwenna. She was, he knew, one of the most skilled mental communicators in Synpla. She had a knack of "listening" before transmitting—a way of knowing when a person was talking to someone. He had never become that adept and usually barged in with a telecom at inappropriate times.

Mac, I'm with Alex now and he's a little perturbed. He says he asked you to find the captain and tell him that he wanted to know the extent of the damage. Alex is irritated because you didn't get back to him on that.

I've been busy, Mac replied quickly. *Tell Alex I learned the captain was killed during the accident. That's why I didn't get to him sooner. I've had to scout around and learn the extent of the damage from several sources. But . . . tell him we're in no immediate danger. The bridge suffered the bulk of damage and all the ship's systems are functioning.*

Hold on . . .

Mac waited patiently. Telecoms usually gave Alex a headache and he preferred to communicate through Gwenna. She would be telling him verbally. Mac reflected that he preferred the arrangement also because Gwenna had a knack of rephrasing things for Alex's digestion and she was often a cushion, softening bad news as it was delivered to their boss.

He buys that, Gwenna responded after a pause. *But now he's frowning because you said you were investigating the cause of the wreck and you didn't get back to him on that. You should see the frown on his face, Mac. It's a BIG frown.*

In the solitude of the conference room, Mac grinned. Gwenna had a way of gently poking fun at Alex.

Tell him we're still investigating the cause. The energy shield failed but we haven't learned why the shield failed. It may be so technical that Alex won't understand it even when we do dig up the reason.

After another pause, Gwenna responded, *He bought that, too, but now he has another chore for you. He's heard that the navigational equipment is not functioning. He wants you to find the navigator and cover the following points: Where is the ship now located? How soon can the navigational equipment be repaired? Will the navigator accept a position whereby he is a direct employee of Synpla, salary negotiable, starting immediately? And, since he has several resources aboard ship, ask the navigator if he needs anything for his comfort or the performance of his duties. You are authorized to negotiate the salary and other items.*

Mac hesitated a few moments, digesting the instructions and then replied, *Okay. I'll find the navigator and take care of that.*

Get in touch with me later, Mac.

Right.

As the telecom conversation ended, Mac rose from his chair and thought, *Since the captain is dead, Alex wants to buy the navigator. It may not be necessary but it's still a clever move.*

He was about to leave the conference room when he received another telecom, this time from the fingerprint expert.

Sir—I checked those prints we found in the maintenance corridor. They belong to two deceased crew members, Harrison and Darnell. The computer, analyzing the drying of the oils in the prints, comes up with a time element of less than twelve hours.

In other words, Harrison and Darnell did something to the energy shield equipment shortly before the accident?

That is correct.

Thank you.

As the SS agent withdrew from the telepathic communication, Mac felt a chill as if the temperature in the room had dropped several degrees. The ship had been sabotaged and he remembered Sheffield's remark:

Harrison and Darnell are our relief operators. Were. They were both on the bridge when the meteor struck. If they did it, they deliberately committed suicide.

The two crew members had sabotaged the ship in such a way that a meteor would destroy the bridge. Then, after doing their act of sabotage, they had deliberately gone to the bridge. That had been like placing themselves under a giant hammer weighing tons.

CHAPTER TWELVE

Eva Hamilton has attempted suicide in her cabin.

The statement burst in Mac's mind loud and clear as he walked toward the navigator's quarters. It was unlike any other telecommunication he'd experienced, but because of the circumstances he did not have time to analyze the sensation.

He found himself running to Eva's cabin and when he discovered the door locked, he drew his SS Special and blasted the lock. Once inside he scooped up Eva in his arms and carried her—once more running—to the dispensary. She was taken from his arms by two interns, a doctor and a nurse who were waiting just inside the open doorway of the dispensary. They wheeled her away to an operating room.

Mac sank into one of the chairs in the waiting room and contacted Krause by telecom:

Did you know Eva tried to commit suicide?

No. When?

About ten minutes ago. I carried her to the dispensary.

How did she try it this time?

I don't know. What do you mean this time? She's attempted suicide before?

Two or three times. Remember . . . I was telling you how she lost

92

her husband and son during an attack by the Pleiadesians? She's been through first degree and second degree mnemonic erasure, but the psychological phase of her alcoholism remained because of the deep emotional roots. Since she refused third degree erasure, we decided to make her an SS operative. She's made a great undercover agent. I hope we don't lose her.

Mac held his breath. For a moment there it sounded as if Krause would hate to lose Eva because of her professional capabilities, like losing a tool rather than losing a friend or fellow human. He decided not to comment. He would seem soft and sentimental and maybe Krause didn't mean it the way it'd sounded.

She's in the dispensary now, Mac said. Maybe we caught it in time. I have a question for you. Who is "we?"

The telecom was silent awhile and then Krause responded, I don't understand . . .

Someone informed me that Eva had attempted suicide, but the person or thing who alerted me didn't identify himself or itself. It was a telecom.

I don't understand what you're driving at.

You know . . . Telecoms from another human being have a certain "sound" the way each human voice has a distinctive sound. When you call me by telecom, I recognize your mental voice. I can recognize most people on the telecoms. The person or thing who notified me of Eva's attempted suicide didn't sound human. The more I think about it, the more I realize it wasn't a human transmission.

If it wasn't human, what was it? An alien?

I think it was a machine . . . a computer. That's what I'm asking you. Does Alex's secret service have a Monitor?

What do you mean by Monitor?

Mac hesitated. Something was wrong. Krause had a good memory. Only a few years ago, when Mac first joined Centrol and it was known he would soon be appointed special assistant to Alex, a liaison between Alex and the secret service division—before the decision was actually made immortal by being put on paper—Krause had taken him to the basement of Synpla's huge office complex and there, in a room protected by armed guards, shown him the computer that would be known as Monitor.

"This will make our job easier," Krause had explained with all the excitement of a boy displaying a new toy with barely restrained enthusiasm.

Monitor, Mac remembered, had been a new style of computer capable of being linked to human intelligences. It would continually record a person's thought, Krause had explained. Those thoughts would be fed into the computer's brain and decisions would be made. The Monitor was to be designed with the capability to transmit to secret service operators. "Like having a Big Daddy," Krause had said.

"Won't you resent the invasion of privacy. . . someone continually reading your thoughts?"

"Ah," Krause had replied. "*Someone* yes. Some*thing*, no. Monitor will be a thing, a computer. Who cares if a machine reads your thoughts?"

You don't remember the name of Monitor?

I don't recall that name. Can you describe it?

It was cancelled at the last minute but it was to be a computer that would be in telecommunication with secret service operatives. It was to have the capability to read thoughts on a continuing basis, make decisions, and communicate those decisions to operatives. It's the type of device that would have been able to read Eva's thoughts of suicide . . .

I don't remember anything of that nature, Krause said. *Let me ask Julia. She does most of my thinking.*

Mac closed his eyes, waiting patiently. Julia was Krause's secretary—a small dark-haired woman who seemed as efficient as the day was long. He remembered—after seeing the Monitor in its metal flesh, they had retuned to Krause's office and Krause had asked Julia for some of the papers describing the new machine. Julia had taken the top secret information from a locked file and they had discussed it in Julia's presence.

Mac heard a faint *click* in his mind. The telecom was now a three-way communication.

Julia, Krause said, *do you remember anything about a computer called Monitor?*

Can you describe it?

Mac gave another brief description of the device and Julia said, *I don't remember anything of that nature.*

I must have dreamed it, Mac said lamely. *Sorry I bothered you.*

Let me know how things turn out with Eva.

Will do.

Shortly after the telecom with Krause ended, the doctor came into the waiting room. He was a tall and slender man with a nearly bald head containing only patches of white hair around the ears, thin white mustache and white eyebrows. *He looks as old as God,* Mac thought absently. He smelled of antiseptics. His flesh had a pale pink, well-scrubbed look as if he purified his body of germs several times a day. *Maybe he does exactly that for all the operations.* Mac remembered vaguely reading about sterilization stalls that surgeons stepped into—much like stepping into a shower. The man wore a white uniform with no buttons but with five large pockets and a small name label that read simply: WINTETROBE.

"She'll live," Wintetrobe said. "It was close. If we hadn't been notified by telecom . . . if we hadn't been waiting . . ."

"*Who* notified you?" Mac asked abruptly.

Wintetrobe frowned. "I don't know. We have a telecom operator the same as a hospital. She receives messages from anyone capable of sending a telecom. The life *was* saved. Is it important *who* notified us?"

"No, Doctor. It's not important." But it was *damned* important, Mac thought. If the Monitor device had been put into use on a top secret basis, he wanted to know about it. As Alexander Stauffer's liaison with the SS, Alex's safety and measures to protect him were his concern.

"The woman will have to undergo third degree mnemonic erasure," Dr. Wintetrobe said matter-of-factly.

"I thought that had to be voluntary."

"Except in cases of attempted suicide or attempted homicide. Then the operation can be made legally without the patient's consent. Our mnemonic surgeon, Wyatt, would like to speak to you. If you'll follow me . . ."

95

Mac followed the tall doctor through the dispensary. He had known that the dispensary had all the capabilities of a small hospital and he had seen some of the injuries suffered because of the collision with the meteor. Still he was shocked at the number of patients crowded into the wards. There were *tiers* of patients—three and four.

Dr. Wintetrobe, catching Mac's surprise said dryly, "Yes. We've been busy."

"I had no idea there were so many injuries."

"We were told not to report the number. So as not to alarm the passengers who were unharmed. It would serve no purpose."

He was ushered into a small operating room and introduced to the mnemonic surgeon. Wyatt was an attractive middle-aged woman with a well-constructed and shapely body, dark hair and eyes. She wore a red lipstick that seemed all the brighter because of the paleness of her flesh and the whiteness of her uniform. Mac decided her paleness was not an unhealthy one. She appeared to be one of those people who rarely ventured into the sunlight and made no effort to color their flesh by artificial means.

After Dr. Wintetrobe had left, Mac said, "You wanted to see me, Dr. Wyatt?"

"My first name is Jane. We may be informal." She raised an eyebrow slightly as if inquiring about his first name.

"Mac. Short for MacPherson."

"I know you are a liaison between Alexander Stauffer and the secret service group that protects him, but I didn't know your name. I wanted to see you because . . . Well . . . Why don't you have a seat and relax?"

Mac sat in one of the two chairs. *She has a great smile,* he thought.

"You'll have to explain to the other operatives that Eva had to undergo third degree mnemonic surgery."

"She won't remember her deceased husband and son?"

"And there was something else that happened to her that she will not remember. The gap in her memory will affect her personality to some degree. I can't predict the exact changes. Will you visit her while she's recuperating?"

Mac nodded his head affirmatively.

96

"Excuse me a moment? I have to prepare for an operation."

Frowning, Mac watched as Wyatt prepared the operating table. The extensions of mnemonic computers were placed near the headrest. She checked several dials and set up a surgical program.

As he waited, Mac wondered if he could check the existence of the Monitor with someone else. He remembered suddenly that his assistant, Addison, should recall the device. Addison had been with Central long before his arrival and the two of them had discussed the Monitor before it was cancelled. Addison was somewhere on the ship—hiding somewhere if not dead. The man had a knack of staying out of sight unless called for.

Addison?

Yes sir.

Where the hell have you been?

The stewardesses have been explaining something to me. You should stop by the stew lounge, Mac. They're great.

Changing the subject abruptly, Mac queried, *Do you remember that computer they were going to call the Monitor? The one that—*

I don't remember anything of that nature, Addison replied, interrupting him midsentence.

Mac felt a chill. Krause and Gwenna and Addison had all given the same response—word for exact word.

That meant they had been programmed. Memory of the Monitor machine had been wiped from their memory and the pat phrase had been planted to cover the erasure.

Thanks, Mac said. *I'll be in touch with you later.*

He took a deep breath as the surgeon named Wyatt turned toward him and said, "Now we're ready for your operation. It will be painless and the item being removed is so small it will not affect your personality. Afterwards you will not remember the operation. Will you make yourself comfortable on the operating table, please?"

Mac felt his muscles move of their own volition. Someone else was moving his body. Monitor. It had to be Monitor. It *was* in existence. It had the power to take over people at certain times, when necessary. It didn't control a person constantly because there was no need to turn everyone into robots.

97

But Monitor wanted its existence kept a secret and now that he had stumbled upon it accidentally, the knowledge had to be removed from his memory.

Settling onto the operating table and making himself as comfortable as possible, he looked up at the surgeon named Wyatt and felt an overpowering sense of futility and frustration.

"It was Monitor who informed me of Eva's attempted suicide?"

Wyatt nodded affirmatively as she applied electrodes to his skull.

"Monitor reads the minds of everyone in Stauffer's employ?"

"Yes."

"And controls our actions?"

"When necessary."

"And . . . as the passengers enter Alex's empire, they . . . will become subjected to Monitor control?"

"Each new employee is told their brainwave pattern must be recorded and the linkage to Monitor is accomplished during that recording." Wyatt extended a slender hand toward a control board. Mac experienced a moment of startling realization:

Monitor controlled *every* secret service agent and *every* Synpla employee. It constantly read all their thoughts and passed them into its central brain. Monitor kept itself concealed. Since it read minds, it could catch any mind at the beginning of awareness of its existence and arrange mnemonic erasure. It was, in essence, an invisible giant of a machine, a computer, an omnipotent god of a machine that would soon control everyone on the ship . . .

CHAPTER THIRTEEN

During the past years Fate has been generous to me and I have been called, among other things, "A Philosopher For the Masses." During the recent day and a half, despite the drama, seriousness of the situation and so forth, I labeled myself, "The Galactic Garbage Collector."

Krause and I headed a program whereby we contacted every single passenger and crew member, soliciting odds and ends, trash, any unwanted or unnecessary items of any type whatsoever. We put forth my invented excuse that we wanted to reduce the load on the gravity machinery by lessening its burden. The passengers accepted this and one irony of the matter is that there will be a beneficial decreased burden on the artificial gravity machinery.

We collected unwanted and unneeded extra clothing, personal items of all descriptions, and some outright junk. Broken instruments, jagged metal, and an assortment of debris in the wrecked bridge were cut free by lasers and torches. One of the mechanics suggested a method of burning and melting the metal fragments so it would appear they had been freed from the ship by an internal explosion. Some bodies from the ship's morgue were requisitioned for what we had now begun to refer to as, Operation Decoy. The storage holds were emptied of all items that would not be useful during the coming weeks or months. There are only a few children aboard the ship but they touchingly gave up some items. One little girl gave up a doll. A small boy gave up his favorite teddy bear. Other children parted with some of their toys.

Some men gave up their wallets with credit cards and currency, some women donated their purses with assorted contents. To make the debris as realisitic as possible, Krause decided to part with a small portion of the ship's food and water. Some bulkheads, compartment floors, ceilings, and stairways were removed, mangled, and burned to again appear as if blown free by explosion.

I have listed here only a portion of the incredible number of items collected for Operation Decoy. Krause made a complete list as a tool to be certain he had not overlooked possibilities. All the items were gathered in the airlocks and in the area of what had been the ship's bridge. At the same instant that the airlocks were opened to jettison the material, the energy shield over the bridge area was released for an instant to simultaneously jettison that material. All the debris was released in the midst of an asteroid belt around a giant red star. In the debris, also, are two types of distress signal devices. One is a visual signal that will flash periodically and the other is an interstellar radio that will transmit an SOS signal.

It is Krause's belief that this action may precipitate action on the part of the hijacker—if there are any hijackers. It will also let us know if there are any space-age civilizations within reach of our signals.

With Starbright in hiding at a considerable distance, Krause has also placed cameras in orbit around the moon of the giant red start, so we will be able to see what our "Decoy" attracts.

Perhaps the most important part of Operation Decoy is the four people who volunteered to be left behind in spacesuits.

Once more Mac was headed toward the navigator's quarters and once more a telecom interrupted him. This time he recognized Krause's telecom voice.

How is Eva, Mac?

Fine. They want to hold her at the dispensary for a day or two. She'll have to undergo third degree mnemonic erasure but the doctors say she'll be all right after that.

I'm in the main lounge. Stop by and I'll buy you a drink.

I was on my way to see the navigator . . .

That can wait.

For Alex.

I know for a fact that Alex will be busy for an hour or two. Besides — my contacts tell me the navigator doesn't have the slightest idea where we are. I had agents spread the word that he's busy working, calculating our position and shouldn't be disturbed. It's worked so far and people have stayed off his back. Come on . . . Stop by for a drink. You've had a hard day and earned it.

You talked me into it.

At the entrance to the main lounge, a man sat behind a desk, stopping each person before he or she went inside.

What the hell is this? Mac wondered.

"Your name, sir?" He was a slender man with a thin mustache, neatly dressed in gray suit, white shirt, dark tie. An atmosphere of bureaucracy seemed to float around him like a tangible fog. *He looks familiar. One of Alex's men?*

"My name is MacPherson."

The slender man consulted a list, made a notation, then reached into a drawer to hand Mac a small booklet.

Mac accepted it but asked, "What the hell is this?"

"Didn't you hear, sir? Alcoholic beverage rationing. Mixed drinks in the lounges are now rationed."

"When did that start?"

"This morning."

Mac accepted the booklet and glanced inside to see neatly printed, perforated coupons.

"How long is this going to last?"

"The ration books being issued now are to last one month. At that time new books will be issued according to the inventory at that point."

"I see." Mac thumbed through the coupons, noting that they had serial numbers and were also numbered consecutively. "Holy cow," he muttered. *"Serial numbers!"*

"Each person has a designated serial number to prevent theft and forgery."

"How many drinks a day?"

"Five."

"Seems generous enough." Shrugging physically and mentally, Mac went on into the lounge. It was crowded. Very crowded. He recognized a man standing near the entrance as one of Krause's secret service men, a tall broad-shouldered man who somehow had a knack of being nearly invisible in a crowd. Since Krause had the task of protecting Stauffer, a byproduct task was often that of maintaining a general orderliness, the theory being that it would be much easier to kill Stauffer under cover of a riot.

"How long has this been going on?" Mac asked the tall man casually.

"It started this morning. All the boozers came out of the woodwork. And, I think, maybe that meteor created some new ones." The tall man grinned.

"Remember all those old movies about the *Titanic,* with the passengers insisting women and children first . . . singing bravely while the band plays? . . ."

"Our passengers may be singing, too," the man said.

Mac nodded in agreement. "I may join them. You know the old saying, 'When in Rome . . .' "

" 'When in Rome . . .' Yes, sir." The tall man grinned again and Mac knew by the *Yes, sir* that he'd been recognized. On the corporation chart, one of the top men at Centrol, he was technically Krause's boss, which made him this man's corporate superior.

"Is Krause in here?"

"Yes, sir. Over there at the end of the bar." He nodded briefly with his head to indicate the direction.

"Thank you."

"Yes, sir."

The *Yes, sirs* annoyed Mac and he thought they were unnecessary but reminded himself that such things were fairly standard within Centrol and corporations such as Synpla. And—hadn't he been saying *Yes, sir* to Alex only a short time ago?

Krause was at the bar with Julia, his secretary, and a young blond-haired girl Mac did not recognize. Krause was sitting at the very end of the bar, with an SS male agent sitting between the two women. At a nod from Krause, the agent relinquished his seat to Mac.

Julia appeared half drunk. The blonde appeared blurry-eyed. Mac withdrew a twenty-credit note from his wallet and placed it on the bar.

"I need one of your coupons, sir," the bartender said.

Mac tore one of the coupons from the book, placed it on the bar beside the twenty, and ordered a Galactic Screwdriver.

Krause leaned forward to speak to Mac and said, "Mac, do you know Lucille?"

Mac looked into the blonde's pretty face and said, "No, I don't know Lucille."

"Lucille, do you know Mac . . . short for MacPherson?"

The blonde's eyes were dark, watery, and blurry—all rolled into one, Mac thought. She studied Mac's face and said, "No, I don't know Mac short-for-MacPherson."

"Maybe someone will introduce you two some day," Julia muttered drunkenly and sipped her drink.

Mac's drink arrived and the bartender took the coupon but slid the twenty-credit bill back. "Everything is on the house except for the coupons, sir."

As Mac gulped his drink, the blonde named Lucille said, "What does a MacPherson do?"

"A MacPherson does as little as he can, tries to stay out of trouble, and sometimes tries to make as much money as he can, although the stuff is most often proven worthless by quirks of fate, as we just witnessed."

"Mac is a big big man at Centrol," Julia filled in. "Special assistant to Alexander Stauffer."

The blonde's dark, liquid eyes twinkled as she smiled and said, "Wow. You must be either modest or . . ."

When she didn't finish and raised her drink to her mouth instead, Mac waited until she lowered the glass. When she acted as if she would not finish the sentence, he prodded, "Or what?"

"Maybe I shouldn't say what I started to say."

"Why not?" The more he looked at her, the more he liked what he saw. *She's really beautiful,* he thought. She was slender with a look of fragility. Her mouth was very red, her lips appearing moist. Her upper lip was nearly straight while her lower lip curved downward, partially exposing perfect white teeth and giving the impression of a continuous smile. She wore two plain gold bracelets on her left wrist and wore no other jewelry, but was wearing a white jumpsuit that fell to her feet, sleeves that concealed the slenderness of her arms above the elbows. The jumpsuit would have been fairly unremarkable, considering some of the costumes and gowns that many of the women aboard ship were wearing, except that it was decorated with confetti-colored ribbon streamers. The streamers were crisscrossed at the chest, stitched tight, but hung loose around the hips and knees, fluttering in the faint flow of an air-conditioner breeze.

"What I started to say would sound terribly self-centered."

Mac grinned. "Now you really have my curiosity up. You have to tell me."

She sighed heavily as if in resignation, turned toward him once more to fix those liquid dark eyes on him, a half-shy smile on her moist red lips. "I almost said that you must be either modest or had no desire to impress me."

Mac waited a few moments before he responded, trying to gather his thoughts. "I have a desire to impress you now that I've had a good look at you," Mac said.

"Thanks."

"How can I impress you?" He sipped his drink again.

She shrugged. "I don't know. If I think of any ways, I'll let you know. Meanwhile . . . maybe you'll think of something. Of course . . ." She toyed with her glass and despite the flirtatious look in her eyes and the teasing smile, her mannerisms seemed shy. "Of course, I'm already impressed by your being a big big man at Central and a special assistant to Alexander Stauffer, the richest man in the universe."

"Thank you, Lucille. I'm glad to hear you're impressed." Wishing to compliment her in some manner, he added unthinkingly, "You know, in that outfit, you look good enough to eat."

Her eyes twinkled, "Is that a promise?"

The flirtatious remark caught him off guard for some reason and he felt his cheeks flushing. It became a vicious cycle. He was embarrassed because of the blush and the embarrassment increased the reaction.

Julia was poking him in the ribs. "If you two lovebirds can spare a minute, my boss has been trying to attract your attention."

Lucille did not notice his blushing or else chose to give the impression she had not noticed it. As she sipped her drink, Mac looked beyond Julia. Krause leaned forward and said, "I need to talk to you for five or ten minutes . . . alone. I have some problems that I need your advice on." He looked at Julia and finished, "Could you girls please visit the powder room for roughly ten minutes?"

"We could disappear for the rest of the day if you want a really long conference," Julia said huffily.

Krause did not answer and when the two girls were a distance away, he said, "Mac, I'm having several problems simultaneously and I don't know what to do about them. I'm taking steps but nothing seems too effective. I need any suggestions or advice you might have."

"What are the problems?"

Krause moved a hand to indicate the lounge around them. "What

105

you see here—the excessive drinking—is only part of the overall reaction of the passengers. Some are going crazy under the strain, literally insane. Although we keep it as quiet as we possibly can, we have a suicide periodically. One of the stews found twelve bodies . . . all victims of a mass murderer. She kept it quiet, locked all the doors to the area, arranged for the bodies to be carried to the morgue on a strictly hush-hush basis. We have to find that murderer before he strikes again—keeping his existence quiet, otherwise we might drive all the passengers into a panic.

"Almost everybody, expecting that the ship might fall apart any minute, has decided to get in one last bang. I always thought I was liberal minded, but, you know, there's so much screwing going on, it's starting to get on my nerves. I suppose that's the least of the problems. One of the worst problems is the drugs floating around the ship. Somebody apparently had a ton of every kind of mind-altering and hallucinogenic pill in existence. The intention must have been to sell them on Algor when we arrived. It sure as hell was a wholesale movement, not the work of a single pusher. After the meteor hit, he or she or they must have decided to unload the pills at bargain basement prices. Pills are floating all over the ship like candy. With so many passengers popping pills that make them behave erratically and unpredictably, control is getting more and more difficult. I've advised Alex to stay in his suite for his own safety because we have an unstable condition everywhere else in the ship. He says he's bored and wants to mingle with the other passengers. I'm trying to save his neck and he's sore at me."

Mac sipped his drink, set the glass on the bar top and said lightly, "I'm glad you don't have any serious problems."

For a long moment Krause looked as if he could not decide whether he wanted to laugh or hit Mac.

"Which type of drug is giving you the worst problem?"

Krause shrugged. "It's a toss up. The one going around the ship in the largest quantities is that brand called Little Red Devils. They make people uninhibited and therefore unpredictable. The ones called

DEMOs zonk people out while they have their favorite hallucination or fantasy or whatever, but some people, one in ten, come out of it with bad effects—seeing giant bugs or snakes or whatever. They're still hallucinating, half conscious, half unconscious—and some of them try to kill the hallucinations. Even if no one is hurt, it rattles the other passengers when they see someone running out into a hall, beating on the walls with a shoe. And sometimes people are hurt. We had a passenger come out of a DEMO trance and grab a gun and start shooting at a giant bug. One of the bullets hit another passenger. Luckily it didn't kill him."

The bad effects of DEMOs were well known, Mac reflected, but the trouble seemed to be that since only one in ten suffered bad aftereffects, most people took the chance that they would be in the lucky nine out of ten. He remembered reading somewhere that some of the people who *did* suffer bad effects went through that spell only a minute or so, and many considered it a worthwhile price for an hour or two of pure fantasy pleasure.

"I think I can cut down on the use of the hard drugs," Mac said thoughtfully.

"How?"

"Let me go ahead and do it and then I'll tell you what I did. The Little Red Devils . . . That's a tough one. Offhand I can't think of any way to get people to stop using them. That would be like trying to get people to stop drinking booze or to stop smoking."

Krause grunted. "Maybe we'll have to live with the Little Red Devils. If we're stranded in space too long, I might start taking them myself."

Mac realized that although he was technically Krause's superior in the chain of command, Krause was subtly assigning *him* various chores. He felt a burst of resentment and then immediately suffocated it. Krause was a natural leader. And, even as he reflected on the situation, Krause was delicately giving him another assignment:

"There's something else you could check into Mac . . . something that might save our necks. We have Nomads aboard."

"Nomads?" All his resentment at their relationship vanished in a wave of new excitement and hope. The Nomads were a secret society of men and women with teleportative ability. Some Nomads could teleport themselves from one planet to another . . .

"How many are aboard?"

"At least half a dozen so far as we can determine. You know how secretive they are. But, considering the spot we're in, they've volunteered to help the other passengers. They're starting meetings at which they'll invite people to join and teach them how to teleport. Their first meeting aboard ship is this evening, eight o'clock. Maybe you could attend, see what's going on, estimate how effective they will be in helping . . ."

Mac nodded yes that he would attend the meeting. All his resentful thoughts about rank were now gone. Not everyone could learn how to teleport, he knew, although he'd forgotten the exact statistics. But if a Nomad could teleport from planet to planet, then a Nomad could obviously teleport from a wrecked spaceship to a planet.

It could be the answer that might save hundreds of lives.

CHAPTER FOURTEEN

Sam Parker slept and dreamed and then awakened into a consciousness that was much like dreaming. He was turning slowly end over end in the midst of an asteroid belt ninety million miles from a red giant star. Debris from *Starbright* surrounded him. Some of the asteroids gleamed with ice like pale moons. The universe was in slow motion, a beautiful but senseless kaleidoscope in shades of black and white on strange objects and the planetoids.

Where am I?

He remembered—

Diane Russell and he had helped in the operation to lighten the burden on the ship's gravity system. They had worked side by side hour after hour. During the work and in between the work periods, they had become better and better acquainted . . .

Then the man known as Krause had asked for volunteers for a dangerous mission.

Diane had volunteered.

He'd volunteered.

And ten others.

They had all been interviewed individually and the twelve had been narrowed down to six.

When they were each informed of the exact nature of the mission, one of the six declined. One was eliminated for reasons unknown.

There were four of them now, in space, with the "wreckage" of the *Starbright*—decoy wreckage that included everything from metal and papers to human corpses . . .

The visual SOS signal flashed brilliantly in a soundless explosion of light that would be seen for millions of miles and also flashed through subspace for a span of indefinite light-years as the ripples on a lake. He thought ironically, *That signal may go on and on across more light-years than I can imagine, eventually to be seen by a race of froglike creatures. By the time they reach us—if they have attained a stage of intergalactic travel—I may be ninety years old. Or they may come here a thousand years after my death, to see what made the strange light so deep in space* . . .

He shoved the thoughts aside. The SOS signal mechanism, as large as an average desk, was now behind one of the asteroids, still flashing but temporarily beyond view.

Diane Russell floated nearby, linked to his spacesuit by one of the tractor beams designed to keep machanics in contact with each other when working on the hull of a ship in outer space.

Are you asleep, Diane? he telepathed.

No answer.

I must be crazy, he thought. He had been attracted to the tall red-head from the first time he saw her. Maybe he was in love with her, but following her into space on this suicide mission was utterly ridiculous. They had not had a real date so far. He had not even kissed her yet. Their most intimate moments had been when she slapped his face and threw him over her shoulder, to land upside down against a wall. Other than that, secondary intimacies had been having quick lunches together and cups of coffee during the short work-break periods. She had started to smile at him, as if she liked him, and he'd thought he detected a kind of half gleam in her eye when she looked at him.

Is that enough to follow a woman into the depths of space? he asked himself. *A smile and a gleam?*

"Are you awake, Diane?" he inquired over the intercom.

When she did not respond, he activated the tractor beam to draw her motionless body closer so he could look through her helmet.

Her eyes were closed, her expression utterly peaceful. He wondered if she was dreaming and, if so, what sort of dreams?

When would she awaken?

Krause's idea, he reflected, had been to make the debris seem as realistic as possible. Real debris. Real parts of the ship. Real corpses. And, Krause had reasoned, it would be likely that in any shipwreck, some passengers might react quickly enough to don spacesuits and somehow escape the ship.

They were here to fool hijackers if there were any hijackers.

If there were no hijackers, their function would be to evaluate any alien patrol ship that might answer the SOS.

In either case, he knew, they could be killed—not by the elements, but by hijackers or aliens.

Four of them— He did not know the names of the other two volunteers and had been told it was not necessary. He could not see their suits now, he could see only Diane.

They were all wearing a very expensive type of spacesuit called the "Stardrifter," specifically designed as a survival unit for someone stranded in space. There had been more than a thousand passengers aboard the *Starbright,* but only a hundred of these expensive suits. The lifeboats aboard the starliner had had a capacity of only a hundred also. Ten boats—each with a capacity of ten. All in all, the ship had contained only enough facilities to save two hundred out of a thousand passengers—scandalous porportions, but legal in this great Intergalactic Age when mankind's science and brains carried him through galaxies on the swift feet of interstellar ships, faster than laws and safety measures could follow. There had been some discussion about launching one of the lifeboats to add to the realism, but no final decision had been made at the time that Diane and he and the others had been set adrift. He wondered now if they had finally decided to add a boat to the debris and glanced in each direction futilely a few moments.

No sign of a lifeboat . . .

He wondered when he would sleep again . . .

The Stardrifter spacesuits were designed to keep each occupant in a languorous state—both physically and mentally—through built-in hypno-electronics. The sleep patterns induced by the hypnos were irregular. It had been explained to Sam that whenever he felt himself drifting off to sleep, he would never know if it would be for a nap of an hour or two hours, or an extended deep sleep of anywhere from a day to four or five days. The pattern was random and unpredictable because it had been proven bad psychologically for a Stardrifter user to know in advance the length of each sleep period. Not knowing resulted in a much greater relaxation. In between sleeps, their bodies were at such a reduced condition that it was nearly identical to the lethargy of being half-asleep.

Because Operation Lightweight had given birth to Operation Decoy, each of the four volunteers had been assigned a link with the ship, a telepath to talk to when necessary in one way or another. Sam's telepath was a dark-haired girl named Olivia. He had met her only once for not more than ten minutes and talked to her face to face. They were not supposed to divulge the names of their private telepaths to the other volunteers but had not been told the reason why they shouldn't.

Sam had not called Olivia since he'd been planted in outer space and she had not contacted him. He decided it would be best to break the ice:

"Olivia? Are you there?"

"I'm here. I was thinking about calling you again. I called you once about an hour ago, but you were asleep. Anything wrong?"

"No. I just wanted to make our first contact."

"Good. Well, hello."

"Hello. So, now we both know everything is working."

"It certainly is."

"The *Starbright* is safely hidden?"

112

"We hope so. No. I shouldn't say *hope*. I know so."

"I feel like a piece of bait out here." And knew he *was* a piece of live bait. And there were three others.

"Don't dwell on that aspect. And whenever you do think of it, consider yourself a decoy rather than bait. How is your Diane?"

"What do you mean, *my* Diane?"

"Your girl friend, Diane."

"We don't qualify as girl friend and boy friend. She's a Virgin."

"Well, she could be a Virgin and still be your girl friend. I've seen the way you look at her. And the way she looks at you."

"You have a vivid imagination. I look at her the way I look at any woman."

"I doubt that. You're not aware of the glow in your eyes when you look at Diane."

The conversation had started to embarrass him. He wondered if he could turn the tide in some way. "Diane is sound asleep, and I have no idea when she'll awaken, since our Stardrifter suits are not synchronized. Incidentally. . . are you married?"

"Yes. Why do you ask?"

"I enjoyed talking to you when we met. You're a very attractice woman. I was thinking about asking you for a date when we return to civilization. But, if you're married . . ."

"I still date occasionally," Olivia answered. "My husband travels quite a lot in his work and I travel in mine. We have an understanding."

"Oh. Then I could ask you for a date?"

"If you could get your mind off Diane long enough."

"What does your husband do?"

"He's an astrophysicist."

As he tried to think of someone else to say, Olivia inquired, "How's the weather out there?"

"Everything is calm. No hijackers or aliens in sight yet. The SOS flashes sometimes in a position where I can see it and it looks like a nova. It would seem that someone somewhere, hijackers or aliens, will see that damned light."

"Or hear the intergalactic radio distress signal."

"I would hate to wait out here forever."

"You won't have to. A Stardrifter suit can keep an occupant alive in outer space for four months, but Krause has decided to cut Operation Decoy short at three months."

For a moment Sam wondered how he would feel at the end of three months but discarded that line of useless thinking immediately. With the extended sleep patterns, being in space that period of time might seem like only three days. And, when conscious, he would have Olivia to talk to. And Diane—whenever their patterns coincided the right way.

"And what do we do if Operation Decoy doesn't work?" Sam asked.

"How do you mean *doesn't*? It is in operation."

"I mean, if it draws neither rescuers—or hijackers."

"In that eventuality, *Starbright* would begin searching for a habitable planet. Not an easy task when done through the auxiliary bridge with fewer controls and instruments . . . But, I've been told, it can be done."

"If we start discovering habitable planets—" The sentence froze in his throat as a woman drifted by. She was middle-aged, a corpse with open mouth and staring eyes, the condition of her body so grotesque that it shocked him as few things in his life had ever shocked him before.

"Are you all right?" Olivia inquired.

"Yeah. Someone floated by. Krause has made this Operation Decoy look realistic all right. How many bodies are out here?"

"I'd rather not tell you. It wouldn't do you any good to know."

"What were we talking about? . . ." Sam watched in fascination as the body of a woman slowly drifted around the side of a planetoid the size of a house. Or was the planetoid drifting between them? It was impossible to tell who was doing what, only possible to see the end effect.

114

"You were talking about habitable planets."

"Oh. That's right. If we discover some livable planets, who will make the decision which one to live on? Stauffer? Or will the passengers be able to vote on it?"

"I don't really know," Olivia reported. "If we should be so lucky as to find a habitable planet, I think—"

Faintly amused that she had stopped midsentence also, Sam inquired, "What happened?"

"I've been keeping an eye on some of the cameras we hid on the asteroids," Olivia said shakily. "Operation Decoy has worked. Someone has bitten. Turn your suit ninety degrees . . ."

Sam turned slowly. Spaceships were appearing between the asteroid belt and the giant red star. He knew by the configurations and elaborate fins that they were alien. No offspring of Terra had ever designed ships with such fins . . .

Aliens, not hijackers, had answered Operation Decoy.

Two things other than their being alien caused Sam to feel a chill . . .

The number of the alien ships. They were winking into existence from subspace by the dozens. There were hundreds altogether—a tremendous *fleet* of ships. From experience he knew that no race capable of intergalactic flight traveled in *fleets* unless they were in conflict.

This was an alien race at war.

The ships were huge. He had seen *Starbright* silhouetted against the giant red star. Checking his perspective, he saw that each of these ships was ten times larger than *Starbright*. Size meant strength of many kinds when it came to measuring the size of an intergalactic ship. And this fleet of aliens had not only size but incredible numbers . . . so many they were blocking his view of the red star.

Without exaggeration, a mighty alien army had answered their decoy!

CHAPTER FIFTEEN

Julia and Lucille returned to the lounge. Mac finished his quota of five drinks—plus the one that Krause "bought" for him. He felt half-drunk but all his tensions had been eased by the alcohol and the association with Lucille, and with Krause and his secretary. He looked forward with interest to his first Nomad meeting—wondered if he could join the group and wondered if he could learn how to teleport from one planet to another. He knew he would soon have to talk to the navigator and then report to Stauffer. He dreaded those particular tasks but knew there would be no way to avoid them . . .

"I have to leave this merriment shortly," Lucille said, glancing at the tiny watch on her wrist. "Troyan has originated some committees. The Entertainment Committee will meet and it's been suggested I should attend."

"Let me walk you part of the way," Mac said. "I have to visit the navigator. He's near the conference rooms . . ."

As they walked toward the set of conference rooms in the center of the ship, Lucille held his hand.

Like a little girl taking the hand of an adult as she is half-frightened while crossing the street?

At first he felt self-conscious, but then he began to enjoy the sensation of holding her hand. Occasionally they passed other couples in the corridor. When some of the men saw Lucille, they looked envious.

She's really beautiful, he thought again, and decided he should learn more about her:

"You haven't told me anything about yourself. What do you do?"

"What do I do? How quaint. I am glad you asked. I, my dear sir, am an entrepreneur and playgirl."

Mac laughed. "I like the way you say that with modesty."

"I love the combination. The entrepreneur half allows me to work hard and accomplish loads of things. The playgirl half lets me have loads of fun."

"What sort of entrepreneuring do you do?"

"Mostly in the entertainment business. I suppose that's why some of my friends suggested I attend this Entertainment Committee. I've produced plays, movies, special events. I owned a circus for a short time. Remind me to tell you about that when you have a spare day."

"Maybe some Sunday," Mac quipped.

"That *is* a date," and he thought her hand tightened its grip around his but the increase in pressure bordered on the imperceptible. "I believe I *do* belong in the Entertainment Committee," she continued easily, "because I have some definite theories and philosophies concerning entertainment. We've had several suicides and attempted suicides since the wreck. Depression and hysteria are increasing and could become epidemic if we're not careful about our entertainment values. I think it will be vital to maintain our morale as we work for survival."

"I agree with you. Wholeheartedly."

"Could you explain something to me?"

"If it's not too complicated," he responded lightly with a grin.

"I know Krause works for Alex Stauffer. And Julia said you're a big man at Centrol. Special assistant to Alex. But I also heard someone say that Krause works for Synpla . . . which is a corporation owned by Alex . . ." She frowned, her pencil thin eyebrows contorting prettily. "But . . . I know Alex owns hundreds of corporations all over the universe. What is Centrol? Someone said something about Krause working for Centrol also? . . . When we were in the powder room,

Julia said something about your working for Synpla. But she'd already said you worked for Central . . . She was drunk, so I didn't push for an explanation, but I was wondering . . ."

Her interest was flattering. He explained, "Central is a type of headquarters organization for all the Stauffer corporations. That's not to say it *controls* all the branches, but it's a headquarters where information and thinking and decision making is more or less pooled. *I* work for Central. Krause works for Central. But . . . Synpla is Stauffer's largest corporation. Someone has to pay our salaries. Although we work out of Central and for Central, we're officially on Synpla's payroll. So, in a sense, Krause and I both work for Central . . and for Synpla. Did that explain everything?"

"No. Not really. Now I'm more confused than ever, but it's not as important because you at least *tried* to explain." She began holding onto his arm instead of his hand. The fragrance of her perfume began to affect his senses. He was conscious of the soft roundness of a breast pressing against him as they walked.

Far ahead in the corridor two men were arguing. They fought briefly. One man was knocked down. The victor hurried away down the corridor. The loser rose slowly and went off in another direction.

"Everyone is going crazy," Lucille murmured. "There are more and more fights . . . Over what I don't know."

They walked in silence awhile. A door opened on one side. A woman emerged, saying to someone inside, "I'll get her . . . wherever she is." She was a slender dark-haired woman wearing a one-piece gown and, to Mac, appeared under the influence of drugs. He looked beyond the woman's shoulder into the room, and saw a maze of naked humans indulging in group sex while others stood on the border, watching quietly. As the dark-haired woman turned to survey them through bleary eyes, she said in a low, slurred voice, "Wanna join our party?"

"Shall we?" Lucille asked, looking up at Mac and smiling mischievously.

"Maybe later," Mac said.

Several minutes later they passed a small sign on the wall that said ASTRODOMES, with an arrow indicating a nearby stairway.

"Let's visit the astrodomes!" Lucille said gleefully. She tugged at his arm.

"You'll be late for the committee meeting . . ."

"Baloney," Lucille countered. "Who cares? It'll take them half an hour to get started."

They went up the stairs and settled into one of the unoccupied astrodomes. There were two chairs side by side, but, when Mac settled into one of the chairs, Lucille settled on the floor by his feet.

"On my first starflight, after I divorced one of my husbands, I saw my first astrodome," Lucille informed him. "I've been hooked on them ever since. Isn't it beautiful?"

She was gazing at the dome above their heads. A small dome physically—perhaps only a yard or so above their heads—but because of certain special effects, the dome gave the impression they were sitting in the open beneath a starfilled sky with galaxies of stars stretching into infinity.

"Beautiful," Mac agreed. As he studied a spectacular spiral nebula, he felt Lucille rest her arm on his knee. Then she was resting her arm on his center thigh. Then on his thigh near his hip. As he continued studying the kaleidoscope of stars, he felt the touch of her fingertips at his crotch, exploring as lightly as the brush of butterfly wings. Shy in their touch but bold in their actions, the pads of her fingers outlined the length and thickness of his maleness. The dimensions were changing, growing as she explored.

When he had reached his maximum, she whispered, "Not bad." Then she was opening his clothing, reaching in, withdrawing his member. He felt the flickering of her tongue, skilled kisses, and then the tight circle of her warm mouth. He looked down once to see her blond head as it bobbed smoothly and expertly above his lap. The sensation was ecstasy. He exploded. Moments later she had adjusted his clothing back to its original status, rose, absently repairing her lipstick. "Maybe we should leave now . . . I should go to that Entertainment Committee meeting."

"Right." He thought a moment and added, "Thanks."

"Pay me back after the meeting," Lucille said casually, eyes twinkling as they went out into the hall.

"You're a bit uninhibited, aren't you?"

Lucille laughed softly. "No. As a matter of fact, I'm a very modest, shy, old-fashioned, inhibited girl." Their eyes met and she could see the question in his expression. She opened her purse and withdrew a large plastic bag of small red pills. "It's the Little Red Devils in me," she said. "Want one?"

This is Olivia, the telecom inside Krause's head said. *We have company. A lot of company. Can you come here to take a look?*

I'll be right there.

Moments later, Krause was standing behind Olivia, studying the images in the screens. They had hidden some cameras on the asteroids and some were floating a few hundred miles on the starward side of the asteroid belt. All the cameras were of an Intergalactic Army type that would self-destruct if tampered with and could also destruct upon telepathic command.

It had been decided that Olivia should set up her observation post near the auxiliary bridge and they had managed to locate an adjoining compartment. Krause knew he would have to tell the *Starbright* crew immediately, so he opened the door to the auxiliary bridge and made the announcement about the arrival of their visitors.

Olivia soon had more than a dozen observers crowded into her compartment.

"We have stirred up some *big* local boys," one of the crew members said. "Look at the size of those ships!"

"Each one is more than ten times the size of *Starbright,*" a crewmember agreed.

"And," another said, "if *Starbright* has a capacity of one thousand passengers . . ."

"Each of those crates could carry *ten thousand.*"

CHAPTER SIXTEEN

When McPherson knocked on the door that bore the label, *Navigator* and received no answer, he turned the knob and went in, not knowing what to expect and prepared for almost anything.

The space beyond was a breathtaking astroglobe. He'd heard of them but had never seen one before. It was immense, possibly one of the largest compartments aboard ship. Adding to the impression of size was the fact that the entire circumference of the globe was a three-dimensional panorama of stars. A clear, transparent floor dissected the globe so that, as Mac walked a few steps, he had the eerie sensation of walking through the emptiness of outer space, surrounded by stars.

The sensation is strange, almost frightening, yet beautiful, he thought.

A small control console with four seats occupied the exact center of the astroglobe. The console itself was constructed in a velvety black material and the four seats, arranged in a tight square—two seats back to back with the other two—were black leather. Since the astrocomputers and telescopes were softly illuminated by faint lights, the arrangement gave the appearance of the navigator sitting in outer space on a pedestal . . .

Like a small god, Mac thought.

The navigator was in full uniform, complete with medals from intergalactic wars.

He looks more like an admiral than a navigator.

A handsome man, in his forties or fifties . . . with a neat beard flecked with gray, sideburns also streaked with gray . . . straight nose . . . cool gray eyes, broad forehead . . .

Unmoving. Staring straight ahead as if in concentration. Dead.

As Mac wondered what could have killed the navigator, he detected a movement of the eyes and realized with some surprise and embarrassment that the man was *working.* The telescope near his head, apparently on some sort of automatic course, was revolving slowly through the bright flecks of a galaxy, displaying fields of stars on a small screen that the navigator studied intently. A small button marked REC flashed quietly, periodically, to show that the visual images were being recorded on a navigational tape.

The navigator turned slowly to look at Mac and one of his eyebrows rose. Mac's knock on the door had activated a small flashing light on the console that the navigator deactivated with a casual movement of his hand.

"Sorry to interrupt you," Mac said. He reached into his jacket pocket, withdrew one of his cards, and handed it to the other man.

After studying the card for what seemed an unreasonably long time, the navigator said, "Special Assistant to Alexander Stauffer . . . How does it feel to be an assistant to the richest man in the universe? Do you help him count his money? . . . Do you help him survey his vast holdings? . . . Do you help in the screwing of all the fine young female things that gigantic fortune must draw like fluttering moths to a bright light?"

Mac was about to answer one of the questions when the man added, extending his hand, "My name is Michael McDunn."

"Glad to know you, Mike," Mac said. It hit him suddenly . . . The expression on McDunn's face, the slightly affected and rambling way of speaking . . .

The navigator is drunk, Mac thought. He inhaled long and slowly through his nostrils, finally detecting the odor of alcohol. *My God. We're wrecked and lost in space and the damned navigator is drunk! The one man who could lead us back to civilization!*

"I'll tell you what I would do if I were special assistant to the richest man in the universe," McDunn said. He gestured expansively. "I'd say, 'Look over here, sir, what do you think of this, sir?' And then, when I had him securely looking over there, I'd move in the opposite direction and relieve him of some of the immense burden of his money."

Drunk talk. Senseless.

"MacPherson? Do they call you 'Mac'?"

Mac nodded yes.

"Mac and Mike," McDumm said. "We should be a team of some sort. A comedy team or news commentators . . ." He changed his voice and said, "And now we bring you Mac and Mike, the funniest team since vaudeville, the wackiest pair this side of Andromeda. Or . . . Stay tuned for the latest and most up-to-date news brought to you by our twin anchormen, Matthew MacPherson and Michael Mc-Dunn . . ." He grinned appealingly, his eyes gleaming in the glow from the millions of stars all around them. "Of course . . . being a team of Matthew MacPherson and Michael McDunn, we could confuse the living bejabbers out of simpleminded folk . . . all those M's, you know . . . them calling us Mike MacPherson, Mac McDunn, McPherson and MacDunn . . . and so forth and so on. But, I think, in actuality, things being what they are, we should at least be great friends."

McDunn paused half a moment and said, "Would you care for a drink?"

Mac nodded yes. McDunn produced a fifth from under his chair and held it up. Mac took the bottle, uncapped it, raised it, gulped a slug. It was good stuff. Smooth, strong, expensive. One of the new blends developed a year or so ago. He couldn't remember the name, but he remembered the taste. McDunn knew how to drink, all right.

"Good stuff," Mac said. "Thanks." He took another slug and felt this second jolt warming his stomach. He began relaxing. "You're right," he said. "We should be at least great friends."

"But did you come today on behalf of Alexander Stauffer?"

Mac returned the bottle and nodded yes.

"And what does the great Alexander Stauffer wish from a lowly navigator?"

"Shortly after the accident, Mr. Stauffer—through one of his assistants inquired about our location. The assistant learned through the *Starbright* central computer that we are in an uncharted galaxy . . . and the navigational equipment is not working. He asked me to cover four points with you. Number one—he would like to know where we are. Number two—how soon can the navigational equipment be repaired? Number three—he would like to offer you a position with his corporation, Synpla, salary negotiable, starting immediately. And, number four—since he has several resources aboard the *Starbright*, Mr. Stauffer has inquired if you need anything for your comfort or the performance of your duties? I am authorized on his behalf to negotiate your salary or any other necessary items."

McDunn drank from the bottle again and passed it on to Mac. "Number four . . . For the performance of my duties . . . I've heard that the onmipotently wealthy Alexander Stauffer has a small army of guards aboard. Correct?"

"Correct," Mac assured him as he finished another slug of the booze.

"Then . . . I would like to respectfully request, for the performance of my duties, two guards to be posted at the door to this place."

"That can be done easily enough. But why? Do you expect someone to try to harm you?"

McDunn gestured with a negligent wave of his hand. "I could tell you stories that would curl the hairs on the back of your neck. I'm sure you've seen the headlines, but doubt you've heard all the gory details. The U.S.S. *Spaceways*, out of Betelgeuse for a short hop to a tourist planet, dipped into subspace and slipped out smack into a meteor field, much as we did, with its energy screen failing also. A meteor struck the ship and the pilot wittily dashed the craft back into subspace and out again. It was a good choice because, otherwise, with the energy screen not working at all, they would have been battered to ribbons. Well, it so happened the gear had been damaged badly and the pilot had dashed them into the middle of nowhere. Saved their lives but only God knew where they were and He wasn't talking right then.

"So the hundred and eighty-six passengers became a wee bit excited and someone got the bright idea of asking the navigator what had happened and where they were. Not the captain or the pilot, or the chief engineer, mind you, but the navigator. So, they crowded around him and said, 'Where are we? Where are we?' He's saying, 'I don't know! I don't know!' Next they're saying, 'You must! You must!' And since they were somewhat worried about drifting through space until they starved to death, they strapped him to his chair and began burning his toes with matches and cigarettes, hopefully to burn some sense into his skull . . . but it didn't work . . . and he died of shock. Ten years later a cruiser found the ship drifting on the beach of a savage planet, a ship filled with skeletons and the diary of a passenger that told the story of the sorry truth.

"Another ship, out of Earth, bound for Sirius, a similar accident, similarly lost in space, the passengers took a different tack and pressed the captain for an explanation, but he, seeing the possibilities of a mob of panicked and unruly passengers, being somewhat unscrupulous, said, 'It's the navigator's fault!' And, realizing they would float in space until they turned to dust, the passengers broke the navigator's bones one by one."

"I see your point. I—"

"But there is one more, milder story. Another ship, out of Cassiopeia, bound for Regulus, a relatively short run, slipped into subspace and the hyperdrive malfunctioned. They emerged into normal space again, in the middle of nobody knew where, safe and sound, but lost as hell. Knowing the navigator was the only one with the ability to calculate their whereabouts and find home again, the passengers stayed with the poor man night and day to see he worked at his utmost to save their necks. They put him to bed at a time voted upon and got him up when they decided best. The poor man couldn't go to the bathroom without a committee of a dozen accompanying him to see he didn't tarry beyond nature's necessary time. They drove the poor man mad."

"I see your point," Mac said. "I'll arrange for guards."

"Ah . . . since I have no desire to have my toes burned or bones broken or a hundred crazy passengers camping at my elbows until I'm driven mad, I am most appreciative."

Activating his telecom, Mac said silently, *Gwenna, will you arrange for two guards to be posted at the navigator's quarters? I'll explain the reason later.*

Will do, Gwenna answered briefly.

"As to the other half of number four," McDunn said. "My comfort . . . The captain had a case of booze in the ship's cargo. He will have no use for it in the hereafter. I will have a great use if you can acquire it . . ." He watched Mac questioningly.

"I think that can be arranged," Mac said. On this one, he decided, it would be best not to use Gwenna. Through the telecom, he contacted Krause and requested, *Will you have one of your men take custody of a certain item in the ship's cargo?*

Sounds easy enough, Krause answered. *What item?*

A case of booze. It should be listed under the captain's name on the manifest. Hold it until I see you again and then I'll tell you the destination.

"Number three may be unimportant except for the prestige," McDunn was saying. "What is the top figure that I could bargain for?"

"I would say around ten thousand credits a day."

"Then . . . that's the figure I want."

"On behalf of Alexander Stauffer and the Synpla Corporation," Mac said, "you are now officially on the payroll."

"Good. Number two—how soon can the navigational equipment

be repaired? The answer to that one is that the equipment is not broken. We are in an uncharted galaxy and surrounded by other unknown galaxies. The result is that the navigational equipment cannot *function*. There is a difference between being broken or in disrepair and simply not functioning. The equipment cannot function because all the computerized data is worthless."

Mac thought aloud in a soft voice, "Like having detailed street maps but being in the wrong city."

"Worse than that," McDunn said. "It is like being in the wrong city in the wrong state in the wrong country, *on the wrong continent.*"

"Then that answers the first point." Mac's throat felt very dry. "Alexander Stauffer wanting to know where we are . . . The answer to number one is that we are lost."

McDunn nodded his head affirmatively.

"This may be a stupid question," Mac said, forcing himself to go on because it was a question he did not want to ask, "but . . . *how* lost?"

"You say it and I'll nod my head if you're correct. What is your guess?"

"Hopelessly lost?"

McDunn nodded his head yes.

"There is absolutely no chance of finding our way back to civilization as we know it?"

McDunn nodded his head yes again.

"And absolutely no chance that anyone will rescue us?"

"One chance in a million," McDunn said.

"What is that one chance?"

"You must know from your elementary astronomy courses that there are millions of galaxies in the universe. Mankind has largely set out on definite intergalactic trade routes with occasional explorations into other galaxies. But the nature of the animal is such that we would not have time to explore and chart all of the universe if mankind had a million years to do so. We are in an uncharted unexplored unknown galaxy surrounded by thousands and thousands of other uncharted unexplored unknown galaxies. We are in one of those corners where

127

mankind has not even set foot previously. There are no familiar stars. None at all. The one chance in a million is if another Earth ship should venture into this unexplored corner of everything and somehow spot us."

"I've heard the intergalactic radio is not functioning. Could it be made operable?"

"No."

"Could you tell me why?"

"I think one of the engineers could explain that better than myself."

"What about a visual signal?"

"A visual signal works fine when you're somwehere along the trade routes or in a galaxy where there's some activity. We could start sending a visual signal, but it would be lost in the maze of stars that surrounds us. If it was somehow accidentally visible to an earth ship or station, it would take anywhere from ten thousand years to a million years for the signal to carry. Chances are that a visual signal would attract any alien races in the neighborhood that have reached the stage of interplanetary travel."

"Isn't that worth a try?"

McDunn shrugged. "We could sit around for hours and have a discussion about what results might be obtained."

"I mean . . . the aliens could help us."

McDunn shrugged again. "That could be argued. Why should they help us? Chances are they wouldn't be humanoid. And they sure as hell wouldn't be speaking English. Communication with aliens is always difficult. In the books it sounds so easy, but in reality it's nearly impossible. An alien race might be inclined to kill us on the spot as troublesome intruders. Or . . . they could decide to eat us for dinner."

Mac grunted. "Any chance of discovering a habitable planet that we could land on?"

McDunn raised a finger, smiling broadly. "Ah . . . that is what I have been working on . . . that and charting the galaxy around us."

Mac was silent and thoughtful for several long moments. McDunn drank from the bottle and handed it to him. After another slug, he said, "Do me a favor?"

McDunn waved expansively in the grand gesture of a drunk willing to do anything for another drink. "Certainly."

"Don't tell anyone else that we're completely lost. I'm afraid that news would cause more trouble than we could handle. If the passengers have to know the truth . . . let them learn the truth gradually. Let's put forth the story that we *are* off course in an uncharted galaxy, but that we have the situation under control and it will take awhile to chart a new course."

As Mac headed toward Alexander Stauffer's quarters a few minutes later, he wondered how he could break the news that they were hopelessly lost.

CHAPTER SEVENTEEN

Alone in his cabin, Krause poured a stiff drink, sipped it, took a shower, slipped into a robe and returned to his bunk where he sat with his back against some pillows. The thinkwriter on the other side of the room chattered softly as it recorded his thoughts—

I could never keep a handwritten diary, because I never had the patience for one. This gadget might work since it's easy to sit here and think and let it write everything down.

The salesman said he had two hundred of these machines that he had planned to sell on Algor. He claimed that he had sold almost every one and would sell the last today or tomorrow. (I told Mac he should get one and also asked the salesman to hold one for him.) Everyone wants to write their last will and testament and/or their last thoughts or farewell letters, and those who believe we will survive this shipwreck have ideas about writing either articles about their experiences or Great Earth Novels. They have the right idea since this is the first time in our history that a ship with as many as a thousand passengers has been shipwrecked in outer space and no doubt there will be millions of people who will want to know what happened.

Does everyone wander so much when they write a diary?

What points do I want to record about today?

One unfortunate incident is that our new captain, James Franklin, committed suicide. Several people had told me that he was incompetent, a weakling afraid of his own shadow. Since he was the senior officer aboard ship, there wasn't much we could do about it. The sight of the alien ships seemed to unnerve him and then someone informed me only a few hours ago that he had committed suicide. We will never know if it was fear of responsibility that forced him into it or simply straightforward fear.

Command of the ship has now officially passed to Technician 1/C Natalaie Farrell. I haven't met her yet but everyone says she is cool and competent.

A stewardess found the bodies of twelve men and women and managed to keep the incident under cover. Only two of the twelve had close friends who began inquiring about their whereabouts and we have managed to keep them quiet to prevent a panic since there is apparently a mass murderer aboard.

We asked the stew to take a Memo-Scan. We had only one of those machines aboard and all it does basically is search a person's mind to focus on an exact memory and do a printout much like an artist's sketch. The 'description' that we got from her enabled us only to narrow the possibilities down to twenty-four men, since she did not look directly at the man's face.

The instructions that came with this machine said that if you want to stress the importance of something such as a diary entry, you think Cap at the beginning and then Uncap at the end.

Cap. OF NUMBER ONE IMPORTANCE FOR THIS DIARY ENTRY I SUPPOSE IS THE FACT THAT THE ALIEN SHIPS WHO APPEARED AS IF IN ANSWER TO OUR DISTRESS SIGNALS—HUGE SHIPS NUMBERING IN THE HUNDREDS—HAVE MADE NO EFFORT TO RESCUE THE FOUR VOLUNTEERS WE LEFT FLOATING WITH THE ASTEROID BELT. IT HAS BEEN A WHOLE 'DAY,' MORE THAN TWENTY-FOUR HOURS SINCE THEY ARRIVED. WHY SHOULD THEY ANSWER OUR SIGNAL AND THEN JUST SIT THERE FOR A WHOLE DAY? Uncap.

Krause deactivated the machine, finished his drink, poured another and then requested the machine to play back what he had dictated. Sipping his new drink he was pleased with everything that the machine had recorded except the words "Cap." and "Uncap." He checked the instructions and saw that to keep the thinkwriter from recording those words, he would have to program it to do so.

He settled down to sleep, turning off the lights, turning on a soft background of music.

When he closed his eyes he once more saw those huge alien ships hovering by the asteroid belt.

Why were they sitting there as if waiting?

Waiting for what?

Why? Why? Why?

Mac stopped by the dispensary to visit Eva. Half because he wanted to see if she was doing all right and half because he wanted to delay his conference with Alex Stauffer.

He bought her some flowers and candy in the small gift shop and found her sitting up in bed, reading. She looked great and gave him a warm kiss on the mouth.

"They tell me you saved my life," she said. "By getting me here so fast. And they said I took an accidental overdose of sleeping pills. They gave me mnemonic surgery to forget the horror of the incident—that is, I remember what happened, but none of the details."

"That's great," Mac mumbled. "And you look great."

"I feel good," she said enthusiastically. "And . . . anxious to get back to work. They say I'll be out of here tomorrow. I've had a change in jobs. Krause has decided to take me off that undercover secretary thing and now I'll work as a liaison between Alex and Troyan. A sort of administrative assistant to both. *Liaison* is the best word for it, I guess."

She studied his face intently. He looked away. The ward was packed with patients. Other than tighter quarters it was nearly identical to an average hospital on Earth. Sometimes it was hard to believe they were on a wrecked starliner, lost in space . . .

"So . . . What's new with you?"

"I met a girl," Mac said.

"What's her name?"

"Lucille."

"Did you get any?" Eva's eyes were twinkling with impish lights. He'd heard that mnemonic surgery could lead to personality changes but this was one he hadn't expected. Eva had always been *sardonic* in the past. Now she seemed so bright and cheerful and—mischievous?

"You aren't supposed to ask that," he countered. "You're supposed to say, 'Is she pretty? Do you like her?' "

"Oh, to hell with those inanities. Getting down to brass tacks, did you get any and was she a good lay?"

"She was good . . . Let's change the subject, Eva."

"All right. What do you want to talk about?"

"The aliens out there. Why are they sitting there, not rescuing the four people we left floating with the asteroids? Do they think it's a trap? If they suspected a trap, why answer the distress signal at all?"

"I know the answer," Eva said confidently. "In college I majored in Business Administration and Alien Psychology. In AP we learned that aliens do not act or react as quickly as mankind. On Earth all living organisms react within certain margins. Alien races from other worlds in other galaxies are often far quicker or far slower. We associated slow reaction with inferior intelligence but in aliens it's often the reverse. I'll bet they're sitting there, focusing their own brand of telescope on the decoy we left . . . studying the debris."

"Why should they study the decoy?"

"They know nothing about us," Eva said. "But . . . you can bet your ass they *are learning* about us. My guess is they're studying the debris with beams we can't detect. They might suspect a trap. That may be why they came in such force—enough to handle anything. In AP we studied hundreds of alien races. When Krause stopped by to visit—"

133

"Did he bring you flowers and candy, too?" Mac asked. For a long time he had been trying to figure the exact relationship between Krause and Eva. They had always spent considerable time together . . .

"Krause? Are you kidding? Krause is a machine, a calculator. He only stopped by because I'm one of his SS agents and he wondered how soon I'd be in operation again. But Krause described the alien ships and I remembered that in AP we studied what the professor called 'Soliary Contacts.' During the past two hundred years there has been *one* other contact with an alien race similar to the one we've just encountered. Only it was a single ship—what appeared to be a scout. It came across one of our radar stations during the first Intergalactic War. The station had run out of food and supplies and sent a distress signal. An alien ship—identical to the ones that Krause described—answered the call."

"Did they help the people at the radar station?"

"The professor called them Colossians. One of the people at the radar station said that their height ranged between seven feet and ten feet . . ." Eva had heard Mac's question. She came back to it, "Help? They didn't give a crumb of food of any kind, not a drop of water. They poked around the station, killed some people with different kinds of weapons as if curious to see which type of weapon in their arsenal would kill humans most efficiently. They dissected a man and woman to learn how we tick—and, when they left, they carried two dozen girls and boys, men and women. The youngest, the healthiest . . . leaving the weak and old behind to tell the story."

Mac felt a chill. Eva seemed so convinced that the hundreds of ships out there were from the same race—Colossians. If so, that meant they were on the verge of contacting one of the most cold-blooded and heartless alien races in the universe.

CHAPTER EIGHTEEN

"Hello." It was Diane, speaking over the spacesuit intercom. He'd been so busy studying the alien ships that he hadn't noticed her awakening.

"Good morning."

"Have we been rescued yet?"

She may have intended it as a joke. He said, "Not exactly."

Diane detected the intense seriousness in his voice. "What's wrong?"

"I don't know *if* anything is wrong. But . . . Look over there." He turned her suited figure so she faced the mass of alien ships.

"My God," she whispered in awe.

Activate your spacesuit distress signals.

Diane and Sam activated the signals. The Stardrifter suits had a visual signal in each leg beneath the knee. The lights began flashing—all four of them—in a nearly blinding intensity.

After several minutes, Sam said, "Turn yours off, Diane, before we blind ourselves. I'll continue mine."

Diane turned her set of distress signals off. A period of time passed during which they both seemed hypnotized by their situation and the panorama. The silence began to gnaw at Sam's nerves. Subtly maneuvering so he could get a closer look at Diane's face, he saw she was staring unwaveringly at the alien ships. Her eyes were wide, her mouth slightly apart, fear evident by the contortion of her features.

To lighten the scene, he said, "I feel like a firefly." He *did* feel odd with the lower portion of his body flashing brilliantly. But—the attempt at levity went unnoticed.

"They're *scary*," Diane murmured. "There's so many of them . . . It must be hundreds. And each ship is so *huge*."

"The bigger they come, the harder they fall." Again Diane did not respond and he began to feel like a comedian with an unreceptive audience.

"What do you think they'll do to us? . . ."

"Probably invite us in for coffee and donuts and ask us what happened to our vehicle."

"Why would so *many* ships respond to the SOS signal?"

"My guess would be they didn't all take off to answer our call for help. I have a feeling it's a fleet of some sort on maneuvers, and just happened to be in the neighborhood when they saw our signal. So they decided to come en masse."

"Maneuvers? What kind of maneuvers?"

Turning his head away from her view, Sam bit his lower lip as he used to do as a teenager whenever he blundered. He had been thinking of *war* maneuvers and had visualized all the ships as an intergalactic army. But how could he tell Diane he thought they were observing the fighting arm of a race at war? She was frightened enough . . .

And, during his hesitation, she guessed, "Those are warships, aren't they?"

"I would say that is most likely."

As if arguing with herself, she said, "But aren't there other possibilities? A fleet of trade ships?"

"That's a possibility. Mankind has never traded in such huge numbers but that doesn't mean some alien races couldn't find it practical. Maybe they trade once a year. Or their equivalent of a year." He said it but when he saw Diane's face, she looked doubtful and he didn't believe it himself.

"Or," she went on, "an intergalactic race leaving its native planet . . ."

"Packing up and leaving because their native sun is dying or about to become a nova?" Sam asked with a smile. He had read that in books but, he remembered, from his classes in Galactic History, it seemed it had not happened in real life to mankind's knowledge. Suns had died and civilizations had withered but never moved on. A sun died in tens of thousands of years. The death was so gradual that the races had usually died of "old age" along with their suns. Some alien races had apparently died when their suns exploded, but in those cases there had been little or no warning.

"But . . . they *look* like warships," Diane continued the self-argument. "If there is a war going on in this part of the universe, it isn't our concern. Mankind isn't involved."

As time went by and their situation did not change, Sam deactivated one of the distress signals. "Now I feel like half a firefly," he joked and was rewarded by half a smile from Diane. He noticed another suit signal miles away and, hours later, saw the signal of the fourth person left in the asteroid belt as part of the decoy.

"Why is it taking them so long to rescue us?" Diane murmured. "It's been *hours*."

"I don't know . . ." At times he had the feeling the aliens were patiently *watching* them—waiting with incredible patience. But watching for *what*?—waiting for what? And there were times when he began to feel the aliens were not moving to rescue them because they did not *care*. After all, they had an intergalactic war going, didn't they? Perhaps they were on the brink of a great battle, with all their hundreds of ships and thousands of combatants gathered. Why should they take time to rescue four insignificant humans?

"I'm frightened, really frightened," Diane admitted.

"Everything will be all right."

"I have an awful feeling it's *not* going to be all right." She moved closer. "Hold me . . . please . . . hold me in your arms . . ."

137

It was awkward because of the bulkiness of the spacesuits, but he wrapped his arms around her. She calmed then. He told himself he was crazy, that if he hadn't gotten hooked on this Virgin, he could be back aboard *Starbright*, this very minute, cuddled in bed with one of those gorgeous stews.

Here I am, he thought, *in a damned asteroid belt with a Virgin— and both of us in spacesuits!*

Still—she had asked him to hold her. That was progress. And, strangely, despite the odd circumstances, he felt content—except for the sight of all those alien warships. They were disconcerting.

CHAPTER NINETEEN

As Mac waited to see Alex Stauffer, he began to feel more and more nervous.

Stop acting like a lower echelon clerk, he chided himself. The self-reprimand helped some but did not do away with his nervousness altogether.

Working for Alex Stauffer had never been easy. Alex had been compared to millionaires of the past such as Howard Hughes—There were similar physical characteristics: Alex in his thirties looked much like the photos of Hughes at the same age. Alex wore a pencil-thin mustache as Hughes had for many years . . .

Similarities ended at that point. Alex was not a recluse. Far from it. He liked to mingle. He was not shy. Whereas Hughes's fortune had grown despite many blunders, Alex rarely made a blunder. He had the reputation of being a cold and often vicious businessman . . .

Mac rose and paced around the small conference room that adjoined Alex's private quarters. Gwenna had announced his arrival but then said that Alex wanted her to act as his telecom on some contacts with various agents concerning the alien ships that had appeared—and Alex would see him immediately afterward . . .

In his pacing, when he neared the half-open door to Alex's quarters, he could hear their voices—

Gwenna: "He said we're not geared to communicate with alien races. After all, he says, we are all passengers on a starliner on a regular flight, not an exploration ship and contact with aliens was not anticipated."

Alex: "Well, damn it, tell him to find some passengers who've had experience in communication with aliens. Somewhere in a thousand passengers, there must be *someone* who's had experience along those lines! Do I have to do his thinking?"

Mac knew from experience that Gwenna would not communicate that last sentence. He continued his pacing, reflecting that the appearance of the alien ships had put Alex in a foul mood.

Alex can be vindictive when he's in a bad mood. Mac remembered the rumors about Synpla IX . . .

It had been the factory farthest from Earth. The ore on the planet had been extremely valuable and the workers transferred there had been paid the highest wages. But things had gone wrong. Far from Alex's stern eye and far from Synpla chieftains, with some lax local supervision, the workers on the planet had set new records for absenteeism and low productivity.

The planet had never been given the dignity of a name—it had always been referred to only as Synpla IX, the designation for the ninth Synpla factory. It had contained no intelligent native life and had apparently not contained anything of real value other than the richness of the ores. It had been rumored that when Alex heard that Synpla IX was losing money, he had ordered the plant shut down—employment terminated—with only one week's advance notice. He did not authorize the use of corporation ships to evacuate the former employees, and commercial starlines were reluctant to make the long journey to the little planet on the outskirts of the known universe. There had been twenty thousand employees on Synpla IX and statistics showed that more than five thousand died of starvation before they could be evacuated. Within the web of the Synpla corporation it had been rumored quietly that Alex had vetoed the sending of sup-

140

plies as well as the sending of company ships for transportation.

Alex Stauffer had indirectly and within the scope of the law murdered five thousand men and women because they had put him in a foul mood.

There had been many other rumors—men and women dying of heart attacks when they had had no history of heart trouble. People dying of mysterious diseases and odd accidents. All when they had caused Alex trouble in one way or another or displeased him or put him in a foul mood . . .

I'm not afraid to die, Mac thought. *That isn't what's making me nervous. It's something else . . . something I can't quite put my finger on . . .*

Alex appeared suddenly, dropped into a chair and waved Mac to a nearby seat. Alex was a tall and slender man with gray eyes that could sometimes glow with emotion when angered. Today they were smoldering with displeasure.

"You talked with the navigator?"

Mac decided to drop the results suddenly. "I talked with him. He says we're lost in space—hopelessly lost."

Alex was silent for long minutes, then asked quietly without looking at Mac, "How can that be?"

"There are millions of galaxies that mankind has never explored. I can remember the navigator's exact words . . . 'We are in an uncharted unexplored unknown galaxy surrounded by thousands and thousands of other uncharted unexplored unknown galaxies. We are in one of those corners where mankind has not even set foot previously. There are no familiar stars. None at all.' When the ship jumped back into subspace after the accident it was out of control, unguided."

Watching Alex's face closely, Mac decided the other did not seem in the least worried—or even impressed by the announcement.

"I expected as much," Alex said. "I have been hearing rumors that we were totally lost, but I did want to hear it from the navigator directly—or at least through an agent such as yourself."

"I understand," Mac said unconsciously and found himself leaning forward in his chair, listening intently for what Alex would say next.

"Krause has been spreading a story that our being lost is only temporary and the navigator will be able to determine our position when he's had enough time to make the necessary calculations. I think we should strengthen the story. Troyan has recommended that each passenger and crew member fill out a brief application blank describing their background and listing their skills. Use those forms to find passengers with some education in astronomy or intergalactic navigation and have them act as the navigator's assistants. It will strengthen the story that we can in time navigate our way out of this uncharted galaxy."

"Yes, sir."

"Krause tells me he's asked you to join the Nomads aboard ship?"

"Yes, sir."

"Keep me informed of your findings."

"Yes, sir."

Walking toward his cabin a few minutes later, Mac felt the familiar resentment returning with greater force. He'd been given another assignment. He felt like a flunky. The homicidal urge that he had felt shortly before the *Starbright's* accident returned with a stronger burst. He wondered if it would keep coming back until he finally eased his tensions by killing someone. *Therapeutic homicide,* he thought bitterly. *Maybe I can find another flunky to kill.*

CHAPTER TWENTY

When Natalaie first heard the news that Jimmy Franklin had committed suicide, she felt a deep sadness. When she learned that she was technically the new captain because Franklin's death had made her the senior crew member, she felt a strange mixture of responsibility and unreality . . .

Captain of the Starbright.

Never in her wildest dreams had she dreamed that she would someday be captain.

Although she would not have the same responsibilities as the captain of a starliner in full operation, she knew she would have some monumental tasks to tackle. Although she would not be in complete control, she would have a definite influence on all decisions.

Her first task—to attend a conference with Alexander Stauffer, one of his assistants named Krause, some other Synpla executives, and representatives from various committees that had been established. First on the agenda: How to handle the contact with the alien race temporarily named the Colossians. Days had passed and the aliens had not made a move. With each passing hour the situation became more and more bizarre. Hundreds of ships out there and not one of them would make a move to rescue the four stranded humans.

My name has always been MacPherson, but I think I will give myself a new name: HIND TIT MAC

Krause told our resident thinkwriter salesman to save me a thinkwriter and he did exactly that. When I went to his cabin I learned that I was obtaining the very last one. The salesman has no others except his personal machine and his demonstration model. He is taking orders for more of the gadgets although there are no more in the cargo. If a person lives, they will be able to use their new thinkwriter when they return to Earth or wherever. The salesman is a born optimist.

But his damned machine is broken. When I checked the printout, I discovered that the goddamned thing prints one paragraph in italics and the next paragraph in straight pica, alternating back and forth for no reason except that the paragraph has changed. When I telecomed the salesman to inquire about this facet, inquiring if there was anything I could program into the thing to correct it, he said that unfortunately the machine was broken.

I have, it seems, a deluxe model that came off the assembly line with a basic flaw. It is intended to print in either italics or pica, at the user's preference, but some of the deluxe models came through with a flaw, a defective relay or something and there is no way to have the thing corrected until we are able to get it in a repair shop.

I wonder if this damned machine will drive me crazy, to suicide. If so, then my soliloquy on this thing will reveal the exact reason. In my eulogy they can say that Mac was a hardworking man with great responsibilities, including liaison for the richest man in the universe, but in the end found himself somehow on the hind tit of life, relegated to running one errand after another while the bright young men such as Krause move steadily up the ladder. And poor Hind Tit Mac suffered his last straw with a defective thinkwriter . . .

I don't know what I should use this damned machine for. As a combination of business and personal usage? On the business side, the secretary I sent to check the Cepheus incident returned with the information. It is an intriguing story of a starliner hijacked and some hundreds of women passengers kidnapped.

The hijacking colony needed supplies aboard the ship but were also starved for female companionship. When the women left the ship, it is reported, they were ushered into a large fenced area where they were raped by the colonists. This is supposed to be the largest mass rape in modern history.

Because of the rape and the political intrigue and the fact that Earth governments do not want to play up the disadvantages and hazards of colonization, the Cepheus incident has been suffocated over the years. Maybe repressed is a more sophisticated word.

But there is a recorded account of how the hijacking was accomplished — how the computer for the energy screen was tinkered with and programmed to go down to demolish the ship's bridge, immediately reestablishing itself. Exactly what happened to us.

Someone did their homework. But for what purpose? Could it be that someone intended to hijack the *Starbright,* but the Colossians have scared them away?

The Colossians. Eva was the first one to give them that name and she may be right. Everyone is calling them "Colossians" now. But whatever their name . . . Why are they sitting out there, waiting, not making any attempt to rescue our decoys?

Josef Kaiser passed the elderly couple, then turned and followed them.

They looked as if they had made it past a hundred with the help of the new longevity serums. They strolled arm in arm as if walking down a boardwalk at a beach resort.

He shot them though the heart so they died simultaneously and fell with their arms interlocked.

During his search for a female companion, he found one in the lounge but when he decided he did not like her well enough to make her a steady companion, he shot her, too, and dumped her body into the ship's trash disintegrator.

CHAPTER TWENTY-ONE

When MacPherson reached the conference room appointed for the first Nomad meeting aboard *Starbright,* he found a figure clad in a dark cloak from head to toe. Printed on the right side of its chest in small letters were the words:

GOLD—EMPIRE

FOURTEEN

You wish to join the Nomads? a voice said inside Mac's skull. His first reaction had been the thought that the costume seemed too dramatic, but there was something forceful about the voice in his head.

And something else.

He had received telepathic communications from thousands of men and women during his lifetime, but this one was *different* than all those thousands—it was more human but still very strong and unique in ways he could not at the moment identify.

Yes.

Behind the screen over there you will find a number of cloaks. There should be a size that will fit you. After you are dressed for the meeting, you may go into the conference room . . . the door to your left beyond the anteroom.

Minutes later, wearing a black robe that covered his entire body, he went into the conference room—and total darkness.

Someone took his arm and began guiding him. *The meeting will start soon*, the someone said. *Sit here. Communication with other new members during the meeting is forbidden.*

Mac felt around in the total darkness, searching for a chair. There was none. His hand brushed someone's head on his left and another head on his right. Everybody was sitting on the floor.

He sat and thought, *This reminds me of a club I joined when I was a kid . . .*

His eyes gradually adjusted to the darkness and he saw the large conference room was packed with dark figures.

A light appeared at the other end of the room and a figure winked into existence beneath the glow of light.

"Welcome to your first Nomad meeting," the figure said. "My name is Jack/Diamond/Empire/Twenty. I'll tell you something about the Nomad traditions, our history, and some of my background . . . and then open the meeting for questions. Since this is your first meeting, you may consider us theatrical, but you will soon see there are reasons for our customs."

The conference room vanished. They were, without any sensation of movement, sitting not on the conference room floor, but sitting on an invisible surface in outer space.

Outer space?

The stars looked different. Space appeared not black, but something else—*as if they transported us into a strange kind of subspace that I've never seen before*, Mac thought.

And . . .

Beneath them—

A flaming star. Incredibly close. So close that its surface appeared flat beneath them—the way the Earth's surface did when in a stratosphere jet.

But the blaze of the star was not blinding. They were so close the brightness should have been too much for their eyes. It was not and Mac found he could look directly at the surface as if viewing it through

147

a strange form of tinted plastic.

"Jesus Christ," a voice next to Mac said. It was a woman's voice. He heard other exclamations—grunts, sharp intakes of breath—and abruptly they were back in the conference room.

"Small demonstration of the seriousness of a Nomad meeting," Jack/Diamond/Empire/Twenty continued. "If a new member does not pay attention or disrupts the meeting in some way—or breaks one of our traditions—we will return here and drop the person or persons into the star."

"Are you *serious?*" the woman on Mac's left asked. "Would you really *kill* someone?"

There was something about the woman's voice that Mac did not like. *She sounds like the kind of person who causes trouble just for the sake of causing trouble.*

"I would like to ask all of you to save all your questions until the end of the meeting at which time we will have a fairly standard question and answer period. First, I would like to tell you something of Nomad history . . .

"There are several groups of Nomads. Origins may vary but our traditions remain basically the same. One group began after a revolution on one of Earth's colonies. Over a period of some generations, the colony had divided itself into two equally fanatical political parties. The party in power had started to persecute the other party. The revolution was violent and bloody, and not only reversed roles but also intensified resentments. Numerous members of the 'minority party' were imprisoned. That is how the Empire group began and, as my name states, I am a member of that group. The political party members imprisoned included several paraphysical students that had begun an investigation into new approaches to the art of teleportation. During their imprisonment, they continued their research and perfected a method of teleportation. They teleported themselves out of their prison and were subsequently forced to learn how to teleport themselves to other planets. They discovered they had to remain anonymous for many reasons. They called themselves Nomads

Anonymous at first, but shortened the name to Nomads. That was the beginning of the Empire group, my home group."

"Are you telling me," the woman on Mac's left said, "that I have to join a political group before I can become a Nomad and learn how to teleport myself?"

Jack/Diamond/Empire/Twenty was silent and although Mac could not see his face, it seemed the black figure seethed with anger and struggled for patience.

"I stated there would be a question and answer period at the end of the meeting."

"But don't you think there are some questions that should be answered as we go along?" the woman inquired in a condescending tone as if talking to a subordinate.

"No. I urge you to save all your questions until the end of the—"

"My memory isn't that good," the woman said and cackled. It was the self-satisfied cackle of a society person unaccustomed to restrictions. Mac saw the hooded head turn in every direction as if seeking approval and applause.

"Then your memory isn't good enough for you to be a Nomad," Jack/Diamond/Empire/Twenty said curtly. The conference room vanished again and they were once more in that strange subspace, above the star. The woman on Mac's left *dropped,* as if the area of "floor" immediately beneath her had vanished. Mac watched as she became a tiny dot and then vanished altogether from view because of the distance. She shrieked a telepathic scream and the scream turned into a senseless, mindless gurgle of thoughts until the instant of her death.

CHAPTER TWENTY-TWO

Natalaie had at first thought that everyone at the meeting would be turning to her for executive decisions.

It didn't work out that way.

They turned to her occasionally for suggestions—and for her vote one way or the other. That was all.

The person who dominated the meeting was a woman named Eva, an attractive but pale-faced woman who qualified for the conference because she had earned a "Master's" in Alien Psychology. Eleven others who had studied Alien Psychology at one time or another had been selected to form a special committee to evaluate the Colossians and make the necessary decisions.

Alexander Stauffer rarely spoke to the participants but occasionally leaned to one side to whisper to his secretary. Other than the woman named Eva, a man named Krause seemed to be the next most powerful figure. Natalaie noticed that most of the conference participants turned in his direction to judge his reaction to various comments. She had the distinct impression that Eva was the most influential person in *this* meeting but, under other circumstances, Krause would be the dominant figure. Eva summarized:

"Considering the high intelligence of the Colossians, I would speculate that their inactivity spreading over a period of days is much more than a slow reaction time. I would like to put forth the theory that they are *studying us,* studying our decoys in the belt, studying the debris we left behind. We have the *Starbright* 'hidden' but there are two threads to the asteroid belt. One is our telepathic contact with the decoys. The second is the transmissions sent by the concealed cameras. The Colossians' science is advanced beyond our own. We've felt safe in our hiding place but I suggest we are *not* safe . . . I suggest the Colossians are backtracking along the telepathic communications and the camera transmissions to learn our exact position. I recommend that we sever telepathic communications and discontinue the camera transmissions."

The recommendation was put before the committee for a vote and received unanimous agreement.

"If we sever all contact with the decoys, how will we know if the Colossians are friendly or not?" Krause questioned. "How will we learn the fate of our four volunteers?"

"I believe there is strong evidence that the Colossians are *not* friendly," Eva said. "If they were friendly and compassionate, would they let our decoys float in space for *days?* But severing the telepathic and camera contacts does not mean we will abandon the volunteers altogether. I believe the Nomads aboard the ship will be able to arrange some contacts in the future."

Krause was thoughtful for long moments and several of the most important figures were watching, waiting for his final comment. "If we sever telepathic and camera contact," Krause said, "then I think we should move the ship again—simultaneously as we break the contacts. If we have betrayed our location to the Colossians through our own carelessness, maybe we can correct that immediately."

Which, Natalaie thought, was one of the most intelligent suggestions she had ever heard.

The meeting ended. As the men and women left the conference room, Krause approached Natalaie.

"Congratulations on your promotion," Krause said with a grin as he extended his hand.

Natalaie shook the offered hand. "Thank you." *I don't feel qualified to be a captain,* she thought. *A few days ago I wasn't even sure how many passengers we had aboard ship.*

Starbright had been designed to carry more than a thousand passengers but in most previous flights had carried only half that amount. This trip to Algor, however, had loaded the ship to its fullest capacity with Alexander Stauffer's retinue and future employees of the new Synpla plant on Algor.

"You are the *prettiest* captain I've ever seen," Krause complimented.

"Thank you."

"Give me a call if there is anything I can do to help you in any way."

"I will. Thank you again." She wondered, *What is there about this man that makes me feel like an awkward schoolgirl? It is nothing superficial, nothing obvious, it is something subtle, indefinable . . .*

"Meanwhile . . ." Krause paused to light a cigarette. He frowned and appeared vaguely worried. "We have some problems aboard ship. Illegal gambling, the use of hard drugs. I want to stop it and dish out some strong punishment. I may need your backing when the time comes."

Was the frown part of an act? If so, he was a damned good actor. "I'm against the use of hard drugs also," Natalaie said. "When the time comes, I think we can agree on a suitable punishment."

As Lamar waited for Natalaie to return, he kept glancing at his wristwatch and found himself becoming anxious. Natalaie had been giving him instructions in recycle engineering and during some of his free time he had been studying the various manuals. At last he was beginning to feel he knew something about the equipment.

His plans had backfired.

Originally he had planned only to become acquainted with Natalaie long enough to learn why she had been buying such large pieces of land on Settle. Interplanetary real estate was a tricky commodity.

CHAPTER TWENTY-THREE

In the conference room again, Jack/Diamond/Empire/Twenty continued as if nothing had interrupted:

"The 'Twenty' of my Nomad name indicates I am the twentith member of the Empire group. Jack and Diamond are my elective names. My friends and close associates call me 'Jack Diamond' and, behind my back, 'The Jack of Diamonds.' When you entered the conference room lobby, you were greeted by one of our newest members, Gold/Empire/Fourteen. Empire is a Nomad group in which the names indicate earned rank. 'Fourteen' joined us recently and has been with us long enough to choose one of his elective names. He chose 'Gold.' The number 'Fourteen' was available since the original number Fourteen was deceased. Group numbers are not always an indication of group size. As an example, the Empire group has twenty members with the designation 'Five.' The number-name 'Five' is being used to designate a particular function rather than sequence of entry. The main point to bear in mind is that our names within the Nomad organization have nothing to do with our identity in what we call 'The Other World.' "

Jack/Diamond/Empire/Twenty paused for breath. In the silence that followed, Mac thought, *It's so quiet you could hear a proverbial*

153

pin drop. No one had commented on the death of the woman. She had been warned at the beginning of the meeting, Mac remembered. He had warned *all* of them by somehow transporting them to that point, close to the surface of the star and clearly stating that if anyone disrupted the meeting, they would be dropped into the star.

He proved his point all right, Mac thought.

"I and some other Nomad members have been aboard the *Starbright,*" Jack/Diamond continued. "Our group includes professional men and women of all classes. We lead dual lives. Being a Nomad, for many of us, is similar to belonging to a secret society that occupies only part of our time. We could save every passenger on this ship. It would take time and involve personal risk to ourselves, but we could possibly 'carry' each passenger to safety. We had a closed meeting and decided not to take that course. Instead we decided to invite all the passengers to join our group. Each person who joins and learned the art of teleportation will save himself or herself. Otherwise he or she will die."

Why? Mac wondered. *When the question and answer period begins, I must remember to make that my first question. Why not save our lives?*

"I will tell you a little about myself. I was in my late teens when my whole family was caught up in the political affairs that I mentioned earlier. We were struggling desperately to master the art of teleportation. My father was tortured and executed before we succeeded. My brother died of malnutrition in a prison cell. My mother disappeared—taken to a prison on the other side of the colony planet and never seen again. My two sisters were held in the prison—supposedly as 'political' prisoners, but the guards held all young and attractive girls in a certain section of the prison where they were used often and also rented out to anyone with the right price. One of my sisters committed suicide. The other . . ." The voice from the man before them did not seem exactly choked with emotion, but it had reached a bitter tone. "I lost my whole family," Jack/Diamond went on. "And then we learned how to teleport. We teleported ourselves

154

out of the prison. It didn't take us long to find weapons. We practiced teleportation and began attacking. Our enemies had no defenses. We could appear in the middle of a group, drop a bomb and teleport away. We could appear at a vantage point and kill with automatic weapons. In one week we slaughtered more than two thousand men and women. That is one of the reasons *I* have to remain anonymous . . . although anonymity is a strict Nomad tradition for other reasons also. If I disclosed my identity for some reason, I would have to face trial for murder. My only regret is that we learned teleportation too late to save my family. Memory of how my family were killed is one reason I take *my* Nomad membership extremely seriously. Being a Nomad for some members may be a hobby, but it is part of my whole life."

Jack/Diamond paused again and then added, "This meeting is now open for questions."

Mac waited a few moments and when no one else started the question and answer session, he said, "Why did the Nomads on the ship decide not to rescue the passengers?"

"We *have* come forth to rescue them. It was a choice of methods. Nomads will occasionally carry someone to safety if they happen to be in a hazardous situation with nonteleportative persons. Our traditions advise against playing 'Superman' and rushing to the rescue of others. If we began that policy, the rescue operations would be endless as well as nonrewarding except in a strictly moral sense. The Nomad society would collapse if we played hero only for the sake of playing hero. You'll gradually understand all the reasons. However, we decided, if we opened our meetings to new members—the passengers aboard *Starbright*—and taught those individuals how to teleport, our Nomad society would grow."

"How many Nomads are aboard *Starbright*?" someone asked.

"That is a confidential matter. We are *always* confidential about the exact number of our members at any location. It's in our traditions."

"Why are Nomads so anonymous?" someone inquired. To Mac's ears it sounded like the voice of a girl in her late teens or early twenties. "You're not *all* criminals, are you?"

"There are many reasons for our anonymity," Jack/Diamond/
Empire explained. "I'll name some but not all because we could
spend hours discussing anonymity alone and I don't want to do that at
this point. Anonymity protects us from outside influences. We have
the power to reach areas beyond the scope of most people. A Nomad
who broke his anonymity would be approached by large corporations
to become an industrial spy. Governments are our worst enemies. If
some politicians could have their way, we would be controlled employees, intelligence agents. Any Nomad who broke his anonymity
would be approached by several governments exerting pressure to
convert the person into an espionage agent. Since there is no bank or
material form of wealth beyond a Nomad's reach, you would also be
approached by criminal elements. In a very literal sense, if you announced your Nomad identity to the world, you would have hundreds of offers and be harassed beyond belief. Our society is
structured so our capacity to teleport is psychologically dependent
upon anonymity. When a Nomad breaks his anonymity, he automatically loses his power."

"How long does it take the average person to become a Nomad?" It
was the voice of a young girl and Mac could sense the hopeful enthusiasm in the tone.

"The average new member needs a year to learn our special skill."

CHAPTER TWENTY-FOUR

The day's game of Stygian Roulette had been going on for more than an hour. A dozen men and women sat in a circle around a table covered with red, white, and blue chips; and the machine called, *The Finger of Fate*.

The machine was nothing more than an ordinary disintegrator mounted on a revolving pedestal, connected to a simple device called a Counter. *The Finger* was spun and when it stopped it would point at one of the twelve players. Bets were made as to whom *The Finger* would indicate on each play. Once the machine was aimed squarely at a person, additional bets were made as to whether the person would be disintegrated or not. The Counter spun randomly when the disintegrator was spun. Similar to an ancient six-chamber revolver, the Counter would fire once in six times, activating *The Finger of Fate*.

Dorothy Sanders had been playing the game every day since it first started. A few more spins of *The Finger* and she would have over a million credits. She had promised herself she would stop at that amount.

Life had not been generous to Dorothy. She had been single all her life with few lovers and drifting from one mundane career to another.

In a search for adventure and excitement, she had decided to take the flight to Algor, to find a job of one sort or another when she arrived . . .

The Finger spun—

It pointed at a young blond-haired girl who could be no more than eighteen. Her eyes were glazed as if she had been taking Red Devils. Her boyfriend was standing behind her . . .

She turned and looked up at him, smiling nervously—the fear of death somehow penetrating the effects of the drug . . .

Her boyfriend smiled down at her . . .

People were betting . . .

"No more bets," the croupier announced. He pushed the firing button at the base of the disintegrator and the machine flared. The blond-haired girl vanished.

For a moment the girl's boyfriend stared in disbelief, motionless as if too stunned to move, then slowly moved away from the table.

The Finger was spun again.

This time it pointed at Dorothy when it stopped. Her heart began to beat faster. The odds were against the machine firing twice in a row, but still there was the faint possibility that she *could* die within the next few seconds . . .

"No more bets." The croupier reached for the firing button—

The door to the gambling room was blown off its hinges. Armed men poured into the room, surrounding the players, gamblers, and spectators.

"You are all under arrest," a masculine voice declared. Dorothy Sanders turned toward the voice and recognized the crewcut hair, the squarish jaw, the cool gray eyes. Krause. A companion in one of the lounges at the beginning of the voyage had pointed him out and described him as Alexander Stauffer's chief of security.

"Arrested for what?" an elderly gentleman inquired.

"Stygian Roulette is illegal," Krause said shortly.

The men and women sitting around the table were rising from their chairs.

158

"Do we get to keep our winnings?" someone inquired.

"Cash in the chips," Krause said. "You can count the money in your cells."

"You're going to imprison us?" the elderly gentleman said huffily.

"We certainly are."

"You can't do that!" The man's face reddened with anger.

"I can. I am acting under the captain's authority . . ."

The elderly man sputtered in protest but there was so much going on that little attention was paid to his complaints. The gamblers and spectators were being ushered out of the room and the croupier was busily cashing in the chips.

As they were about to leave the room, Dorothy said, "Do you mind if I see how that last play would have turned out?"

When Krause did not object, she pushed the firing button.

The disintegrator flashed at the chair where she had been sitting.

The odds were against it but she would have died if Krause and his men had not interrupted the game!

CHAPTER TWENTY-FIVE

The room fell into a stunned silence.

A man was the first to respond, *"A year? We could all be dead by then!"*

"True. But the ship has excellent supplies and recycle systems. A number of us could live on the ship for decades."

"Why does it take so long to become a Nomad?"

Jack/Diamond/Empire/Twenty answered with great patience, "Learning how to teleport is one of the hardest skills that a human can learn. Some say it is the single most difficult skill to learn involving the human mind and body."

"What will we do as . . . students? Is that a good term?"

"As good as any."

"Well? . . ."

"The training is complex. Meetings, sessions. Each . . . student will select a partner—a friend— We use the name, 'telelink.' Each chooses two telelinks—one of the same sex and one of the opposite sex. The first telelinks are also instructors of a special type."

"How much time must be spent each day?"

"An absolute minimum of one hour. We prefer that, under our circumstances, each student set a minimum of anywhere from three to four hours. Eight or ten hours a day studying and absorbing might be a good goal for most of you."

"This may be a silly question . . ." To Mac it sounded like the voice of a middle-aged woman. "If I become a Nomad, can I rob a bank so long as I do not break my anonymity?"

The question brought a ripple of chuckles.

"That is a question everyone thinks of sooner or later and the answer is no. Basically, we cannot teleport unless it is somehow for the benefit of the Nomad society. You *cannot* become a Nomad and become rich by robbing banks. The psychological dependency upon anonymity that I mentioned earlier . . . That same dependency includes a basic and clearly defined moral code. You don't have to be a saint but you cannot use the Nomad power to steal or kill for personal reasons."

"Is there a point of no return?" It was a man's voice, husky, sounding in his fifties or sixties.

"No return from where?"

"We witnessed one murder. I assume that—as we progress in our Nomad instruction—we would reach a point where we would know quote too much unquote. Too much to be allowed to live once we decided to give up the Nomad society. What is that point, the one at which we can walk out of here and still live? Is it shortly before we learn a secret sign or secret process . . . before we learn the identities of top members? . . ." A large figure not far away waved both arms. "You *tell* me. I think you know what I'm driving at."

"All of you are here today because, I assume, you want to save your lives. Becoming a Nomad is the best way. We expect either *no* dropouts . . . or very very few."

"You're evading my question."

Jack/Diamond/Empire/Twenty folded his arms across his chest and Mac wished he could see the man's expression. He noticed black gloves protruding from the sleeves of the black cloak.

"I would suggest that anyone who does *not* wish to become a Nomad leave now. This minute."

Two figures rose. One was the large figure and the other—from the opposite side of the room—was fairly short and slender.

When the two had left the conference room, Jack/Diamond/Empire/Twenty continued, "I would now like to have more questions. Any question at all. Do not be afraid to ask anything for fear it may sound unintelligent."

"What happens if someone fails the course and doesn't learn how to teleport?"

"We have some members who cannot teleport for various reasons. They are still Nomads and help the organization in special ways."

During the following questions and answers, Mac observed that all the students were extremely attentive. One student had been eliminated and the example had been set.

"Concerning anonymity," someone asked. "I understand we are not to reveal our Nomad membership to nonmembers, but it is all right to break our anonymity so far as another member is concerned?"

The voice sounded familiar to Mac. Was that Gwenna?

"Breaking anonymity within the organization is permitted," Jack/Diamond/Empire/Twenty stated.

"Thank you." *Mac?*

Gwenna! That was you who asked that question?

It certainly was. I asked it because you and I have telecommed so long, I thought I felt your mind in here somewhere.

Is Krause here?

Krause is busy breaking up a Stygian Roulette game but I think he wants to join the Nomads later. Oh, oh, maybe I shouldn't have said that.

"Someone is telecomming in the class," Jack/Diamond/Empire/Twenty said. "I'll have to ask you to stop. I want your complete attention."

Outside the conference room, George Katzman removed the black cloak and threw it aside in disgust. Someone else was leaving the room also and he watched with great interest as the person removed their cloak . . .

It was a small redhaired girl who smiled at him nervously.

"Young lady, that was the wisest thing you did today."

"I think so."

"Fanatics!"

"They do take that Nomad thing seriously . . ."

"Murderers!"

"They did kill that woman," the redhaired girl admitted.

"My name is George Katzman," George said. "Young lady, may I have your name and may I buy you a drink?"

"Colleen. Yes, I could use a drink after that experience."

On their way to the lounge, George Katzman informed Colleen that he was a respectable businessman with a chain of one hundred and twenty-six clothing stores on five planets. His intention had been to start an additional store on Algor. The general manager and some vice presidents of his company were aboard the *Starbright* also.

When they reached the lounge, George led the way to a booth and they ordered drinks.

"There's Weldon," George said, spotting someone on the other side of the room. He gestured to the person and a tall gray-haired man rose, crossing the room to join them. "Weldon won't believe we saw someone murdered. Will you back me up, young lady?"

"I certainly will."

The man named Weldon was standing at their booth and George Katzman handled the introductions, inviting the tall gray-haired man to join them.

"Weldon," George began as the other settled into the booth. "The most incredible—" He felt the young girl's hand touch his thigh and move toward his crotch. Hidden beneath the table, Weldon could not see her hand. Despite his sixty-five years of age and a couple of medical difficulties, George Katzman had an instant reaction. Young girls today were so bold. He remembered the young girl in the restaurant in San Francisco, the girl who'd sat beside him at the anniversary party, a young secretary to one of the executives. The table had been crowded and everyone had been busy eating and drinking and the pretty little thing— What was her name? Virginia. He had only met Virginia two minutes before they sat at the table. It had always been his custom to sit with local executives and their staff when attending branch anniversary celebrations. And the young secretary named Virginia had boldly slipped her hand to his lap while smiling at him sweetly and innocently and while everyone ate and chatted, she had slipped her fingers inside his clothing and given him some extremely pleasurable moments . . .

"What's incredible, Katz?"

Only his closest friends and associates had the nerve to call him Katz to his face. He liked it.

"The most incredible thing happened not more than ten minutes ago . . ." He slipped a hand to the girl's soft thigh. Her hand was now at his crotch and he suddenly discovered she was *not* like the girl named Virginia in San Francisco, not out for kicks with the boss, for the large ring on her finger was vibrating soundlessly, apparently from an amazingly strong battery and the vibrations were shuddering through the hulk of his body—

And his heart stopped beating.

Those vibrations stopped his heartbeat.

He looked at the girl in astonishment. She was one of the Nomads, she had followed him out of the conference to execute him, to keep him from talking about what had happened during the meeting.

And she had done it.

I'm dead, he thought, closing his eyes, feeling himself slump forward.

CHAPTER TWENTY-SIX

When Mac returned to his cabin after the Nomad meeting, he found Lucille sitting there in the chair, legs crossed.

"Make yourself at home."

"I did," Lucille said. Her top leg began to swing idly.

"To what do I owe the honor of your visit?" he asked, sitting on the edge of the cot. He still felt depressed. Hind Tit Mac. Depressed and frustrated, and filled with that strange urge to kill someone. Anyone.

Plus something else. Something else was inside him—an emotional or mental thing he couldn't define . . . *The Mysterious Something*, he thought. What the hell is it?

"I'm mad at you," Lucille said, pretending to pout.

"Oh? What for?"

"You were supposed to meet me after the Entertainment Committee meeting. You didn't."

"I'm sorry," Mac apologized, taking off his jacket and throwing it to one side with an untypical carelessness. *Maybe it will do me good if I talk to her. Get it out. Therapy.*

"You don't look sorry."

"I am. Really. I had to talk to the navigator and that took longer than expected. Then I had to have a conference with Stauffer."

"Excuses, excuses."

"The truth."

"Did you take the Little Red Devils I gave you?"

"Too busy. I still have them in my pocket . . ." He reached into his pocket and dug out the handful of pills she'd given him. The damned things were supposed to be what everybody called *zoomers* in contemporary lingo. To zoom you up high.

He swallowed one.

"Hey," Lucille said, grinning at him. "Good boy."

He swallowed another.

"Great."

He swallowed a third.

Lucille applauded.

He swallowed a fourth.

"You will be above the clouds," Lucille said and he knew she had taken some of the things not too long ago because her eyes were very bright and she was bubbling with an unnatural cheerfulness.

The things were starting to take effect.

"They're quick," he said.

"Quick-quick-quick," she said. *"The Little Red Devils are quick!"* She made it into a song. The room was transforming before Mac's eyes. The colors were bright—they had turned from drab and depressing to cheerful glowing tones. Now he could see Lucille's true beauty. Before—only moments ago, without the Red Devils—she had been only an attractive woman. Now she was a raving beauty.

"You're beautiful," he murmured in awe.

"You're saying that partly because of the Little Red Devils in you, but that's okay. I love it, anyway."

"Could I seduce you?"

"Maybe. Apologize some more, first. You hurt my feelings when you didn't look me up after the Entertainment Committee meeting."

"After the conference with Stauffer, I had something to attend to," Mac explained. "Something very important. I'd promised Krause that I would do something about the hard drugs—the DEMOs. So I

166

stopped at the dispensary and talked with the doctors and nurses there and persuaded them to pass out the false information that DEMOs aboard ship were . . ."

He rubbed his forehead. He felt wonderful but he was having trouble thinking.

". . . Were fatal," Lucille supplied. "I heard the rumor. Everybody has. So you're the one who started it."

"The doctors and nurses were supposed to say their autopsies showed that DEMOs were responsible for a large number of deaths . . ."

"They did, they did," Lucille was laughing as if they were telling each other a tremendous joke.

He took another pill.

Lucille laughed. "Don't take any more! You'll get up so high you'll never get down!"

"I don't want to come down!" Mac said, laughing. He crossed the room quickly, grabbed her, pulled her back to the bed but only sat there with her, holding her in his arms, kissing her cheek. She turned her head, wanting to be kissed on the mouth. They struggled because he was in the mood to kiss her cheek and ears.

He started to take another pill and, laughing, she knocked it out of his hand. It fell to the floor and rolled a short distance. He laughed. "Little Red Devils roll," he said, doubling over with laughter. It was like being drunk, he realized. This was his first time on the devils but it was similar to being intoxicated with alcohol . . .

No, he thought. *Somehow better.*

"Your trick about the DEMOs didn't work," Lucille said, laughing. "Nobody believed the rumors . . ."

"Lost again," Mac said, laughing also. "I'm a failure." But it didn't bother him now. Nothing bothered him. "Errand boy failure," he said with a drunken pride.

"I like you," Lucille said. "You know that?"

"I didn't know it. I was hoping you did."

"What I did for you in the astrodome . . . I don't do that for every-

167

body."

"You don't?" Mac queried seriously.

"No. Only someone I like. You're cute. You're nice. You're gentle, intelligent, considerate, handsome and an all-around good fella." She punched him on the shoulder. "Let's make love."

She began undressing. Mac rolled to the floor and began crawling around, pushing the Little Red Devil with his nose.

He picked up the pill and was about to once more pop it into his mouth but she again knocked it from his hand.

"I want it," he said.

"You're taking them too close together. When you come down you'll be in trouble if you're not careful."

"I'll stay up forever," Mac said happily.

"You can't. You make a lousy pillhead, a rotten junkie." She was undressing him. His arms felt pleasantly warm and useless.

"Junkie, junkie, junkie," he babbled.

"You're not so bad when you're zoomed up. When you're natural, you're nice and all that but kind of grouchy."

"I want to zoom higher." He reached for the pill on the floor.

"Let me get your damned clothes off first." She finished undressing him.

He sat there on the edge of the bed, nude. She was nude. He asked thoughtfully, "You're the boss?"

"Damned right I am, Buster," she said.

"Give me the fifth pill."

"Five is too many for a person of your build and weight."

"You sound like a professional."

"I am," she said, kissing him on the mouth, running her hands through his hair. "In the cargo of this ship I have enough Little Red Devils to keep everyone on this ship happy for years. I was going to sell them on Algor. I have *tons* of the things!"

"You're a drug dealer!"

"Damned right I am."

He shook her hand. "You are a real entrepreneur," he said. "I'm

168

proud of you. He dropped to his knees and reached for the fifth pill. The room was spinning like an old-fashioned merry-go-round and he could hear tinkling music.

Lucille moved faster and grabbed the Little Red Devil. Holding it between her two fingers, she sat on the edge of the cot and slid it between her blond-fringed labia. "Come and get it," she teased. "You said I was good enough to eat."

Mac crawled over to her and in a short time Lucille was running her fingers though his hair, moaning with pleasure. She shuddered with violent orgasms and, afterwards, he pushed her down on the cot and made love to her.

When he finished, she looked up at him and said, "Eat, drink, and be merry, for tomorrow the Colossians will kill us."

"I want to go higher," Mac said. He hadn't felt this happy in years.

"You can't go higher on Little Red Devils," Lucille informed him. "The only thing higher is a DEMO if you want to risk a bad comedown."

"Give me one."

"How do you know I have one?"

"You have everything."

"True," she said with a pleased smirk.

"Everything a man could possibly want. Give me a DEMO."

She shrugged and went to her purse, reached inside and removed a silver flask.

"Take a gulp of this," she said.

"What is it?"

"Gin."

"Gin? Who wants gin? I want a DEMO!"

"It'll smell up your breath. If you're caught later, people will think you're drunk . . . only drunk . . . if you're lucky . . . You know, taking DEMOs is illegal."

"Listen who's talking. The little girl who sells Little Red Devils like candy."

"There's a difference."

He took the silver flask and swallowed some. He took another mouthful and swished it around in his mouth before swallowing.

"Is there any danger in mixing Little Red Devils and gin and DEMOs?"

"To use medical phraseology," she said, "there is no danger at all if you manage to live through it."

"You are one smart cookie," he complimented. "A real professional drug-taker."

"You betcha." She giggled and took a long drink from the flask of gin.

"Where's my DEMO?"

She reached into her purse, removed a gold cigarette case, disclosed a concealed compartment and handed him a large black pill. "I don't smoke," she said, wrinkling her nose in distaste as she replaced the secret compartment. "Bad for the health. But it makes a good hiding place for DEMOs."

"These things are *big*," Mac complained happily, staring at the large black pill.

"Nobody takes a DEMO by mistake," she said. "The way nobody takes a golf ball by mistake."

"I don't know if I can swallow this thing," he said.

"You can."

"If I can't swallow it, maybe I should be an interplanetary engineer instead. When I was a kid I wanted to be an interplanetary engineer and build roads through alien jungles and cities on mountain tops on strange planets." He paused and added dreamily, "Cities or castles."

"I think you're drunk," Lucille said. "Swallowing that pill has nothing to do with being an interplanetary engineer. You can be an engineer regardless."

"I may be a little drunk," Mac conceded and giggled.

"You are."

"But, nevertheless, I can't swallow this thing."

"Sure you can. I'll help you." She sat on his lap and gently took the pill from his hand, placing it between his lips. "Under the tongue.

170

Now . . . here . . . gulp the gin . . . wash it down . . ."

He struggled to swallow the pill. She bounced on his lap, shouting, "Swallow! Swallow! Swallow! Go! Go! Go!" Her naked breasts jiggled enticingly.

"The pill is not going down but something else is coming up," he informed her unnecessarily.

"Is that all you men ever think of? *Beasts! Beasts!*" She clamped a hand over his mouth and beat a tiny fist against his chest. *"Beasts! Beasts! Beasts!"* she screamed. When he tore her hand away from his mouth and managed to hold both her wrists, twisting them painfully, she looked up at him and tilted her head to one side, smiling sweetly, fluttering her eyelashes coyly and murmuring, "But I have to admit life would be incredibly boring for a girl without beasts such as yourself and such things as sex and so forth. As my philosophy professor in college said, 'Birth and Death would be only meaningless brackets for meaningless life if man and woman could not screw around in between the two ultimate brackets.' "

"I think you're drunk, Lucille."

She kissed him on the mouth. "I have an idea."

"What?"

"Let's get married."

"All right."

"We're perfectly suited for each other. I love you. You love me. Why fight it?"

"All right."

"You're serious?"

"I'm drunk but I'm serious," he said.

"It's a deal. We'll get married if the Colossians don't kill us first."

She rose from his lap and began dancing, humming softly to herself, "Cha-cha-*cha!* Cha-cha-*cha!*" with much swinging of hips.

"How long does it take a DEMO to work?"

"They're slower than Red Devils. Another five minutes. The gin is gone. Do you have anything to drink?"

"There's some bottles behind the books in the bookcase."

171

"Mac?"

"My God," Mac said. "It's Gwenna on the telecom!" Then, with studied calmness, *What is it, Gwenna?*

Alex wants you to report on the Nomad meeting.

You were there. Can't you tell him what happened?

He doesn't want me to tell him. He doesn't know I attended that meeting. I'm not supposed to break my anonymity. He ordered you to go to the Nomad meeting, so your anonymity was broken before you went.

Alex didn't order me. Krause—

Whoever. Alex knew about it through Krause. Can you come see him right away?

Gwenna. I—Oh, my God, he thought. *I've taken five Little Red Devils, half a pint of gin, and a DEMO which is just about to take effect! I can't see Alex now!*

"What is it, Mac? Your mind sounds strange.

Gwenna. I'm busy. I—

Other things are about to break fast, Mac. Krause is about to move the ship. He thought you might be able to help synchronize some of the elements. Krause wants—

Get out of my mind!

"What is it?" Lucille asked, looking at him, frowning.

"Alex Stauffer's secretary!"

Who is that with you, Mac?

A woman, for God's sake, Gwenna!

He's in bed! Lucille shouted telepathically.

Ouch! Sorry, Mac! And my apologies to your friend, whoever—

Lucille.

Pleased to meet you, Lucille.

Pleased to meet you, Gwenna.

Hope I didn't disturb—

No problem. Give us another half hour.

Mac felt Gwenna's telepathic tendril leave his mind.

Lucille resumed her dancing, chanting once more. "Cha-cha-*cha!*

Cha-cha-*cha!*"

"They're going to move the ship," Mac mumbled, watching the sway of Lucille's hips. "Big things are happening and here I am, zooming up." It was a disaster but he felt happy. The Devils were keeping him up.

"No one is indispensable," Lucille said wisely. "They can move the ship without you."

"What do you do when you take a DEMO? This is my first time. I don't know how."

"You create your favorite fantasy. Think of something you want to fantasize about. The DEMO will take you there."

Mac decided he would fantasize about dinosaurs. As a little boy, dinosaurs had always fascinated him . . .

"Dinosaurs," he said, feeling the room fade away.

"Oh, good," Lucille said. "It's starting to hit you. While you're away in DEMO dreamland, I think I will"—She sprawled at his feet, giggling—"lick your toes while you don't know what I'm doing. It's one of my little fetishes, it's so deliciously degrading, decadent, and depraved."

Mac looked down at the nude girl, watching her pretty blond head as her pink tongue flickered over his toes. It aroused him tremendously and he muttered, "Do that sometime when I'm conscious."

"It's a deal."

Then the DEMO was taking effect on his mind and the world slithered away . . .

He was standing in a prehistoric jungle, watching a Diplodocus swing its snakelike head from tree to tree, munching at the vegetation with its tiny head.

He watched as a Brontosaurus walked along a beach . . .

Thirty tons of animal! he thought excitedly.

The Brontosaurus was attacked by an Allosaurus . . .

He watched the battle in fascination and then watched a Tyrannosaurus devour a Pachycephalosaurus . . .

He came out of the drug to find himself flat on his back, Lucille

173

above him. She was making love to him.

"Damn," she complained. "I thought I'd rape you while you were out of your head, but you came out too soon."

He placed his hands on her hips and they climaxed simultaneously.

He was still high from the drugs when he remembered the strange mental voice that had warned him about Eva's attempt to commit suicide. Then he remembered his thoughts about the Monitor machine.

Lucille rolled away. "Great," she said. "When I come down a bit, I'll find the ship's new captain and get her to set a time to perform our wedding ceremony."

He remembered the incident in the ship's dispensary when the surgeon had performed the mnemonic erasure.

Monitor had established a procedure to keep itself invisible. It could read the minds of its servants. If one of its servants remembered Monitor, it arranged to have that memory removed!

How can I remember it now? he wondered.

Lucille was on her side, studying him. He could see her from the corner of an eye but he didn't want to interrupt his chain of thought—

Because my mind has been altered by the drugs. Mnemonic erasure must not remove all *of a memory.*

It must remove only the portion that the conscious mind could contact. But—the mind-altering capacities of the drugs he had taken were strong enough to raise the memory from the depths of the subconscious . . . bring it up to the conscious mind?

"You're a thoughtful type, aren't you?"

"Solving a problem," Mac said.

"What did you do in DEMO land?"

"Saw some dinosaurs."

"To each his own," Lucille muttered, shrugging her shoulders. "Change your mind?"

"About what?"

"Getting married."

"No," he said, amazed that he could remember their decision to get married. "Let's do it."

174

He wondered how long it would take Monitor to send someone to drag him off to the dispensary for another mnemonic surgery?

He didn't like the idea of the mind-controlling machine. It existed to assure Alexander Stauffer's protection but he hated the idea of a machine constantly reading his mind and sometimes controlling his actions . . .

I wish I had a way of killing the damned machine.

CHAPTER TWENTY-SEVEN

"You are *all* going to be arraigned and prosecuted and convicted for the felony of conspiracy to commit homicide," Krause told the prisoners. "Because Stygian Roulette *is* a felony by international law. The players will receive a first degree charge. The gamblers will receive a second degree charge. The punishment will be either solitary confinement or suspended animation."

A chorus of moans and groans rose from the gathering.

"Shut up," Krause barked, glowering at them. The group fell silent.

After a long pause, he continued, "Stygian Roulette *may seem* only a *game* to you, but a dozen passengers died during your little game."

No one in the group commented.

"And you will be punished unless . . ."

The prisoners were eagerly awaiting his words now.

". . . unless four of you volunteer."

"Volunteer for what?" a husky man with a cigar inquired.

"You're all gamblers," Krause said. "I want someone to gamble. Four volunteers to take over the telepathic contact to our decoys. How many of you are telepathic?"

Eight of the prisoners raised their hands.

"Step forward."

The eight stepped forward.

"Do I have four volunteers to send a telephatic message to our four decoys?"

"You said you wanted someone to gamble. Where's the gamble?" It was the man with the cigar.

"What is your name?"

"Mikhail Rasumny. M-i-k-h-a-i-l R-a-s-u-m-n-y."

"The gamble lies in the fact that I do not trust the Colossians," Krause stated. "A committee formed of passenbers with some knowledge of alien psychology has decided that the Colossians could be tracking our telepathic contacts with the decoys. And possibly tracking the camera transmissions. We've hidden *Starbright* several light-years from the asteroid belt. Our technology is not advanced enough to trace a telepathic contact across that distance. But there's the possibility that the Colossians can do it. Or have done it. I want to place four volunteers in a lifeboat. Then we'll move the *Starbright*. After we've moved the ship, I want the four volunteers to tell the decoys that we will have to discontinue telepathic contact until further notice. If the Colossians are aware of our location . . ."

When he did not continue. Mikhail waited awhile and then prodded, "What?"

"The Colossians may regard us as a potential enemy. If they know our location, they might blast it when they learn we're breaking telepathic contact. That might be an indication to them that we're wise to what they're doing."

"Doing what?" one of the prisoners asked.

"Using the telephathic contact to zero in on our location."

"If that's their tactic, haven't they had time enough to accomplish it?"

Krause nodded his head negatively. "I don't think so. We are *alien* to them. They know nothing of our telepathy. Or *did* know nothing at the origin of our contact. I have a feeling they've been watching and studying and learning. With our comparatively retarded technology, it would take us months or years to trace alien telepathic communications to establish a location across several light-years. We could use standard interstellar radar in microseconds, but it would take us a long long time to define an alien's mental emanations and learn how to trace them to a receiving point."

"It all sounds farfetched to me," Mikhail criticized. "I think the Colossians are friendly . . . but cautious. Why should they want to blast us? You're saying you think they're so dangerous, they'll try to blow our ship apart the moment they think we're moving?"

"In essence that's what I think."

"But if they know our location, why haven't they blasted us before this?"

"Because," Krause said, "I think they may know where we are but they're still studying us. I think we're like—to them—a strange animal within their grasp. And I have a strong feeling they'll keep studying us until they feel we're about to slip out of their reach."

"I'll volunteer," Mikhail said. "I think you're one hundred percent wrong."

"Three more volunteers?"

It began to happen so slowly that at first Diane was not aware of the movement . . .

"They're drawing us toward one of their ships, Sam."

"At last."

"I'm frightened."

"But this must mean they're friendly, they're going to rescue us. Look— Over there. The other two volunteers . . ."

"It looks as if we're all being drawn into the same ship."

Olivia, Sam telepathed. *Have you been reading me?*

Absolutely. We're changing shifts, Sam. A man named Mikhail will be your new contact. We're changing all four contacts so we can have some relief.

It seems a hell of a time to change, he thought, but telepathed, *Okay, see you later.*

178

He told himself to stay calm but despite all his efforts at composure, his heart began to beat faster and faster. He held Diane's hand as they were pulled steadily toward one of the huge alien ships. A section of the hull slid aside to reveal an immense airlock.

Hello. Sam? It was a new telepathic voice.

Hello.

My name is Mikhail. M-i-k-h-a-i-l. I'm your new contact.

Hello, Mikhail.

What's happening?

They're drawing us into the ship. All four of us. It's like being swallowed by a huge black whale!

CHAPTER TWENTY-EIGHT

As he entered the conference room, Rian Thornfield felt someone touch his arm. Looking to one side he saw a girl in a tight-fitting black Nomad uniform. On her chest was the name—

PRINCESS
DIAMOND—EMPIRE
TWENTY-ONE

"Will you follow me, please?"

Rian followed the girl out of the conference room and down a hallway to a door which led to a narrow utility hall. Halfway down that hall, the girl unlocked an unmarked door and he followed her inside.

It was a small office crowded with two chairs, a slender couch, a desk, a memo-rec filing cabinet, recording equipment, and some other equipment Rian did not recognize. A second door now closed obviously led to one of the main hallways that ran through the ship and Rian knew that door probably bore the name of the person sitting opposite him.

For this *was* the office of a ship's crew member. Unmistakably. The walls were decorated with several paintings and photographs. One was a dramatic photograph of the *Starbright* in space, a remarkable shot that showed both the moon and Earth also; catching the cratered surface of the moon in stark black and white contrast while showing the Earth in soft hues of green and brown and blue, and layers of white clouds with edges frosted pink by sunlight. The sun was not visible in the photograph but the velvety darkness of space was captured—the dark velvet of infinity sprinkled with specks and clusters of stars shown as sparkling diamond dust. *Starbright* was shown as a magnificent manmade artifact and the impression was given that it was gracefully clawing its way into outer space, a powerful metal creature with all the stamina and intelligence of mankind behind it . . .

"I'm glad you like the photo," the girl said. "It's my favorite. Oh. In all politeness I should inform you I am a peeper."

Rian nodded that he understood. During all the Nomad meetings he had occasionally felt someone peeping into his mind. It had seemed natural. At the meetings they were being instructed and what was more natural than for some of the teachers to peek into their minds occasionally to see how they were progressing? On his way here with this girl—and during the few seconds they had been in the office, he had felt her mind peeking into his. He was an expert telepath and more sensitive to peepers than the average person. Still, despite all his above average powers, he could not peep into the girl's mind. He did not have the power to "peep" as such, and the girl had not so far opened her mind to him.

The photograph was so good it did not look real but appeared as if it might be a composite with some of the colors painted in.

"Is it an actual photograph?"

"I don't know," the girl admitted. "I don't care, really. It's beautiful as it is and I am one who prefers beauty rather than stark reality when it comes to artwork."

Rian nodded again that he understood and quickly scanned the other photographs and paintings. One of a waterfall and pool surrounded by a dense jungle not of Earth was the only other wall decoration that caught his attention. There were few standing ornaments. A brass statuette of a man fighting an alien animal resembling an octopus served as a paperweight. On a bookshelf were tiny glass figures of birds and animals. On the top of one shelf was a metal replica of an ancient English double-decker bus . . .

Having quickly surveyed the room, he turned to face the girl. She sat casually with her legs crossed, watching him.

"You appear to be our most exceptional student," she said. "And we want to give the leading students special instructions rather than holding them back to the level of the class . . ." She changed her position, resting her elbow on the edge of her desk. "I think you can teleport on your own—*now*—without further instructions. You've done it several times with our help. Try it. To the conference room. Stay there half a minute. And return here."

Rian closed his eyes. He had been a telepath since birth. His mother had talked to him in the cradle with her mind and claimed they had communicated telepathically while he was still in her womb. She claimed she had sung to him and comforted him and kissed him with the warmth of her mind. She claimed he had learned to say, *Mama* and a few other simple baby things with his mind while still in the womb. His father had taught him to carve soft woods with his mind—carve his own toy building blocks with his mind before his legs were strong enough for him to walk.

He had been, literally, a sculptor and a telepath all his life. His mind had carved all types of wood and stone into objects of art. He had worked his way up from soft woods to woods nearly as hard as rock, to actual rock and stone. His great-great-grandfather and grandmother had settled on a strange planet named Gytha where the native humanoid race were much like humans but had mastered certain phases of telekinetic energy.

Gythans were handsome but relatively weak with dwarfed and nearly useless arms and hands. Primitive Gythans since the beginning of their recorded history had burrowed their tunnel homes into solid rock *with their minds,* creating "doors" of massive rock that fitted tightly enough to keep out the planet's marauders. Gythans had learned how to use their minds as a defense—not as a complete shield for the entire body but as small strategical shields to parry the thrust of claws and fangs. Gythan hunters had learned the proficiency to kill with their minds—a slash with the mind to sever a throat, a blow to the skull to crush, a thrust of divergent forces to snap a spine, or a spearlike lunge to pierce a heart or other vital organ. The best Gythan hunters were not the strongest physically, they were the strongest *mentally.*

The skill of the Gythans had been somehow absorbed by Rian's great-great-grandparents and passed down from generation to generation. With the gradual increase of interstellar trade, the Thornfield family had become wealthy with the objects of art that they sculpted with their minds. Rian had sculptured small animals and flowers in soft woods as a young boy. In his teens he had formed statuettes from metal and stone; usually working with his eyes closed, his mind open in the strange Gythan way, feeling the surface, carving, disintegrating the spaces that had to be removed—molding, shaping until he had an artistic object that would sell for its beauty and the fact of being a Thornfield creation.

His mind had served as a great implement all his life, greater than his hands and he had suspected from the very beginning of the Nomad classes that he would have a tremendous advantage over the others . . .

Teleporting with the help of the instructors during the Nomad classes had seemed to him much like leaping across the width of a yawning chasm. They had been instructed to visualize their destination—not the endless gulf. To concentrate on the goal fully, send the mind first—and use the mind as the bridge to carry the physical body.

In the past exercises there had been the shadow of a Nomad at his side—at the side of each student—holding his mind symbolically, sometimes holding hands physically.

Here! Here we go! This is how you do it!

Push and shove and drag . . .

He had sometimes visualized it as an older brother or close friend helping you as a child in a playful jump across a big ditch . . .

Now, he thought. *Now! Do it by yourself. Jump the big ditch! It's only as wide as you think it is. Remember what your father said—You can do anything with your mind. Anything. If you only think you can and practice and build your strength. Jump, jump, jump. JUMP!*

He jumped—teleported—to the conference room.

He sat there a moment among the other students. The room was darkened. Jack/Diamond/Empire/Twenty was lecturing:

"Confidence is the all-important factor in teleporting. We can help you in the beginning . . . take your minds and lead the way, but in the end you must feel confident you can do it alone. Second to confidence, a *very* close second, is motivation. You have one of the greatest motivations here aboard. To save your lives. That may seem the greatest motivation possible but you may learn it is not always *sufficient* to drive a person to teleport from—"

Rian jumped back to the office. He was sitting in the chair again, sweating, shaking—

Not with fear.

With an excitement he had not known since childhood.

Teleporting was a fascinating new world!

CHAPTER TWENTY-NINE

We're inside the ship, Sam informed Mikhail.

What's it like?

The outer airlock is being closed . . . it's like being in a gigantic warehouse.

Can you see the aliens?

Not yet.

Can you feel any vibrations? If any of these questions seem goofy, Sam, don't blame me. A character named Krause is telling me what to ask. He and a dozen other people. Don't blame me if I get confused.

No vibrations.

Did they change your contact, Sam? Diane asked. *They changed mine. It was a man named Stanley, now it's a woman named Wanda.*

They changed my contact, too. I don't know why. It's a poor time to change. My new contact isn't as skilled as the first. He's asking me something now but I can't understand what it is. I'll have to get him to repeat it.

What did you say, Mikhail?

I said—can you see any of their machinery?

Nothing that looks like machines.

Any clue as to their size?

Not yet.

Can you—

Something's happening. We're being guided into a smaller room . . .

The four humans found themselves standing in a small group in the center of a gray room featureless except for several black circles that lined the walls.

We're in a gray room now. Circles on the walls—

What size?

Each is about three feet wide.

How many?

Two on each wall. Sam judged by the expression on the faces of the other three that they were also in constant communication with their telepathic contacts aboard *Starbright*.

YOU MAY TAKE OFF YOUR SPACESUITS NOW. YOU WILL FIND THIS SECTION OF THE SHIP CONTAINS YOUR OXY-GEN.

Holy cow, Sam said. *Did you hear that? It was like having a giant shout inside your skull!*

Hear what? Mikhail questioned.

Our first telepathic contact with the Colossians. They said "You may take off your spacesuits now. You will find this section of the ship contains your oxygen." But it was crude telepathy.

The *Starbright* had slipped away through subspace to a new position even more light-years away from the asteroid belt, and left one of the lifeboats in its previous location. Olivia was in contact with Mikhail who now maintained the steady contact with Sam Parker. Three more telepaths sat with Olivia and kept up communications with the other "volunteers" in the lifeboat, but it was Olivia who relayed information to Krause.

When she informed him about the alien telepathic contact, Krause slammed the fist of one hand into the palm of another.

186

"Those bastards *were* studying us! So—they learned a variation of our telepathy? What else did they learn?"

The other two volunteers are taking their spacesuits off, Sam relayed. *I don't know their names. One is a man . . . the other is a woman.*

Are they having any trouble breathing?

No. Doesn't seem so.

TAKE OFF YOUR SPACESUITS.

We're being reminded.

Well, Diane, I suppose we should join the crowd . . .

Natalaie appeared at the doorway to the auxiliary bridge. "Krause . . . I think you'll want to see this . . .

"See what?"

"One of their ships is swallowing the asteroid belt."

"What?"

Krause hurried into the small control room where one of the few viewscreens showed an alien ship squarely in the asteroid belt. An airlock yawned as the ship moved steadily, the asteroids disappearing in the area of the airlock.

"Can that be magnified?" Krause asked.

An operator turned a knob slowly and the image on the screen magnified to the point of blurriness but still showing the process: The Colossian ship was not *swallowing* but was *disintegrating* the flotsam and jetsam of the asteroid. The *Starbright* debris, however, was being passed on into the ship.

"They studied us long enough to distinguish asteroid material from *our* material," Krause mused. "No great feat, maybe, but it shows we're not dealing with a bunch of dummies." Lost in thought, he returned to the other room to stand by Olivia.

Mac? Krause wants you in the auxiliary bridge.

Right away.

"I have to go," Mac told Lucille. He had been stalling—sobering up gradually, but still wondering why Monitor hadn't sent someone to drag him off for another mnemonic surgery . . .

"It takes twenty-four hours for the effects of a Little Red Devil to wear off," Lucille told him. "You're so new at this . . ." She bit her lower lip. "Look . . . Don't smile too much. You'll feel *great* . . . really high, but you'll have to put on an act. Are you a good actor?"

"No."

"Try, damn it. Do everything you can to act normal."

On his way to the auxiliary bridge, Mac wondered if it was possible that the Monitor machine could no longer read his thoughts because his mind had been *altered*.

Altered by drugs.

If so, he would be free to wreck the Monitor machine.

I want to wreck it, he thought, *but . . . wouldn't that be considered an act of treason against Stauffer?*

CHAPTER THIRTY

"I would like to be your telelink," the woman said. "Do you have any objections?"

"No."

"Then I'll reveal my identity . . . if you haven't guessed it already." She removed the black hood that had completely concealed her head.

She was blond, blue-eyed.

"My name is Laurel Austin, I'm the ship's psychologist . . . and a peeper."

Rian nodded.

"Take off your hood."

He removed the black garment and placed it on the floor by his chair. "What function does a telelink perform exactly? That wasn't made entirely clear in the classes."

"A telelink is an experienced Nomad who coaches a beginner. That's all. Part friend, part instructor."

"Sounds reasonable."

"As telelinks, we should become better acquainted." Laurel took a form from her desk and began making notations on it. "Mind if I ask you a few questions?" And then, without pausing, went on, "Age?"

"Twenty-five."

"Married?"

"No. Single."

"Occupation? Artist, isn't it?"

"Yes."

"I peeped that. Sculptor, to be exact. Right?"

"I've been a sculptor all my life."

"How do you do it?"

As best he could, Rian explained how he carved materials with his mind.

"I have some of your work in my apartment on Earth," Laurel said. "True confessions. I recognized your name. I've admired your art for years."

"Which pieces did you buy?"

"An eagle in flight. A tree. One large one of an island. It's quite detailed. Beach, hills, dead volcano."

"How wide?"

"About three feet. I have it in the center of my living room. It's quite a conversation piece."

"I remember that one."

"And some others. But, we shouldn't get too engrossed in a talk about your art. That could come later. Telelinks work together best when they *understand* each other. I love your art but there are many things I don't know about you. Do you like music?"

"I like music but I'm not an authority on it."

"I'll be helping you on your first jump through subspace. That's quite different than the jump you just made through normal space. It'll be important for us to be thoroughly familiar with each other and to know each other better than the average brother and sister and most husbands and wives. I'll ask you a string of personal questions and make notes and then you'll have a chance to ask me similar questions. All right?"

"All right." He would have preferred to be practicing teleporting, but if this was a necessary preliminary . . .

"Favorite color?"

"Orange."

"Favorite food?"

"Singular or plural?"

"Make it plural."

"Fried chicken, watermelon, crabs . . ."

While he tried to think of other favorite foods, she had moved on to another question, "Like dancing?"

"With the right girl."

"What is your concept of the right girl?"

"Intelligent . . . beautiful . . . compassionate . . . gentle . . . and passionate."

Are you blushing? he wondered. His cheeks felt flushed. He didn't like the line of questioning and wondered if he could interrupt it awhile with some questions of his own:

"What do Nomads *do?*"

She stared at him and did not answer. Did she have her head tilted to one side as if listening to something or someone? Her eyes were focused. Was she *peeping* someone? Listening in to someone's mind?

"I mean . . ." Rian went on awkwardly, not knowing if she was paying attention or not. "If we become telelinks, what will we *do?*"

"I'll teach you how to teleport. I'll teach you everything I know."

"Is it too much to ask . . . After I've learned . . . what would we do then?"

She took a deep breath and her expression was grim. She placed the paper to one side. "We would go on . . . We have a simple word for it in Nomad language. *Missions*. We would go on missions together, traveling and working side by side."

"What type of missions?"

"There are all kinds. Carrying supplies from one Nomad station to another. Serving in one of the communications or information networks. Nomads have fundraisers. And researchers. We're quite like the French Underground during the Fourth Intergalactic War. We live

191

for our teleportive art and—I don't mean this to sound dramatic, but it is the truth—we live to serve mankind. We devote our lives to using our teleportive powers for the best causes that we can find. We stay clear of human politics and we can't take part in intergalactic wars between our colonies. You can understand that would be disastrous. As an extreme case, we could side with Democrats, fighting Republicans . . . or vice versa. Or find ourselves on the side of such-and-such a colony fighting its neighboring colony. That type of thing is against our traditions. But Nomads are best at understanding aliens and fighting them when necessary. We move quickly and we have no homes as such. No real homes. Excuse me. I have to go . . . Something's happened. I'll be in touch with you later. Why don't you jump to your cabin? Wait for me there. . . ."

He rose from the chair, knowing he could jump—teleport—through space to his cabin with no problem. Each time would be easier and easier.

"You peeped something while we were talking, didn't you?"

"Yes."

"Something unpleasant."

"The Colossians did something . . . something horrible to one of our people. I'll tell you later. I don't want to tell you now. You'll hear soon enough." She smiled and it was a grim sort of smile, and the bitterness of her next words surprised him:

"If you learn the Nomad way fast enough, you can go with me on a mission to kill some of those Colossian alien bastards."

CHAPTER THIRTY-ONE

Sam and Diane removed their spacesuits. They waited for another communication from the aliens and when they received none for the next hour, became acquainted with the other two volunteers, Mike and Kay.

"I'm not frightened now," Kay said. "I think everything will be all right."

"They had a chance to kill us if they had wanted to," Mike pointed out.

"They *did* rescue us from the asteroid belt," Sam agreed.

TAKE OFF THE REMAINDER OF YOUR CLOTHES AND PREPARE FOR ANTISEPTIC SHOWER

The four undressed and their clothes were gathered by a flat machine with tentacles that appeared to be made of a flexible metal . . .

What's going on? Mikhail queried.

We were just asked to undress and prepare for an antiseptic shower. Diane is thoroughly embarrassed. Kay is taking the nudity in her stride . . . Now . . . a doorway appeared. I feel something pushing us.

What? Can you describe it?

Feels like an invisible hand on the back—warm, firm, insistent.

Now we're in a small cubicle that must be the shower room.

Excuse me, Kay, Sorry!"

Ouch! Whatever it is, it's too hot! It's driving Diane down to her hands and knees . . . we're all in pain . . . the shower substance, whatever it is, is so strong it feels like a burning acid . . . I think Kay and Diane are screaming with the pain but I can't hear them because of the noise of the shower. If this goes on much longer, we'll lose consciousness . . . Oh. It's stopped.

When Olivia informed Krause of the latest development, he said, "I don't like it. They must have some inkling as to the human pain index, but they did not stay within comfortable range . . ."

From the corner of an eye, Krause saw Mac enter the room. "Where the hell have you been?"

"I'll explain later."

Krause telecommed, *Gwenna said something about you being in bed with a blonde. Lucille?*

I do have a private life, Mac said. *Ten minutes here and there.*

Gwenna? Why did you tell him about—?

I thought he would understand that. Sorry, Mac.

Are you drunk, Mac? You look smashed.

How could he hide it from Krause? *Not drunk,* he telecommed. *I had a few drinks, that's all.*

You picked a hell of a time for it. Right when the Colossians decided to take action and when we decided to move the ship.

I didn't know the Colossians would start perking and I didn't know you would move the ship, Mac retorted. *I'm not a mind-reader.* As he telecommed that to Krause, he was also wondering wordlessly in concepts alone when they would come to get him because he had remembered Monitor.

But I am a mind-reader, someone said in his head, *and you must stop thinking about Monitor.*

A peeper?

Right. As I said, stop thinking about it before someone else peeps it out of your dumb skull. There are other peepers aboard Starbright.

Who are you?

None of your business at this point. I'll let you know who I am after Monitor *is destroyed. Get away from Krause as soon as you can and stop at the conference room where the Nomads have their meetings. There's a new meeting starting now. I'll contact you there and we'll go someplace where we can talk.*

The woman named Olivia was saying, "Now they're being moved into another room . . . *They're getting their first look at the aliens!*"

"What do they look like?" Krause—eagerly.

"Seven feet tall . . . eyes glowing . . . humanoid in shape but eyes fiery as if there is some sort of energy inside . . . Color of skin varies . . Some are dark . . . as if deeply tanned. Others are pinkish. Still others are green . . . Some yellowish . . . Sam says they wear no clothing except what looks like belts. But he can't understand what the tools are for. Now they're being asked to sit down and eat."

Mac wondered how he could get away from this gathering of intent people and reach the conference room without arousing questions.

"They're sitting down and eating," Olivia said. "Sam says it tastes like shit."

"What?"

Olivia laughed. "Sam says it may be nutritious but it tastes like shit."

"That does it. All of you. Listen. Tell each contact in the lifeboat to relay this message—exactly— 'Sorry. We have to break contact. We're going to move the ship.' "

As Olivia relayed the message, Krause went to a viewscreen that showed the lifeboat as seen from a camera floating a thousand miles away.

The lifeboat became a nova.

"They had it zeroed in," Krause stated.

"And they exploded it as soon as they thought they would lose us altogether," Olivia whispered in awe. "If *Starbright* had been there . . . if you hadn't moved the ship . . ."

"No more transmissions to the four decoys," Krause ordered. "We'll

195

peep them occasionally. But I want the peeping done from another lifeboat. Mac, check with Troyan and find the names of all the peepers aboard ship. Get a volunteer to go off in a lifeboat and peep the decoys. Drop the lifeboat at a safe distance from the Colossian fleet and then tell the captain to move *Starbright* to a new location."

Mac nodded affirmatively and hurried off. The first lifeboat being novaed meant that the Colossians had somehow—with their superior technology—been able to send a nuclear missile along the path of a telepathic communication.

If they could track a peeper, they would lose another life boat and another volunteer.

CHAPTER THIRTY-TWO

Gwenna, where is Troyan? Mac was hurrying along the corridor outside the auxiliary bridge.

I'm not sure where he is right now. It might take awhile to find him . . . What's the problem?

Krause wants me to look at the list of peepers . . . and find a volunteer for a job.

Eva can take care of that for you. She's been handling more and more things that Troyan would ordinarily handle. What does Krause want exactly?

Mac explained the need for a volunteer peeper to scan their four decoys aboard the Colossian fleet and when Gwenna said she and Eva could take it from there, he went on to the conference room.

Most of the Nomad cloaks had been taken and he couldn't find one that fit properly, so he chose an extra large one that was at least half-way comfortable to wear. He went into the conference room as quietly as possible and stood in the rear . . .

"We lead dual lives," the Nomad instructor was saying. "In the 'other world' as some of us call it, I am a lawyer. I have a wife and two children. My Nomad life-style does not interfere with my profession or my personal life. I keep the two separate. The point I am making is that there is no reason to think that by becoming a Nomad you will have to give up either your profession or your family."

It sounded like a class slanted toward beginners and the voice was not that of Jack/Diamond/Empire/Twenty. As he wondered how many separate classes would be initiated aboard *Starbright*, the peeper contacted him:

Ready?

Yes.

Brace yourself. I'll teleport us to a safe place where no one can peep our minds while we're talking . . .

During his first Nomad classes, Mac had received a brief taste of how it felt to teleport through normal space, when the experienced Nomads "carried" each student on a brief jump. This, however, was much different—a leap through subspace. He had the feeling he was being carried hundreds or thousands of light-years to—

Dropping through subspace toward normal space, feeling the mote of a planet far below, feeling it grow larger and larger until it appeared to his senses monstrously large, seemingly filling the universe—

He could sense the Nomad close, very close as they traveled, with the feeling of sticking near a friend in strange territory . . .

From somewhere on the surface of the planet still far below, he could detect a babble of primitive telepathic emanations. They passed through the emanations with the sensation of passing through a roar of voices.

They were standing in a small cell formed of stone blocks. The cell had no windows, but an arched doorway with thick metal bars looked out upon a darkened area that reminded Mac of an arena with row upon row of other dimly seen cells. Creatures were crawling out there—in some of the cells with open doors, on the shadowy platforms, up and down the stairways—creatures far from human.

"We can talk safely here," the Nomad said. "Even the best of peepers cannot penetrate the noise of those things out there."

"What are they?"

"A freak of nature. Carnivorous animals with telepathic powers.

198

There are two theories. One theory is that they developed telepathy because many of the other forms of life on the planet were telepathic and the other theory claims that their masters trained the animals to be telepathic and it passed from generation to generation partly by heredity and partly by the young learning from the old. Whichever theory is correct, they are still animals and their chatter blocks peepers. I come here whenever I want to be certain I am not over-heard by another peeper."

Mac went to the metal bars and stared out at the shadows. From where he stood none of the creatures were close enough to see clearly, but they appeared to resemble Earth's lions.

"If they're animals, how does their telepathy do them any good?"

"In more ways than you might guess. Originally they were able to communicate with the dominant life-form. When that race died away, they had to become hunters again. Their telepathy allows them to track prey. They could read your thoughts—your emotions at least. If you were in combat with one, it could anticipate your every move a microsecond before you put your muscles in use. But we can't spend too much time talking about them. We have to talk about *Starbright* and the Monitor . . ."

"I remembered it," Mac reviewed. "I don't quite understand how that happened . . ."

"You had your first contact with Monitor *before* you were hired . . . a unique occurrence."

"I had been hired," Mac corrected.

"The decision had been made, but all the papers had not been processed and your employee status was not registered in the computers. At that particular point, Monitor was put into operation and memory of its function removed from the minds of the few SS agents who knew of its existence. Only Krause and a few other top agents knew. The memory was eliminated from their minds. SS agents hired from that point on were linked to the Monitor without knowing of its existence."

"Incredible."

"And it went as smoothly as giving each employee an invisible tattoo during their physical examination upon hiring. The range of the Monitor was expanded beyond the secret service protective agents to other Synpla employees, in a wider and wider range."

"Monitor feeds all thought into its central computer?"

"Yes."

"And makes decisions?"

"Yes."

"And can control physical actions in some cases . . ."

"Yes."

"It warned me that Eva was attempting suicide because it could read her mind . . ."

"And it didn't want her to die because she is a valuable agent."

"So—it notified me that she had attempted suicide, without revealing its identity. And I went rushing off to save her if possible. And then, when I remembered hearing about the Monitor shortly before being hired, it arranged for the mnemonic erasure. It controlled my muscles, my body, through my mind—forced me to climb up on the operating table . . ."

"Yes."

"Then the memory came back when I took those drugs. They altered my mind. I don't understand how that happened. I can understand part of it but not all the—"

"Mnemonic erasure is in effect a numbing of certain electrical synapses in the mind. Strong drugs such as the ones aboard *Starbright* upset the results of a mnemonic erasure and nullify the results in some cases. Monitor is fighting a losing battle right now. There are so many drugs aboard *Starbright*—"

"You mean, what happened to me is happening to other SS agents?"

"Yes. Other agents have remembered Monitor. And Monitor has had to put them through new mnemonic erasure. Monitor is fighting use of drugs on *Starbright* for several reasons and one of the main reasons is that such drug usage endangers its own secrecy. It—"

Screams of fear followed by screams of pain echoed through the dark chambers beyond the cell. They were brief in duration but startling in their intensity. Mac froze, a chill running up and down his back.

"Nothing important," the Nomad said. "The strongest of the telepathic species captures weaker animals and keeps them prisoner in some of these cells until feeding time."

"And—feeding time arrived?"

The Nomad nodded yes and moved over to a stone slab apparently designed to serve as a bench. Mac sat also and began to wonder if the Nomad was a man or woman. Should he ask? It didn't matter, really, except for personal curiosity. So far he could not remember anything in the conversation that had implied either a feminine or masculine personality.

"What is this place?" he asked abruptly.

"It served as a prison for the criminal elements of the dominant race, but when that race died away, the telepathic animals began using it."

"I had the urge to kill Monitor," Mac said, abruptly changing the subject again. "I didn't like the idea of a machine reading my mind, controlling my actions . . . But I suppose Monitor serves a bona fide function, the protection of Alex Stauffer . . ."

"It did serve a proper function originally," the Nomad said. "When Monitor was originally designed and put into operation, it was geared to detect attempts on Stauffer's life. If an SS agent became a traitor, Monitor was designed to detect that immediately. It was also designed to coordinate the efforts of all SS agents. Presidents of many countries use Monitors. What one guard sees and thinks is computerized with all the visual images and thoughts of all other guards. Protection becomes much more efficient. No one had any objection to Monitor as originally intended. But— Have you heard of the Jubilee machines?"

"Yes." He remembered reading about the Jubilee corporation, the "Rolls Royce of the Entertainment World" that designed a computer attuned to its owners' needs for diversion and entertainment.

201

"The Jubilee machines were designed to be sold only to wealthy clients. Alexander Stauffer purchased a Jubilee Nine model. The ninth version included telepathic communication with servants, secretaries, relatives, and employees. By law the linkages had to be voluntary. A Jubilee machine ordinarily did such things as arranging surprise birthday parties or meetings with exciting or interesting people.

"Someone—and it may have been Alexander Stauffer himself—conceived a method of *combining* the Jubilee Nine machine and Monitor. Not combining exactly but linking them together." The Nomad hesitated and nodded toward the sounds coming from the darkened area beyond their cell. "Those are living telepathic *animals* out there. But someone created another type of telepathic monster—a telepathic monster machine, without conscience, seeking only to entertain Alexander Stauffer in any way possible. We believe the monster combination of Monitor and Jubilee Nine arranged the wreck of the *Starbright* because Stauffer was bored during the trip and bored with the whole idea of going to Algor. The shipwreck injected something exciting into his life—something far more exciting than a surprise birthday party."

Mac found himself stunned for many long moments. His mind whirled as he struggled to digest the concepts. A Jubilee machine and a Monitor *combined?* Both telepathic, both able to read minds and direct actions? He knew the results would be unique—*had been* unique because the Nomad was saying the union had been accomplished.

He had read somewhere that the new genre of telepathic machines such as Jubilee and Monitor invariably reflected the personalities and mentalities of their owners and users. And Alex had long had the reputation of being ruthless and cold-blooded beneath the polite and socially acceptable veneer. Mac remembered the rumors of all the people Alex had "eliminated" during his lifetime, the five thousand men and women who died on Synpla IX because of Alex's decisions . . .

"It's hard to believe Alex could have been responsible for the *Starbright* being wrecked," Max said. "It—"

202

"Alex Stauffer did not arrange it personally," the Nomad reminded. "If that is what happened, it happened because his *machines* arranged it without his foreknowledge."

"Why did you begin investigating the Monitor? What aroused your suspicions?"

"I belong to a group that has been investigating Alex Stauffer's activities for several years. There have been indications that Alex arranged the second and fourth intergalactic wars for commercial reasons."

Mac could not think of any comment. It was general knowledge that Stauffer's corporations had prospered immensely during the second and fourth wars. With his control of politicians and influence in so many governments, it would have been possible for Alex to exert influence to start the wars.

If this Nomad had been investigating Alex's activities as related to the wars, then that meant the Nomad must be a member of one of the intergalactic investigative agencies.

"How do I fit into everything?" Mac inquired.

"We want you to destroy the Jubilee and Monitor machines aboard *Starbright*. It has to be timed. We will tell you when."

"Destroy by what means?"

"Your laser. A blast for each machine will be sufficient."

"Where are they aboard *Starbright*?"

"They are located in the same maintenance corridor where you and Krause checked the energy screen equipment. There are compartments there reserved for the use of starliner passengers and Alex Stauffer. The Jubilee and Monitor machines are located in unmarked compartments but they are the only two colored green."

Mac thought he remembered seeing the two compartments although, at the time that he went through the maintenance corridor with Krause and the engineers, he had been engrossed in the problem of how the ship's energy screen had been sabotaged; too engrossed to give much thought to the other equipment that might be in the corridor.

"When do you want the machines destroyed?"

"It has to be timed carefully. Stauffer will be aware of their absence the moment it happens. You know he has a large number of SS agents aboard *Starbright* . . . Many of them are telepaths and some are peepers. We will have to choose the right time to strike. We will let you know when the right time arrives."

"How can I get into the maintenance corridor? The ship's crew have keys, but I—"

"You have access," the Nomad said. "You are a Nomad and when the time comes you will know how to teleport yourself."

CHAPTER THIRTY-THREE

Krause settled on his bunk, propped pillows beneath his back, and the thinkwriter on the other side of the room began to chatter—

This type of daily diary is easy because all you do is sit and think at the end of a day.

Today was a bitch, but some things did get resolved. The Colossians blasted our lifeboat when we sent the message to our decoys that we had to break contact because we were moving the ship. It resolved the question of whether the Colossians are friendly or unfriendly.

They are not only unfriendly, they are murderous bastards.

Speaking of madmen, the team of agents tracking the killer who's been wandering around the ship, murdering anyone he catches alone and who once murdered twelve people at a clip, has narrowed the possibilities down to one man they consider THE MAN.

Josef Kaiser.

They will arrange a meeting. He has not yet signed to be on Alex's staff. The agents will try to persuade him. If he joins, fine. During the physical he will be placed under sedation and a peeper will read his mind to see if he is actually the killer. If the probing is affirmative, proper steps will be taken. If he refuses to join the staff, chances are that he may have an accident.

We now have another volunteer in a lifeboat, a peeper who will see if she can scan the decoys' minds and more important in some ways, the minds of the Colossians. If they believe they destroyed the Starbright when they destroyed the lifeboat, our situation will be more tenable than if they realize we tricked them.

Gwenna will let me know the news of the peeping but I do not expect good news.

Mac has been falling apart. He is now taking drugs. His actions are off character but not sufficiently to warrant a reprimand.

At one point today when I tried to reach him by telecom, the telecom switchboard came up with a complete negative. Not sleeping. Not unconscious. Not on Starbright at all.

The only answer to that is that Mac is either a skilled Nomad and teleported himself off the ship or else a Nomad carried him off for a while.

Why?

That's enough thinking for one day.

Krause was sound asleep and deep in a dream when, two hours later, Gwenna contacted him by telecom. She was certainly an expert telepath. He had been awakened in the past by some telepathic messages that had felt like someone shouting in his ear.

Gwenna was so smooth about it that she seemed to be in the room, sitting on the edge of his bunk, gently touching his shoulder and softly speaking into his ear—

You said you wanted to be notified of the first peeper results, even if you were asleep.

That's right, Krause affirmed, yawning.

The peeper had difficulty peeping the Colossian minds. She could not read distinct thoughts but the fragments and impressions seem to be that the Colossians are generally of the opinion that they destroyed our ship. Only a very few think it may have been a trick to draw their fire. Since the majority of the aliens agree that Starbright has been destroyed, they are making preparations to move on to another galaxy, their original destination before they received our distress signal.

Good. He kept his eyes closed and remained turned toward the wall to maintain the feeling that she was sitting there with him.

Do you want me to tell you some information that may disturb your sleep—or hold it until you awaken?

Tell me.

One of the decoys, a man, was dissected.

Krause's stomach turned but he forced himself to shove the horror from his mind, forced himself to be objective. He said, as calmly as he could, *Then that ties in with what Eva has been saying about the Colossians who dissected humans when they came across a radar station during the First Intergalactic War. We've been calling them "Colossians" because the description was close. I'd say that clinches it and they are definitely the Colossians. What happened to the other volunteer decoys?*

The woman named Kay was separated from the others and taken to a laboratory aboard the ship and the peeper says her mind is in a state of shock. She has not been able to get any complete thoughts—only the smallest fragments. The peeper thinks Kay may have been raped but she's not absolutely certain. The impressions she's received do indicate that she is being experimented with—like a guinea pig in a laboratory.

Any indication as to the purpose of the experiments?

None so far.

Tell the peeper to keep at it and dig up what she can. What happened to the other two volunteers?

They have not been harmed but some of the aliens are in nearly constant telepathic contact with them. The peeper has the feeling that the aliens are practicing telepathy.

Practicing, Krause echoed and groaned. The Colossians were heartless, thorough bastards all right. Dissecting one of their volunteers, experimenting with another, and practicing telepathy with two others. *That's dangerous,* he said bitterly. *Telepathy was not a real art back in the days of the First Intergalactic War when the Colossians*

207

made their initial contact with our race. I doubt if anyone there was a real telepath. But if they study some of us enough to learn the knack of our telepathy, they can create their own peepers. If they do that, mankind will never be safe from them in any galaxy.

Two more items . . . Gwenna began. *Diane Russell and Sam Parker have been assured they will not be harmed. One of the aliens said they will be taken to—the peeper told me the alien words but I can't retain their complexity. Translated to our language they mean cosmic menagerie.*

Menagerie? That's a synonym for zoo, isn't it?

Yes.

Krause felt his blood begin to boil. *You mean—they dissected one of our people, they're experimenting with another, and they're going to put the remaining two in a zoo as if they're some kind of uncivilized animals?*

Gwenna did not answer the question as such but elaborated, *The peeper received the impression there are hundreds or thousands of humans at the cosmic menagerie . . . descendants of the people the Colossians kidnapped from the radar station and from unrecorded contacts with our race.*

Mmmmm. Krause struggled to calm himself.

Last bit of information, Gwenna went on. *The Colossians are involved in an intergalactic war. The peeper couldn't get any details, but they are definitely in a conflict.*

I hope the other side wins, Krause said bitterly. It was a simple statement, partly facetious, but he had started to wonder if they could somehow use the Nomads to launch an attack and kill at least *some* of those alien bastards.

They had been talking for hours and the lounge had closed. When Josef looked around, he saw three people sitting at the bar—a man by himself and a couple.

The three men in the booth with him had been putting on pressure for him to join Alexander's staff and he had been refusing on the grounds that he preferred to remain independent.

"There are only six people who haven't joined so far," the tallest of the trio stated again. "One of those six is ninety years old. The other five are—" The man shrugged. "Frankly, I think the other five lack normal mental capacities. It makes sense to join Synpla at this point in time. You'll be *paid* for working toward your own survival."

Josef opened his mouth to say *no* one final time—

And noticed something strange. The three at the bar were looking in his direction. Supposedly they had not been paying attention but now they were sitting there, watching him, waiting.

"One last time," the tall man said. "Will you join?" He smiled faintly and there was no overt threat but Josef detected something.

His senses told him that they would kill him if he said no. This had been arranged carefully—this meeting late in the evening, the stretching of the talk until after closing time. The three in their booth were watching him unwaveringly although the ones at the bar had again looked away.

They must know, he thought. Somehow they knew he had been killing passengers. Without saying so in precise words, they were offering him a choice. Join Stauffer's staff or be killed.

But if they knew the truth, why were they so anxious for him to be in Stauffer's employ?

They act like undercover cops, he thought. But the ship had a police force of sorts. If they suspected him of killing some of the passengers, it would be an easy task to turn him over to the *Starbright* security police . . .

Could it be? . . .

An incredible possibility occurred.

His instincts told him they knew the truth about himself and also warned him that they would kill him if he didn't accept their offer . . .

Could it be that Stauffer wants to hire an assassin?

He shrugged. "You're very persuasive. You win. I'll join."

CHAPTER THIRTY-FOUR

They were sitting motionless in the cell on that alien world—wherever it might be—but Mac's mind had started on an accelerated swirl of thoughts.

The Nomad had confirmed his deductions that the Red Devil drugs had raised the memory of the Monitor from his subconscious. And that same drug-induced alteration in his mind was what prevented Monitor from reading his thoughts at the current time. He would be safe from Monitor scanning, the Nomad had explained, so long as he remained in a drugged state. To protect his supply of drugs, the Nomad had given him a prescription bottle complete with his name on the label and the one-a-day dosage information along with the proper pharmaceutical coding. The pills were white instead of red.

"The effect is almost identical to that of the Little Red Devils," the Nomad had informed him, "but the chemicals are designed to cause a stronger neurological change. That change will protect you from Monitor probing so long as you take one a day."

"Any side effects?" he'd inquired.

"Only a sense of euphoria similar to that caused by the illegal Red Devils. This way you'll be protected until we decide to make our move against Monitor. If anyone questions the medication, tell them it was issued by the ship's automedico for a slight nervous condition."

After that explanation, the Nomad had suggested they simply sit and wait awhile until the neurological medication had time to take effect.

He had decided the Nomad was a woman. The voice was muffled by the black costume and the person seemed to be making a deliberate effort to disguise it, but it *did* have feminine tones. He thought he detected the faint odor of perfume. He had been under the impression that Nomads all had their designation on their uniforms, but this individual did not. He had toyed with the idea of asking the person's name—at least the Nomad name—and decided against that. The plan was to be undercover as much as possible until the Monitor-Jubilee machines were destroyed and if something should go wrong, with himself being caught it would be disastrous to know the name of someone else involved.

"Shortly before we return to *Starbright*," the Nomad had informed him, "I'll give you a limited hypno to keep you from thinking about Monitor until we're ready for you to make your strike."

He had also been informed that he would be placed in an accelerated Nomad class—a specially selected group of the most promising telekinetic students. In the class, along with the group, he would practice teleportation through normal space as many hours each day as he possibly could and still function in his liaison capacity.

"The accelerated group will move rapidly into studying the ability to teleport through hyperspace," the Nomad had informed him, "and that limited group may be able to teleport from the *Starbright* in approximately three months."

The three-month period had intrigued him. Jack/Diamond/Empire/Twenty had stated that the average new member of the Nomad society needed a year to learn the telekinetic skill. Certainly the average person did not have the same incentive to learn as the passengers aboard *Starbright*. They would be learning the skill in an effort to save their necks! But if the training period could be reduced from a year to three months, could it be further reduced to a single

211

month if the training sessions were intensified right up to the point of human endurance?

"How long do we have to sit here?" Mac asked, suddenly beginning to feel impatient to be on the move again.

"Not too long. That medication is almost as fast as the Little Red Devils. We can leave as soon as you begin to feel that sensation of euphoria."

Mac sighed silently. He felt like a pawn, a puppet being manipulated by others—

But, he thought suddenly, *what's so bad about that? When you're a puppet, you don't have to think. You don't have to evaluate and make decisions. In the final analysis, isn't it more comfortable to be a puppet and let the others do the thinking and solving of problems, to just drift along—this way, that way?*

He smiled, shifting his position. Looking around at the cell, he admired the architecture. The sensation of solidity was amazing, like being in a comfortable, warm womb, protected from *all* outside elements. The sounds of the alien telepathic animals were intriguing, soothing, and pleasant somehow . . .

"How do you feel?" the Nomad inquired.

"I like it here," Mac said with a broad smile. "Let's stay as long as we can. It's very comfortable here. Doesn't it have a cozy feeling?"

The Nomad laughed and, muffled beneath the black cloak, it sounded like the laughter of a strange dark alien. "I think we can leave now."

As soon as Josef Kaiser closed the door to his cabin, he felt the entity in his mind.

Entity. That was the name he gave it immediately. It was not a person—it was a telepathic *thing,* overpowering, much stronger than any person he had ever known—a nonhuman entity.

And the thing was delving into his mind stronger than any human . . .

As a young man in his teens, he had tried to be a telepath. He had

212

studied, taken lessons, practiced hour after hour, night after night. No amount of effort had succeeded in making him a fluent telepath. The most he had ever been able to do was crude blunderings.

The ambition to be a good telepath had been born, ironically, because of a fervent passion for a delicate girl in high school English Advanced classes. It had been a revolutionary era for education and the EA courses had just begun to teach elementary telepathy in addition to written and spoken English. That painful year he had learned two things almost simultaneously: One—the teenage boys who could telepath smoothly were the ones who scored with the prettiest girls. Telepaths of the opposite sex could "talk" across the width of a city on a moonlit night, or any night, or any time at all. The right kind of telepathic communication exceeded any type of flirtation possible verbally or by body language. Two—telepathy would be, for some, forever out of reach. As some would never be able to run or swim because of physical restrictions, some individuals would find it forever impossible to communicate telepathically because of mental limitations. And he was one of those so restricted.

The girl he admired in school had become the girl friend of a talented telepath in EA classes and the looks passed between the two during school hours had been, for Josef, a frustrating reflection of the male-female courtship that passed between the two telepathically. He had had very few dates, no steady girl friends. He had not been born physically attractive, had come from a lower middle-class family, and had found himself with little to offer a potential girl friend.

He had, however, developed in other ways. He had strengthened his body and quickened his reflexes. He'd joined the First Galactic Army at eighteen, served a four-year hitch and learned how it felt to kill both humans and aliens. After the tour of duty in the First Galactic Army, he had become a mercenary, hiring himself out to whichever government needed him the most or could pay the highest. During all his years in the army and as a free-lance soldier, he had practiced the skill that earned its adepts the name of *ironhead*.

An ironhead could block any telepath and any peeper. No one

could read an ironhead's thoughts. Blocking your thoughts completely to everyone else was, ironically, a talent as valuable as a skilled peeper's.

In between mercenary hirings, he had occasionally performed the duties of a hired assassin. On a few occasions, he had allowed women to penetrate his mind, telepathically just to see how it felt—an exotic food to be relished only once or twice a year, because once an ironhead had learned his skill, letting down the unconscious defenses for only a moment required great effort.

On three memorable assassinations, he had allowed the female victim to touch his mind telepathically only moments before he killed her. He remembered those female mental probings clearly. In combat he had often allowed scouts and points to enter his mind—and he clearly remembered those male communications.

This *thing* in his mind now was neither male nor female. It crushed through all his ironhead barriers as if they were flimsy cardboard. It delved into his memories—he could feel it probing relentlessly, finding all the facts he would have hid forever . . .

And he could feel that the thing was very interested in how he had killed a number of people aboard *Starbright* . . .

Very interested.

He was taking the laser from its hiding place . . .

Why am I taking the gun out of hiding?

As his arm raised the gun to his head, he screamed mentally, WHO ARE YOU?

The thing in his head answered, *Monitor.*

WHAT ARE YOU?

No answer.

Monitor was controlling his muscles, moving the gun up to his head . . .

How did it get inside my mind?

The gun brushed his ear. In a moment it would be placed squarely against his temple. Monitor would make him kill himself.

They planted it in me when they measured my brainwave pattern.

They did much more than measure the pattern — they planted this monster in my mind or somehow paved the way for it.

He tried to block Monitor with his mind and his body. His hand trembled with the strain . . .

They arranged my suicide because they discovered I was killing some of the passengers. They tracked me down and Monitor is my assassin!

His finger was tightening on the trigger.

At the last moment — with one of the greatest exercises of willpower that he had ever generated, he managed to move the gun away from his temple but not away from his head completely. The blast of the laser burned away his left ear.

He did not scream from the intense pain. He had been wounded dozens of times in combat and never cried out in pain.

The laser was coming up to his head again . . .

As the weapon rose, he went to the cabin door and opened it with his free hand . . . There were people in the corridor outside and he shouted, "Help! Monitor! Help!"

The gun was against his head again. The people were staring at the blood gushing from the rip in flesh where his left ear had been . . .

"Help! Monitor! Help!"

At the last moment he again managed to deflect the laser. The shot seemed to tear the top of his skull apart. He fell and moaned, "Monitor . . . Monitor . . ." His mind was tracing back to the heart of Monitor. He sensed that what he was doing would have been impossible for an ordinary telepath. Any other human would have been too sensitive mentally. His mind was tough beyond description . . .

But, when he reached Monitor, *it* was beyond description; cold, mechanical, all powerful, heartless. He sensed it was constantly reading the thoughts of hundreds of people, feeding the thoughts into its computer, sometimes controlling their actions . . .

This time Monitor was making him place the gun in his mouth. Once more he managed to swerve the aim at the last moment . . .

He did not die but the blast blew his jaw off.

215

His ears were ringing with screams. Women were screaming, had been screaming since they first saw him.

He felt himself slipping into unconsciousness and even as the darkness closed about him, he felt his hand moving once more, lifting the gun to his head again. He knew that this time he would be unable to swerve the aim. He thought, *It must be the most cold-blooded, deadliest machine in the universe . . .*

CHAPTER THIRTY-FIVE

The several days of teleporting within the ship had seemed, to Mac, endless. Not entirely unpleasurable, but not entirely pleasant either. It reminded him of how he had felt when he first studied spatial tennis. He had practiced hour after hour with some attractive teammates, but swirling through the air on antigravs for prolonged periods had proven tedious and tiresome.

In his advanced Nomad class, he had progressed from teleporting *with* a telelink to teleporting absolutely under his own power. He could now reach any place of the ship that he had been to previously—teleport there in less than the blinking of an eye—and it was developing into a skill that he performed nearly as automatically as walking. One of the restrictions of teleporting was that a Nomad could only teleport to a place that he or she had seen previously—or a place that they could telepathically connect in another person's memory. He understood the principle involved—it would be like using someone else's memory, but he was having trouble with those classes.

When he returned to his cabin after a particularly grueling day of practicing teleporting and studying some of the advanced techniques, he groaned inwardly when he found Lucille and her friend, Selma, chattering away. Lucille had moved into his cabin and he had enjoyed living with such a beautiful girl. There were a few disadvantages and the worst disadvantage so far had turned out to be Selma who would stop by unexpectedly and chat for hours with Lucille. Mac had nicknamed Selma, *motormouth*, because she was talkative and she seemed to infect Lucille during her visits.

"Hello, Mac," Selma greeted, immediately turning back to Lucille and the conversation.

Mac did not answer, but gave a brief wave of his hand, went to the portable liquor cabinet that Lucille had brought with her and poured himself a stiff drink. Selma was saying:

"—and this man was standing in the doorway of his cabin with a laser in his hand. He'd shot one of his ears off! He yelled something. I couldn't understand it, but someone said later he yelled, 'Help. Monitor. Help.' He was yelling for help, but he didn't seem really *afraid*, just sort of angry and calling for someone to help him. As we stood there in the hallway and watched, he shot himself in the head. He fell down and I thought he was dead, but he put the gun in his mouth and would have killed himself but twisted at the last moment and blew his jaw off. Then he put the laser to his skull and *that* shot ended it. Eric had seen suicides before but said it was the strangest one he'd ever seen. I'll introduce you to Eric. You'll love him. He's tall and handsome and says he's just a cop, but he's had the most fantastic experiences being a Federation Sheriff on all kinds of weird worlds."

And on and on it went. As Mac felt a growing resentment and tenseness at Selma's chattering, he remembered to take one of the little white pills the Nomad had given him. Selma talked so long that the damned pill had time to take effect. He felt his mood change from resentment at Selma's presence and talkativeness, to acceptance, to an actual enjoyment of her motormouth. In a far corner of his mind, he knew it was the effects of the white pill that caused the change, but he didn't care. He joined in the conversation between the two women and Selma left about an hour later.

"Alone at last," Lucille said, sitting on his lap, putting her arms around him, and giving him a kiss.

"You didn't seem too anxious to get rid of her."

"I know you like her company."

"True," he lied.

"So I let her stick around. She keeps me supplied with all the ship's news and gossip. Wasn't that a fantastic story about the man killing himself?"

"Fantastic," he muttered, running his fingers through her blond hair.

"What do you think he was yelling? Who is Monitor?"

"I don't know." He nibbled her ear and, wanting to change the subject, said, "When are we getting married? Did you see the captain?"

"Are you kidding? We're living together. Why do you want to spoil it by getting married."

"It was your idea."

"I know. I was drunk. But then, when I sobered, I realized that although I might love you, you didn't love me."

"Why do you love me?" he asked.

"Because you're like a big dumb ox and easy to manipulate."

"You're dumb, too. I love you and you're too dumb to see it."

"Do you really love me? I thought it was all an act on your part, to keep me around so you'd have somebody to screw. Why do you love me?"

"Because you're a crazy sexy blonde," he said affectionately, ruffling her hair. "I always wanted a nutty blonde."

"In that case," she said, running a fingertip along the line of his jaw, "since we both love each other, maybe we *should* get married."

They began a long passionate kiss and the peeper was suddenly in his skull, telepathically breaking the hypnosis that had made him forget Monitor for several days. All the memories were back—of Monitor, of the talk with the unidentified Nomad, and of the plan to destroy the Monitor and Jubilee machines.

The peeper telepathed firmly, sharply:

Destroy Monitor and Jubilee. Now!

You're wrecking a romantic moment, Mac said lightly, but lifted Lu-

219

cille from his lap, saying, "Excuse me a moment," and teleported from a sitting position, straightening his body while in the fleeting instants of subspace, drawing his laser, landing in a standing position in the maintenance corridor and blasting at the mteal panels that concealed Monitor and Jubilee. From the microsecond that triggered his mind to jump through space, the peeper was shouting in his mind, *Fast! Fast! Fast!* and he understood the need to be lightning quick before other peepers learned his intention. The laser in his hand fired again and again and the panels burned away, the beams from the gun ripping into the hearts of the two machines. He had the strangest sensation of telepathically hearing silent screams—the death cries of two strange machines that had *lived* in the way that no machine had ever lived before . . .

Then he was back in his cabin again, the laser still in his hand, a wisp of smoke curling from the barrel. When Lucille looked at him wide-eyed and gasped, "What was that all about?" he realized he was trembling not with fear but with intense nervous tension.

"I just killed two machines," he said in near awe. "Two machines that were"—he fought the impulse to shudder—"*alive.* It was like killing two *giants.* Not physical giants, but giants in their powers and—"

The words froze in his mouth. Two Nomads had appeared in the cabin. The laser fell from his hand as it went numb and he and Lucille and the Nomads were hurtling down a long dark tunnel through the universe while stars and galaxies were dim blurs roaring by on every side, Lucille screaming in unadulterated fear, screaming inside his mind . . .

CHAPTER THIRTY-SIX

They landed at an office unlike any office Mac had ever seen before. It was immense, shaped, like an asterisk, luxuriously furnished and incredibly varied in both equipment and decorations. The arms of the asterisk shape were cul-de-sac areas roughly in the form of large rectangular rooms, each specialized in various ways. One of the nearest asterisk cul-de-sacs contained comfortable seats between floor to ceiling aquariums with exotic alien fish. Another asterisk arm contained row upon row of antique filing cabinets, another resembled a bedroom, another appeared to be a dining area, and another was a library with countless shelves of books, the area decorated with the heads of wild animals.

The center of the room contained an antique from the twentieth century, a massive oak desk in the form of an O, surrounded by semicircular couches. Max recognized the style of central furnishings immediately—it was the way Alexander Stauffer had arranged his main Earth City office. Mac had attended a few conferences and would never forget how Alex sat in the center of his circular desk, surrounded by dozens of high echelon executives who sat on the couches and waited while Alex slowly revolved in his swivel chair, conferring with those present on a mind-boggling succession of corporation topics.

This was a scaled-down version of Alex's main office and the antique desk was considerably smaller than the sparkling modern one. The semicircular couches did not have accompanying low-level desks for papers and reports as in the main office . . .

Alexander Stauffer appeared in the center of the desk, sat in the large swivel chair. He held the Nomad black hood in one hand and tossed it casually onto the desk top. Mac had arrived at this destination standing but Lucille was sprawled on the floor and shifted to a sitting position. Mac helped her to her feet. She stared at Alex.

Mac looked at the Nomad standing to Alex's right, at a chair near the circular desk . . .

Gwenna had a chair in a similar arrangement in the Earth City main office—a position where she could be closest to Alex, handing him papers and memo-recs across the width of the desk when necessary, close at hand when he needed her . . .

Gwenna?

Yes. To Mac her voice seemed sad.

You wrecked the Monitor and Jubilee aboard Starbright. *We knew it immediately. Alarms went off when the machines stopped.*

How did you know it was me who wrecked them?

A peeper. An expert peeper on our staff caught you a split second later.

"Have a seat," Alex said casually, waving at the couches. Numbly, Mac settled onto a couch. Lucille sat beside him. Gwenna remained standing.

Gwenna, you and Alex have been Nomads for years, haven't you?
That is right.

And you never told me.

We never told anyone, Mac. You're starting to understand that through your classes. A Nomad can only teleport if he maintains his anonymity outside the society.

Mac remembered how Alex had taken the news of their being lost in space. He had not appeared worried at all. Of course. Alex was a

Nomad and had not been trapped aboard the *Starbright*. He could teleport himself off the ship anytime.

Alex is a skilled teleporter, Gwenna telepathed.

You were reading my mind, weren't you?

I want to stay in the closest touch with you, Mac. You're in trouble—

You're a peeper.

Yes.

Secretary to the richest man in the universe. A Nomad. A telepath. A peeper. Is there anything you can't do?

Mac . . .

Alex Stauffer was sitting with his elbow on the desk, resting one cheek against the upturned hand of that arm, frowning thoughtfully. "Why did you do it?"

"I wrecked Monitor and Jubilee because they caused the *Starbright* wreck, they caused us to be lost in space, they killed dozens of people and their actions may result in hundreds of deaths."

"What makes you think Monitor caused the accident?"

"A Nomad told me."

"Which Nomad?"

"I don't know her identity." And as soon as the words left his mouth, he knew he had slipped and identified the person as a woman.

"You accepted her statements?"

"I believed them."

"Why?"

Mac hesitated. He could feel himself sliding into a defensive stance. Alex had always intimidated him in many ways. Alex was rich beyond imagination—a man who could buy, and did in fact own, cities and worlds and spacefleets and armies of men and women. He, on the other hand, was one stumbling not-too-bright lackey who . . .

Don't knock yourself so much, Gwenna said. *You're one of the most intelligent men I've known. And you're far from a lackey. You have one of the highest positions in Synpla.*

"I believed what the Nomad said because," Mac explained to Alex,

223

"I had heard of the Jubilee machines and I had heard of the Monitor. I understood how the two combined could result in a heartless telepathic machine capable of wrecking the *Starbright*, killing dozens of people all to create diversion—an interesting adventure—for its owner—you."

"You're an expert on telepathic machines?"

"Well, no. But I—"

"Come over here." Alex teleported himself to one of the cul-de-sacs. Mac followed on foot. Alex stood before the faces of a dozen tickertape machines. "These are the first telepathically controlled teletypers," Alex said. "Real antiques. I keep them here to keep me posted about the financial positions of some of my key companies. Over here . . ."

As Alex wandered around the room, showing Mac both antique and new telepath machines, Mac telecommed to Gwenna:

Where in hell are we?

This is what Alex calls his den. You can only reach this office by teleportation. There are no doors or windows . . .

"Are you telecomming to Gwenna?" Alex asked suddenly. Mac winced. Something in his expression had betrayed him.

"I asked her where we were . . . but I was still paying attention to what you were saying . . ."

"This is my den," Alex said gruffly, turning abruptly and heading back toward his desk. "Gwenna and I come here quite often. We're out of reach here, safe from phones and telecoms and peepers. I do my best thinking here. Gwenna and I have solved some gritty corporate and personnel problems here. And I doubt you were paying attention. My point was that *I* was a young boy when the first Telmech machines came out on the market. My father bought me the first models. I have always kept up with the Telmechs and I own the three top companies that manufacture them. You may not be aware of that since you're so wrapped up in Synpla and the picayune details of your own life."

Mac felt a flush of anger at Alex's last statement. *How dare he refer to part of my life as picayune!*

"You have become a gritty personnel problem," Alex said sharply. "What makes you think I would own and maintain machines capable of cold-bloodedly arranging a spaceliner accident costing lives?"

Mac was holding his breath. The anger was boiling in him, sweetened somewhat by the medication he'd been under, but still boiling and suddenly bursting past restraints as he poured it out:

"Everyone knows you let five thousand people die on Synpla IX. You arranged two intergalactic wars in which hundreds of thousands of people died. You—" Mac's point would have been that Alex was personally conscienceless. But the galactic tycoon had been standing with his arms folded across his chest, shaking his head ruefully, and interrupted:

"The events at Synpla IX have always been totally misinterpreted. The factory had to be shut down because the workers were criminally negligent and unproductive. It was an experimental factory staffed by ex-criminals and social misfits. The intention was to see if a manufacturing enterprise could also be a rehabilitation center. The project failed miserably. After the plant was shut down, we offered transportation back to Earth. Thousands of the Synpla IX employees turned down the opportunity. They wanted to remain on that planet. They didn't want to come back to society as we know it on Earth. They couldn't survive. They weren't intelligent enough or industrious enough to manage their own survival. I could not have brought them back to Earth unless I kidnapped them, yet I am blamed for their deaths."

Mac did not comment. If he lived long enough, he could check on Alex's version. He countered:

"You caused two intergalactic wars so you could prosper financially."

"The intergalactic wars were on their way," Alex stated. "They were inevitable. Do you know what that means? *Inevitable?* Every sociological and socioeconomical analyst in the world said that nothing could stop the war with the colonies and the one with the so-called

225

Galactic Federation. I had some political influence. When those two wars were proven to be inevitable, I fought a delaying action with my political influence. I managed to assist in the holding off of the actual conflict until the Synpla plans were in maximum production capacity. Our plastics—stronger than any metal known previously—went into the starfighters and hundreds of weapons that eventually won both wars. If I could have stopped the wars, I would have. Since I couldn't prevent them, I arranged the timing as best I could. We won those wars but since Synpla profited financially, rumors blame me for their origin."

During the silence that followed, Mac stared absently at the nearby aquarium. It contained pink and black fish with silver filigreed fins. In the mass of water as high as the ceiling and at least twenty feet in width, there were ivory pagodas and Torii gates, coral reefs of gold and a village of oriental houses carved from the huge slabs of ruby and jade found on the planet called Almarado.

"Do you believe me?" Alex queried.

"Partly."

"Did it ever occur to you that the wreck of the *Starbright* may have been part of an elaborate plot to discredit me—or to gain control of my empire?"

"No. That didn't occur to me."

"We've been here long enough."

Mac knew they would be teleporting somewhere—within brief moments—

He telecommed to Gwenna, *Is he going to kill us?*

You'll be kept in a safe place until Alex feels it will be safe to release you.

Once more Mac felt himself hurtling down a long dark tunnel through the universe while stars and galaxies roared by on every side. Lucille was beside him, Gwenna and Alex leading the way, forcing the way . . .

Suddenly he sensed the presence of other Nomads. Gwenna screamed telepathically while Alex shouted in anger. Whereas the

226

four of them had been together—Lucille, Alex, Gwenna, himself—now they were divided; Alex-Gwenna; Lucille-himself.

Alex and Gwenna were in the control of a group of Nomads that dwindled beyond contact down another long dark tunnel. Lucille and himself were in the control of other Nomads, suddenly in his cabin again.

They would have killed you, someone said in his mind.

What's going to happen to them?

That will be decided later on.

The Nomads left the cabin as abruptly as they had appeared.

Mac thought, *They rescued us halfway to the chopping block.*

EPILOGUE

Graduation Day.

That's what it is, Mac thought. *Graduation day for the first class.*

Three months, one week and four days of Nomad instruction. They had all, during the past weeks, teleported from *Starbright* to the ship's lifeboats arranged in varying distances—teleported first with the assistance of telelinks, and then jumping alone. They had all practiced hour after hour until, for most, passing through subspace had started to seem as natural as walking.

But this was The Big Jump. Graduation day jump to places in their memories.

Rehearsal had been impossible.

You do it or you don't.

Diamond/Starbright/Thirty-Two—

The class had been divided, with roughly half jumping through subspace alone and half making what they all called "The Big Jump" with their telelinks, experienced Nomads.

I was one of the top students in the class, Thirty-Two thought proudly. *That's why they decided I could try The Big Jump alone.*

He focused his mind on a memory of his parents' home in San

Francisco and stepped into subspace with confidence.

Stepping with your mind, he thought. *That's how you do it. The mind goes first. What was it Jack of Diamonds said? Instead of thinking in terms of putting your left or right or best foot forward, tell yourself that you're going to take a giant step by putting your mind forward and the body will follow . . .*

He concentrated on his parents' home—

The living room, so comfortable with the thick rug where he had stretched out as a teenager, watching the video with his sisters, the kitchen, warm and smelling of the spicy things his mother loved to prepare, the garden in the rear of the house . . .

No, no. You're doing it wrong. You're supposed to concentrate on one location — one room. Thinking of different places within the house is as bad as thinking of all the various places your parents lived. When Dad had that job as guide on Khairasthan and you were only eleven or twelve, you lived in those clay huts . . .

And, abruptly, he was there—he felt himself slipping out of subspace, once more in "real" space . . .

Khairasthan, not San Francisco.

You goofed it! he thought angrily. *You let your thoughts wander from the home in San Francisco to Khairasthan . . .*

He was standing on a windswept hill covered with the remnants of clay huts. This is where he had lived with his parents for two years. Someone had had the bright idea of turning the planet Khairasthan into a New Africa complete with safaris and wild game preserves. It had worked for a while but the tourist trade proved to be too small to maintain the planetary economy, so the whole enterprise had disintegrated.

The jungle stretched endlessly in every direction beyond the hill. He studied it a moment and thought, *If this happened to me, possibly the best students in the class, what's going to happen to the others? One second's wavering in concentration and you—*

He heard the animal behind him—heard its paws on the ground as

229

it leaped. He started to turn but then the beast was on his back, its teeth ripping at his throat . . .

Sapphire/Starbright/Twelve—visualized subspace as a chasm and was leaping across that chasm when she suddenly found herself falling.

What did I do wrong?

There were no answers.

She tried to return to *Starbright* and found that somehow impossible.

Locked into a fall that would last for all eternity, she began to scream . . .

Ruby/Starbright/Fifteen—teleported to his home planet. It was a perfect jump and he landed in the patio of his home where he had lived for many years.

And landed in the middle of a war. He never saw the missile that exploded only a few hundred feet above his head. The explosion left a crater in the ground and following missiles demolished the town but caused little damage to the underground military installation not far away.

Tiger/Starbright/Four—*All I have to do is make this one jump through subspace and I'll earn my fourth name. What should I choose?*

He liked the name of Tiger. Should he take his own first name as his fourth name? No. Something else, he decided. Something that would go along with Tiger and sound manly and colorful, but not too flashy . . .

Jump, he told himself.

Jump!

Jump!

Jump!

He had jumped ever-increasing distances to the lifeboats with no trouble.

This was The Big Jump. So what? The instructors had said it was all in your mind. If you weren't afraid . . .

Jump!

He found he couldn't jump. He was paralyzed. He opened his eyes . . .

The class had gathered in the conference room and, as instructed, all had closed their eyes for the intense concentration necessary. As he looked around, he saw his Nomad classmates disappearing one by one as they teleported into subspace.

He, however, found himself immobile, paralyzed by unreasonable fear . . .

Princess/Starbright/Ten—made The Big Jump by concentrating on her bedroom in the small town where she had lived all her life.

Coming out of subspace, she saw the room in detail but with the objects blurred as if seen through fogged glass.

She tried to clarify the familiar room in her mind and her efforts resulted in a further distortion.

Realizing she could not delay the transition any longer, she attempted to step into the room and found the way blocked as if shielded by an invisible but solid wall.

Something's wrong. I did something wrong and I'm not going to make it.

Arrow/Starbright/Thirteen—had originally been undecided about where to teleport to. He had toyed with the idea of making The Big Jump to his summer cottage at the beach. Which would give him a chance for a quick swim, a bit of sunbathing. He'd also toyed with the idea of jumping to his office. He owned a small company which he'd closed down, sending everyone on vacation. The recorder might have some important calls on it. That would give him a chance to check the calls and see if there was anything he should attend to right away. A person in business for himself had to work extra hours. Or— he could jump to Vera's apartment. Vera and he had lived together the past half year. She'd been unable to take a vacation when he did and it would be good to see her again.

Wrestling with the indecision of the three destinations, he had decided on the summer cottage.

In subspace, during those fleeting seconds, he changed his mind and decided he should go to the office.

And changed his mind again, deciding to go to Vera's apartment . . .

When he felt himself coming out of subspace, he saw—the summer cottage—his office—Vera's apartment.

One, two, three.

Saw them again, one, two, three, in rapid succession, and again and again until the images and sensations blurred beyond recognition.

He remembered one of the Nomad instructors saying that indecision could be fatal. And he had let indecision creep into his mind at the last instant.

Like steering a car, one of them had said. As simple as that. Steering with a firm grip . . .

The images blurred and his mind blurred as he knew he would die somewhere in hyperspace, not reaching any of the three destinations . . .

Dagger/Starbright/Nine—made The Big Jump into hyperspace and realized an instant later that he had not concentrated on his destination properly.

He had decided to return to the apartment he'd been maintaining in New York City for business purposes. The experienced Nomads had said that anonymity must be maintained. They wore the cloaks whenever teleporting for several reasons. It formed a solid psycho-

232

logical association and aided concentration. But it had the disadvantage that when you arrived at your destination, you arrived in your cloak, and therefore, had to, like Superman finding a place to return to the Clark Kent identity, find a place to remove the cloak.

The apartment would be ideal.

But he did not visualize the destination clearly enough. He'd been there a few times but had not paid much attention to the place, walking through it in an absent-minded manner.

Now he found himself hurtling through the grayness of subspace at an unimaginable speed with no destination in mind. When he tried to visualize the apartment again, he found it impossible.

At the instant when he should have visualized the destination, he had let his mind slip into a visualization of hyperspace itself.

He found he couldn't return to *Starbright*.

I'm lost! he screamed mentally.

Silver/Starbright/Twenty-One—sent his mind leaping ahead to his destination as the Nomads had instructed.

He faltered somehow and did not know how or exactly why, the way a person can trip and fall and not see or know the object that caused the tripping—and, incredulously, found his mind at the destination with his body lagging behind, somehow trapped in subspace, dying—his consciousness winking out of existence like a light blinking away when the power has been cut—

Gold/Starbright/Fifteen—arrived at the destination but felt something wrench at the last instant. He was too quick closing the mental-physical door to hyperspace. The Nomads had said to centralize *all* thoughts on the destination during arrival and release the sensations of hyperspace smoothly, gradually.

And he'd done it wrong, being nervous at a crucial time, hurrying too much, doing several things incorrectly—found most of himself at his destination but found he'd incredibly shut the "door" of teleportation on his arm and, moments before losing consciousness from shock, stared down at the stump of his arm as it spurted blood.

He'd left an arm in hyperspace!

Spear/Starbright/Eight—felt her mind being *diverted*.

She had chosen a difficult destination, the outpost where her husband was stationed. A colonel in the Galactic Army, he'd described the place to her while on furlough; she'd telepathically shared his memories—knowing it was thousands and thousands of light-years beyond the mainstream of civilization as they knew it, on the fringe of human exploration.

Creatures were diverting her—alien, horrible things beyond description, pulling her mind and body down, down, down—to a cage—

Rose/Starbright/Two—caught herself in the gulf of subspace and felt as if she had stepped into an endless ocean.

I can't do it!

She returned to *Starbright,* to the conference room, to find several of her class had not been able to make the leap . . .

Bear/Starbright/One—concentrated as hard as he could, thinking, *This is the only way we can save ourselves. By teleportation. Discovering a habitable planet will be impossible. However, if enough of us can teleport to civilization and return to* Starbright *with food and supplies and help carry others to safety . . .*

He jumped, telling himself, *Go! Go! Go!*—and exerted so much mental pressure that he landed in the lobby of his hotel in Chicago, screaming.

His mind and body arrived safely, intact, but something had snapped in his mind with the tremendous exertion. Two bellboys and two bellgirls managed to drag him off to the hotel physician who instantly gave him an injection to knock him out—and removed the black cloak, muttering, "These damned secret societies are cropping up like weeds. What the hell did they do to this poor man?"

Minutes later an ambulance carried unconscious Bear/Starbright/One to a hospital.

Lila Hartnett teleported to her apartment in Los Angeles, collapsed on the rug, sobbing.

She felt exhausted—totally exhausted. The Nomad instructors had advised that the students who succeeded in teleporting themselves should return to *Starbright* immediately.

"Learn the return trip," one of the Nomads had stated, "while the route is still fresh in your mind."

Route? It was like . . . Like what?

I can't make the trip back to Starbright, she realized. *I'm out of nerve . . . completely out of nerve . . .*

Green/Starbright/Fourteen—with the help of his telelink reached his destination and returned instantly to *Starbright*. It was so easy with the help of the experienced Nomad. He wondered if he could do it alone.

You'll have a chance to try it alone, his telelink said.

He looked around at the conference room. Moments before it had been crowded to capacity. The occupants had teleported themselves away singly and in pairs. He had been one of the last to leave and the room had contained only nine or ten who'd apparently found themselves psychologically or physically unable to make the teleportive leap.

More people were returning . . . but not nearly as many as there had been.

Accidents? he asked his telelink.

We expected some casualties, the response came. *Everyone was warned of the dangers.*

Green/Starbright/Fourteen kept counting as the experienced and novice Nomads returned.

In the end he was shocked at the figures.

They had lost half of their class. Dozens of men and women had died while trying to learn how to teleport themselves to safety.

Having successfully completed the Nomad course of instruction, I wonder if I will be the only teleporting philosopher in the universe. It is a shame the Nomad society is a secret society. If not, I could have business cards printed:

Hans Steiger
Nomad Philosopher

It is our graduation day and we are about to leave on our Big Jump. I am dictating this to my thinkwriter and will try to continue dictating while in hyperspace. I wonder if the machine will be able to receive the transmissions?

My destination will be my study on Earth . . .

I wonder if I cannot only project my thoughts to the thinkwriter while in hyperspace, but also project them from my study on Earth, through the emptiness of subspace, so the machine can record them.

Here we go. Our instructor is asking us to take the jump, wishing us luck . . .

Subspace — so far — feels no different than it did when we made those assisted practiced jumps to the lifeboats . . .

My study!

My wife is sitting at the desk, reading my notes . . . Her back is to me . . . She never enetered my study before . . .

Of course!

She received word that Starbright met with an accident and she must believe I am dead.

I . . . cannot stop and talk to her now. The Nomads suggested it would be wisest to return to Starbright immediately.

Maria is turning . . .

I must have made some sound.,

Into subspace.

Appears and feels no different than before . . .

Nomads are popping back into the conference room . . .

The teleporting wasn't as hard as I anticipated. Some people find it difficult to teleport, others find it impossible — but I find it less strenuous than jogging. Perhaps the reason is because I have always exercised my mind and it is strong while my body is, sorry to say, too old for jogging . . .

So — now that I have made the return trip — I think I will make a quick teleportive jog back to Maria for a brief visit and hope she doesn't have a heart attack when she sees me materialize. She knows about the Nomads and their techniques of teleporting, so if she survives the initial shock . . .

Natalaie and Lamar arrived on the planet Settle with no problems. They had traveled together through hyperspace and were holding hands when they materialized.

"I wish we could stay," Natalaie sighed. "I wish they hadn't instructed us to return to *Starbright* immediately."

Lamar winked. "Any good motels here? We could jump back later and spend the night."

Krause made a routine jump to his private office on Earth, picked up the handful of mail from the incoming box and jumped back to his cabin aboard the *Starbright*. He had made several trips to Earth since the meteor first struck the starliner but had not communicated with anyone.

It was damnably ironic, he reflected. He could jump back and forth with ease. Yet he could do little as an individual to help the *Starbright* passengers. They had to help themselves. Few Nomads could "carry" another person through hyperspace. Those few who did have the strength to carry someone else could only do so when the spatial co-ordinates in "real space" were only a few light-years apart. *Starbright* was floating too far away for even an experienced Nomad to carry someone to Earth or any of the other planets inhabited by mankind.

He had been a Nomad since his teens.

Removing the black hood, he sat at the small desk in his cabin and went through the personal letters.

Olivia telepathed to him before he finished the mail:

Our losses on that first big jump are high. Very high.

Give me a percentage?

Fifty percent.

Half!

We rushed some of them, pushing them into it before they had enough training.

Olivia broke the telepathic contact and Krause stretched out on the cot, thinking.

Half. So many lives . . .

There is more at stake than individual survival, he reminded himself.

The intergalactic wanderings of mankind were bringing it face to face with powerful alien enemies—and some conflicts with those aliens had proven unavoidable.

In some of the wars with alien races, mankind had come dangerously close to being the loser.

Losing an intergalactic war quite often meant extinction for the losing race.

Mankind has to forward itself, he thought. It has to keep on learning how to fight aliens—continue expanding and improving its teleportive skills . . .

Survival of the race, not of individuals.

And so far *Starbright* was proving to be a remarkable recruiting ground.

Laurel Austin and Rian Thornfield made a teleportive jump to Laurel's apartment, not holding hands or physically joined in any way, but with their minds and telepathic faculties closely attuned.

In the apartment they rested awhile before returning to *Starbright*. They did not make love physically but Laurel, with her peeper skills, eased into his mind in such an intimate manner that the result to Rian was a sensation of making love mentally and emotionally.

When they were ready to return to *Starbright,* Laurel said, "You asked about Nomad missions . . . Close your eyes and look at this."

Rian closed his eyes and saw the mental projection she eased into his mind.

It comprised images and thoughts that Laurel had peeped from prisoners in a Colossian zoo—men and women treated as the lowliest animals, placed on exhibit for the inquisitive of the alien race.

Our next mission will be to free them, Laurel explained. *It will be our hardest mission to date. We will need you . . .*

Gold/Starbright/Nineteen—made the jump exactly as he had been instructed, with great skill. He had been a telepath from the earliest origins of his human brain. While still in the womb, he had sensed the warmth of his mother's mind gently reaching out to him.

His mother, a superb telepath, had nursed him physically and mentally during his infancy. He had developed into not only one of the most talented telepaths in the universe, but also one of the few male peepers. His paraphysical strength exceeded most so far as telepathic abilities were concerned.

But he concentrated too hard and put too much mental force behind The Big Jump. He had the sensation of being in a vehicle and inadvertently pushing the accelerator too far, bursting through the destination—crashing into a fantastic place.

Mind and body. Complete. Alive. But—*where?*

Something in his teleportive skills had died of exposure to tremendous strains and forces he could not fully comprehend. He instinc-

239

tively knew he would not be able to teleport away from this place . . .

Where was he?

He sensed with his mind rather than his physical senses, and he felt as if he were stretched endlessly in every direction. Something towered above him, something gigantic, omniscient. Not God, but a godlike entity that had grown in this strange cosmic place and now looked down upon him like an adult who looks down upon a lost child who stumbles into the wrong room. *It* knew him instantly and he felt a mental warmth as his mother's mind had felt during infancy, but stronger, immeasurably stronger—and he knew *It*, like a cosmic father, would protect him and care for him for all eternity.